Praise for Colin Dexter and his most recent Inspector Morse novel, THE DAUGHTERS OF CAIN

"Colin Dexter, that puzzlemeister without peer, has devised another infernal brainteaser."
—*The New York Times Book Review*

"Audacious and amusing . . . May be the best book yet in this deservedly celebrated series."
—*The Wall Street Journal*

"Very cleverly constructed . . . Dexter writes with an urbanity and range of reference that is all his own."
—*Los Angeles Times*

"Dexter combines an erudite, literate writing style with a story line that is easy to follow. All of his characters are interesting."
—Associated Press

By Colin Dexter:

LAST BUS TO WOODSTOCK*
LAST SEEN WEARING*
THE SILENT WORLD OF NICHOLAS QUINN
SERVICE OF ALL THE DEAD*
THE DEAD OF JERICHO*
THE RIDDLE OF THE THIRD MILE
THE SECRET OF ANNEXE 3
THE WENCH IS DEAD
THE JEWEL THAT WAS OURS*
THE WAY THROUGH THE WOODS*
THE DAUGHTERS OF CAIN*
MORSE'S GREATEST MYSTERY and Other Stories*

*Published by Ivy Books

LAST
SEEN
WEARING

Colin Dexter

IVY BOOKS • NEW YORK

Ivy Books
Published by Ballantine Books
Copyright © 1976 by Colin Dexter

http://www.randomhouse.com

Library of Congress Catalog Card Number: 96-94819

ISBN-13: 978-0-8041-1491-2

ISBN-10: 0-8041-1491-9

This edition published by arrangement with St. Martin's Press, Inc.

Manufactured in the United States of America

First Ballantine Books Edition: April 1997

For
J.C.F.P. and J.G.F.P.

Prelude

The Train Now Standing at Platform One

He felt quite pleased with himself. Difficult to tell for certain, of course, but yes, quite pleased with himself really. As accurately as it could his mind retraced the stages of the day's events: the questions of the interviewing committee—wise and foolish; and his own answers—carefully considered and, he knew, well-phrased. Two or three exchanges had been particularly satisfactory and, as he stood there waiting, a half-smile played across his firm, good-humoured lips. One he could recall almost verbatim.

"You don't think you may perhaps be a bit young for the job?"

"Well, yes. It will be a big job and I'm sure that there will be times—that is if you should appoint me—when I should need the experience and advice of older and wiser heads." (Several of the older and wiser heads were nodding sagely.) "But if my age is against me, there isn't much I can do about it, I'm afraid. I can only say that it's a fault I shall gradually grow out of."

It wasn't even original. One of his former colleagues had recounted it to him and claimed it for his own. But it was a good story: and judging from the quietly-controlled mirth and the muted murmurs of appreciation, apparently none of the thirteen members of the selection committee had heard it before.

Mm.

Again the quiet smile played about his mouth. He looked at his watch. 7:30 P.M. Almost certainly he would be able to catch the 8:35 from Oxford, reaching London at 9:42; then over to Waterloo; and home by midnight perhaps. He'd be a bit lucky if he managed it, but who cared? It was probably those two double whiskies that were giving him such a glowing sense of elation, of expectancy, of being temporarily so much in tune with the music of the spheres. He would be offered the job, he felt—that was the long and the short of it.

February now. Six months' notice, and he counted off the months on his fingers: March, April, May, June, July, August. That would be all right: plenty of time.

His eyes swept leisurely along the rather superior detached houses that lined the opposite side of the road. Four bedrooms; biggish gardens. He would buy one of those pre-fabricated greenhouses, and grow tomatoes or cucumbers, like Diocletian . . . or was it Hercule Poirot?

He stepped back into the wooden shelter and out of the raw wind. It had begun to drizzle again. Cars swished intermittently by, and the surface of the road gleamed under the orange streetlights . . . Not quite so good, though, when they had asked him about his short time in the army.

"You didn't get a commission, did you?"

"No."

"Why not, do you think?"

"I don't think I was good enough. Not at the time. You need special qualities for that sort of thing." (He was getting lost: waffle on, keep talking.) "And I was, er . . . well

I just hadn't got them. There were some extremely able men joining the army at that time—far more confident and competent than me." Leave it there. Modest.

An ex-colonel and an ex-major nodded appreciatively. Two more votes, likely as not.

It was always the same at these interviews. One had to be as honest as possible, but in a dishonest kind of way. Most of his army friends had been ex-public-schoolboys, buoyed up with self-confidence, and with matching accents. Second lieutenants, lieutenants, captains. They had claimed their natural birthright and they had been duly honoured in their season. Envy had nagged at him vaguely over the years. He, too, had been a public-schoolboy . . .

Buses didn't seem very frequent, and he wondered if he would make the 8:35 after all. He looked out along the well-lit street, before retreating once more into the bus-shelter, its wooden walls predictably covered with scrawls and scorings of varying degrees of indecency. Kilroy, inevitably, had visited this shrine in the course of his infinite peregrinations, and several local tarts proclaimed to prospective clients their nymphomaniac inclinations. Enid loved Gary and Dave loved Monica. Variant readings concerning Oxford United betrayed the impassioned frustrations of the local football fans: eulogy and urination. All Fascists should go home immediately and freedom should be granted forthwith to Angola, Chile and Northern Ireland. A window had been smashed and slivers of glass sparkled sporadically amid the orange-peel, crisp-packets and Cola tins. Litter! How it appalled him. He was far more angered by obscene litter than by obscene literature. He would pass some swingeing litter laws if they ever made him the supremo.

Even in this job he could do something about it. Well, if he got it . . .

Come on, bus. 7:45. Perhaps he should stay in Oxford for the night? It wouldn't matter. If freedom should be granted to Angola and the rest, why not to him? It had been a long time since he had spent so long away from home. But he was losing nothing—gaining in fact; for the expenses were extremely generous. The whole thing must have cost the Local Authority a real packet. Six of them short-listed—one from Inverness! Not that *he* would get the job, surely. Quite a strange experience, though, meeting people like that. One couldn't get too friendly. Like the contestants in a beauty competition. Smile and scratch their eyes out.

Another memory glided slowly back across his mind. "If you were appointed, what do you think would be your biggest headache?"

"The caretaker, I shouldn't wonder."

He had been amazed at the uproariously-delighted reception given to this innocent remark, and only afterwards had he discovered that the current holder of the sinecure was an ogre of quite stupendous obstinacy—an extraordinarily ill-dispositioned man, secretly and profoundly feared by all.

Yes, he would get the job. And his first tactical triumph would be the ceremonial firing of the wicked caretaker, with the unanimous approbation of governors, staff and pupils alike. And then the litter. And then . . .

"Waitin' for a bus?"

He hadn't seen her come in from the far side of the shelter. Below her plastic hat tiny droplets of drizzle winked from the carefully-plucked eyebrows. He nodded. "Don't seem very frequent, do they?" She walked towards him. Nice-looking girl. Nice lips. Difficult to say how old she was. Eighteen? Even younger, perhaps.

"There's one due about now."

"That's good news."

"Not a very nice night."

"No." It seemed a dismissive reply, and feeling a desire to keep the conversation going, he wondered what to say. He might just as well stand and talk as stand and be silent. His companion was clearly thinking along similar lines and showed herself the slicker practitioner.

"Goin' to Oxford?"

"Yes. I'm hoping to catch the 8:35 train to London."

"You'll be all right."

She unfastened her gleaming plastic mac and shook the raindrops to the floor. Her legs were thin, angular almost, but well-proportioned; and the gentlest, mildest of erotic notions fluttered into his mind. It was the whisky.

"You live in London?"

"No, thank goodness. I live down in Surrey."

"You goin' all that way tonight?"

Was he? "It's not far really, once you've got across London." She lapsed into silence. "What about you? You going to Oxford?"

"Yeah. Nothing to do 'ere."

She must be young, surely. Their eyes met and held momentarily. She had a lovely mouth. Just a brief encounter, though, in a bus-shelter, and pleasant—just a fraction more pleasant than it should have been. Yet that was all. He smiled at her, openly and guilelessly. "I suppose there's plenty to do in the big wicked city of Oxford?"

She looked at him slyly. "Depends what you want, don't it?" Before he could ascertain exactly what she wanted or what extra-mural delights the old university city could still provide, a red double-decker curved into the lay-by, its near front wheel splattering specks of dirty-brown water across his carefully-polished black shoes. The automatic doors rattled noisily open, and he stepped aside for the girl to climb in first. She turned at the hand rail that led to the upper deck.

"Comin' upstairs?"

The bus was empty, and when she sat down on the back seat and blinked at him invitingly, he had little option or inclination to do otherwise than to sit beside her. "Got any cigarettes?"

"No, I'm sorry. I don't smoke."

Was she just a common slut? She almost acted like one. He must look a real city gent to her: immaculate dark suit, new white shirt, a Cambridge tie, well-cut heavy overcoat, and a leather brief-case. She would probably expect a few expensive drinks in a plush four-star lounge. Well, if she did, she was in for a big disappointment. Just a few miles on the top of a number 2 bus. And yet he felt a subdued, magnetic attraction towards her. She took off her transparent plastic hat and shook out her long dark-brown hair. Soft, and newly washed.

A weary-footed conductor slowly mounted the circular staircase and stood before them.

"Two to Oxford, please."

"Whereabouts?" The man sounded surly.

"Er, I'm going to the station . . ."

She said it for him. "Two to the station, please." The conductor wound the tickets mechanically, and disappeared dejectedly below.

It was completely unexpected, and he was taken by surprise. She put her arm through his, and squeezed his elbow gently against her soft body. "I 'spect he thinks we're just off to the pictures." She giggled happily. "Anyway, thanks for buying the ticket." She turned towards him and gently kissed his cheek with her soft, dry lips.

"You didn't tell me you were going to the station."

"I'm not really."

"Where are you going then?"

She moved a little closer. "Dunno."

For a frightening moment the thought flashed across his mind that she might be simple-minded. But no. He felt quite sure that for the present time at least she had an infinitely saner appreciation of what was going on than he. Yet he was almost glad when they reached the railway station. 8:17. Just over a quarter of an hour before the train was due.

They alighted and momentarily stood together in silence beneath the TICKETS: BUFFET sign. The drizzle persisted.

"Like a drink?" He said it lightly.

"Wouldn't mind a Coke."

He felt surprised. If she was on the look-out for a man, it seemed an odd request. Most women of her type would surely go for gin or vodka or something with a bigger kick than Coke. Who was she? What did she want?

"You sure?"

"Yes, thanks. I don't go drinkin' much."

They walked into the Buffet, where he ordered a double whisky for himself, and for her a Coke and a packet of twenty Benson & Hedges. "Here we are."

She seemed genuinely grateful. She quickly lit herself a cigarette and quietly sipped her drink. The time ticked on, the minute hand of the railway clock dropping inexorably to the half hour. "Well, I'd better get on to the platform." He hesitated a moment, and then reached beneath the seat for his brief-case. He turned towards her and once again their eyes met. "I enjoyed meeting you. Perhaps we'll meet again one day." He stood up, and looked down at her. She seemed more attractive to him each time he looked at her.

She said: "I wish we could be naughty together, don't you?"

God, yes. Of course he did. He was breathing quickly and suddenly the back of his mouth was very dry. The loudspeaker announced that the 8:35 shortly arriving at Platform One was for Reading and Paddington only; passengers for . . . But he wasn't listening. All he had to do was to admit how nice it would have been, smile a sweet smile and walk through the Buffet door, only some three or four yards away, and out on to Platform One. That was all. And again and again in later months and years he was bitterly to reproach himself for not having done precisely that.

"But where could we go?" He said it almost involuntarily. The pass at Thermopylae was abandoned and the Persian army was already streaming through.

Chapter One

Beauty's ensign yet
Is crimson in thy lips and in thy cheeks,
And death's pale flag is not advanced there.
SHAKESPEARE, *Romeo and Juliet*, Act V

Three and a half years later two men were seated together in an office.

"You've got the files. Quite a lot of stuff to go on there."

"But he didn't get very far, did he?" Morse sounded cynical about the whole proposition.

"Perhaps there wasn't very far to go."

"You mean she just hopped it and—that was that."

"Perhaps."

"But what do you want me to do? Ainley couldn't find her, could he?"

Chief Superintendent Strange made no immediate answer. He looked past Morse to the neatly-docketed rows of red and green box-files packed tightly along the shelves.

"No," he said finally. "No, he didn't find her."

"And he was on the case right from the start."

"Right from the start," repeated Strange.

"And he got nowhere." Strange said nothing. "He wasn't a fool, was he?" persisted Morse. What the hell did it matter anyway? A girl leaves home and she's never seen again. So what? Hundreds of girls leave home. Most of them write back to their parents before long—at least

9

as soon as the glamour rubs off and the money has trickled away. Some of them don't come home. Agreed. Some of them never do; and for the lonely waiters the nagging heartache returns with the coming of each new day. No. A few of them never come home . . . Never.

Strange interrupted his gloomy thoughts. "You'll take it on?"

"Look, if Ainley . . ."

"No. *You* look!" snapped Strange. "Ainley was a bloody sight better policeman than you'll ever be. In fact I'm asking you to take on this case precisely because you're *not* a very good policeman. You're too airy-fairy. You're too . . . I don't know."

But Morse knew what he meant. In a way he ought to have been pleased. Perhaps he was pleased. But two years ago. Two whole years! "The case is cold now, sir—you must know that. People forget. Some people need to forget. Two years is a long time."

"Two years, three months and two days," corrected Strange. Morse rested his chin on his left hand and rubbed the index finger slowly along the side of his nose. His grey eyes stared through the open window and on to the concrete surface of the enclosed yard. Small tufts of grass were sprouting here and there. Amazing. Grass growing through concrete. How on earth? Good place to hide a body—under concrete. All you'd need to do . . . "She's dead," said Morse abruptly.

Strange looked up at him. "What on earth makes you say that?"

"I don't know. But if you don't find a girl after all that time—well, I should guess she's dead. It's hard enough hiding a dead body, but it's a hell of a sight harder hiding a living one. I mean, a living one gets up and walks around and meets other people, doesn't it? No. My guess is she's dead."

"That's what Ainley thought."

"And you agreed with him?"

Strange hesitated a moment, then nodded. "Yes, I agreed with him."

"He was really treating this as a murder enquiry, then?"

"Not officially, no. He was treating it for what it was—a missing person enquiry."

"And unofficially?"

Again Strange hesitated. "Ainley came to see me about this case several times. He was, let's say, uneasy about it. There were certain aspects of it that made him very . . . very worried."

Surreptitiously Morse looked at his watch. Ten past five. He had a ticket for the visiting English National Opera performance of *Die Walküre* starting at half-past six at the New Theatre.

"It's ten past five," said Strange, and Morse felt like a young schoolboy caught yawning as the teacher was talking to him . . . School. Yes, Valerie Taylor had been a schoolgirl—he'd read about the case. Seventeen and a bit. Good looker, by all accounts. Eyes on the big city, like as not. Excitement, sex, drugs, prostitution, crime, and then the gutter. And finally remorse. We all felt remorse in the end. And then? For the first time since he had been sitting in Strange's office Morse felt his brain becoming engaged. What *had* happened to Valerie Taylor?

He heard Strange speaking again, as if in answer to his thoughts.

"At the end Ainley was beginning to get the feeling that she'd never left Kidlington at all."

Morse looked up sharply. "Now I wonder why he should think that?" He spoke the words slowly, and he felt his nerve-endings tingling. It was the old familiar sensation. For a while he even forgot *Die Walküre*.

"As I told you, Ainley was worried about the case."

"You know why?"

"You've got the files."

Murder? That was more up Morse's alley. When Strange had first introduced the matter he thought he was being invited to undertake one of those thankless, inconclusive, interminable, needle-in-a-haystack searches: panders, pimps and prostitutes, shady rackets and shady racketeers, grimy streets and one-night cheap hotels in London, Liverpool, Birmingham. Ugh! Procedure. Check. Recheck. Blank. Start again. *Ad infinitum.* But now he began to brighten visibly. And, anyway, Strange would have his way in the end, whatever happened. Just a minute, though. Why now? Why Friday, 12th September—two years, three months and two days (wasn't it?), after Valerie Taylor had left home to return to afternoon school? He frowned. "Something's turned up, I suppose."

Strange nodded. "Yes."

That was better news. Watch out, you miserable sinner, whoever you are, who did poor Valerie in! He'd ask for Sergeant Lewis again. He liked Lewis.

"And I'm sure," continued Strange, "that you're the right man for the job."

"Nice of you to say so."

Strange stood up. "You didn't seem all that pleased a few minutes ago."

"To tell you the truth, sir, I thought you were going to give me one of those miserable missing person cases."

"And that's exactly what I am going to do." Strange's voice had acquired a sudden hard authority. "And I'm not *asking* you to do it—I'm *telling* you."

"But you said . . ."

"*You* said. I didn't. Ainley was wrong. He was wrong because *Valerie Taylor is very much alive*." He walked over to a filing-cabinet, unlocked it, took out a small rectangular sheet of cheap writing paper, clipped to an equally cheap brown envelope, and handed both to Morse. "You can touch it all right—no fingerprints. She's written home at last."

Morse looked down miserably at the three short lines of drab, uncultured scrawl:

Dear Mum and Dad,
    Just to let you know I'm alright so don't worry. Sorry I've not written before but I'm alright. Love Valerie.

There was no address on the letter.

Morse slipped the envelope from the clip. It was postmarked Tuesday, 2nd September, London, E.C.4.

Chapter Two

On the left-hand side sat a man of vast proportions, who had come in with only a couple of minutes to spare. He had wheezed his way slowly along Row J like a very heavy vehicle negotiating a very narrow bridge, mumbling a series of breathless "thank yous" as each of the seated patrons blocking his progress arose and pressed hard back against the tilted seats. When he had finally deposited his bulk in the seat next to Morse, the sweat stood out on his massive brow, and he panted awhile like a stranded whale.

On the other side sat a demure, bespectacled young lady in a long purple dress, holding a bulky opera score upon her knee. Morse had nodded a polite "good evening" when he took his seat, but only momentarily had the lips creased before reassuming their wonted, thin frigidity. Mona Lisa with the guts ache, thought Morse. He had been in more exhilarating company.

But there was the magnificent opera to relish once again. He thought of the supremely beautiful love-duet in Act 1, and he hoped that this evening's Siegmund would be able to cope adequately with that noble tenor passage—one of the most beautiful (and demanding) in all grand opera. The conductor strode along the orchestra pit, mounted the rostrum, and suavely received the plaudits of the audience. The lights were dimmed, and Morse settled back in his seat with delicious anticipation. The coughing gradually sputtered to a halt and the conductor raised his baton. *Die Walküre* was under way.

After only two minutes, Morse was conscious of some distracting movement on his right, and a quick glance revealed that the bespectacled Mona Lisa had extricated a torch from somewhere about her person and was playing the light laterally along the orchestrated score. The pages crinkled and crackled as she turned them, and for some reason the winking of the flash-light reminded Morse of a revolving lighthouse. Forget it. She would probably pack it up as soon as the curtain went up. Still, it was a little annoying. And it was hot in the New Theatre. He wondered if he should take his jacket off, and almost immediately became aware that one other member of the audience had already come to a firm decision on the same point. The mountain on his left began to quiver, and very soon Morse was a helpless observer as the fat man set about removing his jacket, which he effected with infinitely more difficulty than an ageing Houdini would have experienced in escaping from a strait-jacket. Amid mounting shushes and clicking of tongues the fat man finally brought his monumental toils to a successful climax and rose ponderously to remove the offending garment from beneath him. The seat twanged noisily against the back rest, was restored to its horizontal position, and groaned heavily as it sank once more beneath the mighty load. More shushes, more clickings—and finally a blissful suspension of hostilities in Row J, disturbed only for Morse's sensitive soul by the lighthouse flashings of the Lady with the Lamp. Wagnerites were a funny lot!

Morse closed his eyes and the well-known chords at last engulfed him. Exquisite . . .

For a second Morse thought that the dig in his left rib betokened a vital communication, but the gigantic frame beside him was merely fighting to free his handkerchief from the vast recesses of his trouser pocket. In the ensuing struggle the flap of Morse's own jacket managed to get itself entrapped, and his feeble efforts to free himself from the entanglement were greeted by a bleak and barren glare from Florence Nightingale.

By the end of Act 1, Morse's morale was at a low ebb. Siegmund had clearly developed a croaking throat, Sieglinde was sweating profusely, and a young philistine immediately behind him was regularly rustling a packet of sweets. During the first interval he retreated to the bar, ordered a whisky, and another. The bell sounded for the start of Act 2, and he ordered a third. And the young girl who had been seated behind Morse's shoulders during Act 1 had a gloriously unimpeded view of Act 2; and of Act 3, by which time her second bag of Maltesers had joined the first in a crumpled heap upon the floor.

The truth was that Morse could never have surrendered himself quite freely to unadulterated enjoyment that night, however propitious the circumstances might have been. At every other minute his mind was reverting to his earlier interview with Strange—and then to Ainley. Above all to Chief Inspector Ainley. He had not known him at all well, really. Quiet sort of fellow. Friendly enough, without ever being a friend. A loner. Not, as Morse remembered him, a particularly interesting man at all. Restrained, cautious, legalistic. Married, but no family. And now he would never have a family, for Ainley was dead. According to the eye-witnesses it was largely his own fault—pulling out to overtake and failing to notice the fast-closing Jaguar looming in the outside lane of the M40 by High Wycombe. Miraculously no one else was badly hurt. Only Ainley, and Ainley had been killed. It wasn't like Ainley, that. He must have been thinking of something else . . . He had gone to London in his own car and in his own free time, just eleven days ago. It was frightening really—the way other people went on living. Great shock—oh yes—but there were no particular friends to mourn too bitterly. Except his wife . . . Morse had met her only once, at a police concert the previous year. Quite young, much younger than he was; pretty enough, but nothing to set the heart a-beating. Irene, or something like that? Eileen? Irene, he thought.

His whisky was finished and he looked around for the barmaid. No one. He was the only soul there, and the linen wiping-towels were draped across the beer-pumps. There was little point in staying.

He walked down the stairs and out into the warm dusking street. A huge notice in red and black capitals covered the whole of the wall outside the theatre: ENGLISH NATIONAL OPERA, MON., 1ST SEPT–SAT. 13TH SEPT. He felt a slight quiver of excitement along his spine. Monday the first of September. That was the day Dick Ainley had died. And the letter? Posted on Tuesday, the second of September. Could it be? He mustn't jump to conclusions though. But why the hell not? There was no eleventh commandment against jumping to conclusions, and so he jumped. Ainley had gone to London that Monday and something must have happened there. Had he perhaps found Valerie Taylor at last? It began to look a possibility. *The very next day* she had written home— after being away for more than two years. Yet there was something wrong. The Taylor case had been shelved, not closed, of course; but Ainley was working on something else, on that bomb business, in fact. So why? So why? Hold it a minute. Ainley had gone to London on his day off. Had he . . . ?

Morse walked back into the foyer, to be informed by a uniformed flunkey that the house was sold out and that the performance was half-way through anyway. Morse thanked him and stepped into the telephone kiosk by the door.

"I'm sorry, sir. That's for patrons only." The flunkey was right behind him.

"I *am* a bloody patron," said Morse. He took from his pocket the stub for Row J 26, stuck it under the flunkey's nose and ostentatiously and noisily closed the kiosk door behind him. A large telephone directory was stuck awkwardly in the metal pigeon-hole, and Morse opened it at the A's. Adderley . . . Allen . . . back a bit . . . Ainley. Only one Ainley, and in next year's directory even he would be gone. R. Ainley, 2 Wytham Close, Wolvercote.

Would she be in? It was already a quarter to nine. Irene or Eileen or whoever she was would probably be staying with friends. Mother or sister, most likely. Should he try? But what was he dithering about? He knew he would go anyway. He noted the address and walked briskly out past the flunkey.

"Good night, sir."

As Morse walked to his car, parked in nearby St. Giles, he regretted his childish sneer of dismissal to this friendly valediction. The flunkey was only doing his job.

Just as I am, said Morse to himself, as he drove without enthusiasm due north out of Oxford towards the village of Wolvercote.

Chapter Three

At the Woodstock roundabout, on the northern ring-road perimeter of Oxford, Morse took the sharp left fork, and leaving the Motel on his right drove over the railway bridge (where as a boy he had so often stood in wonder as the steam locomotives sped thunderously by) and down the hill into Wolvercote.

The small village consisted of little more than the square stone-built houses that lined its main street, and was familiar to Morse only because each of its two public houses boasted beer drawn straight from the wood. Without being too doctrinaire about what he was prepared to drink, Morse preferred a flat pint to the fizzy keg most breweries, misguidedly in his view, were now producing; and he seldom passed through the village without enjoying a jug of ale at the King Charles. He parked the Lancia in the yard, exchanged a few pleasantries with the landlady over his beer and asked for Wytham Close.

He soon found it, a crescented cul-de-sac no more than a hundred yards back along the road on the right-hand side, containing ten three-storey terraced residences (pompously styled "town houses"), set back from the adopted road, with steep concreted drives leading up to the built-in garages. Two street lamps threw a pale phosphorescence over the open-plan well-tended grass, and a light shone from behind the orange curtains in the middle-storey window of No. 2. The bell sounded harsh in the quiet of the darkened close.

A lower light was switched on in the entrance hall and a vaguely-lineated shadow loomed through the frosted glass of the front door.

"Yes?"

"I hope I'm not disturbing you," began Morse.

"Oh. Hullo, Inspector."

"I thought . . ."

"Won't you come in?"

Morse's decision to refuse the offer of a drink was made with such obvious reluctance that he was speedily prevailed upon to reverse it; and sitting behind a glass of gin and tonic he did his best to say all the right things. On the whole, he thought, he was succeeding.

Mrs. Ainley was small, almost petite, with light-brown hair and delicate features. She looked well enough, although the darkness beneath her eyes bore witness to the recent tragedy.

"Will you stay on here?"

"Oh, I think so. I like it here."

Indeed, Morse knew full well how attractive the situation was. He had almost bought a similar house here a year ago, and he remembered the view from the rear windows over the green expanse of Port Meadow across to the cluster of stately spires and the dignified dome of the Radcliffe Camera. Like an Ackerman print, only alive and real, just two or three miles away.

"Another drink?"

"I'd better not," said Morse, looking appealingly towards his hostess.

"Sure?"

"Well, perhaps a small one."

He took the plunge. "Irene, isn't it?"

"Eileen."

It was a bad moment. "You're getting over it, Eileen?" He spoke the words in a kindly way.

"I think so." She looked down sadly, and picked some nonexistent object from the olive-green carpet. "He was hardly marked, you know. You wouldn't really have thought . . ." Tears were brimming, and Morse let them brim. She was quickly over it. "I don't even know why Richard went to London. Monday was his day off, you know." She blew her nose noisily, and Morse felt more at ease.

"Did he often go away like that?"

"Quite often, yes. He always seemed to be busy." She began to look vulnerable again and Morse trod his way carefully. It had to be done.

"Do you think when he went to London he was er . . ."

"I don't know what he went for. He never told me much about his work. He always said he had enough of it at the office without talking about it again at home."

"But he was worried about his work, wasn't he?" said Morse quietly.

"Yes. He always was a worrier, especially . . ."

"Especially?"

"I don't know."

"You mean he was more worried—recently?"

She nodded. "I think I know what was worrying him. It was that Taylor girl."

"Why do you say that?"

"I heard him talking on the phone to the headmaster."

She made the admission guiltily as if she really had no business to know of it.

"When was that?"

"About a fortnight, three weeks ago."

"But the school's on holiday, isn't it?"

"He went to the headmaster's house."

Morse began to wonder what else she knew. "Was that on one of his days off—?"

She nodded slowly and then looked up at Morse. "You seem very interested."

Morse sighed. "I ought to have told you straightaway. I'm taking over the Taylor case."

"So Richard found something after all." She sounded almost frightened.

"I don't know," said Morse.

"And . . . and that's why you came, I suppose." Morse said nothing. Eileen Ainley got up from her chair and walked briskly over to a bureau beside the window. "Most of his things have gone, but you might as well take this. He had it in the car with him." She handed to Morse a Letts desk-diary, black, about six inches by four. "And there's a letter for the accountant at the station. Perhaps you could take it for me?"

"Of course." Morse felt very hurt. But he often felt hurt—it was nothing new.

Eileen left the room to fetch the envelope and Morse quickly opened the diary and found Monday, 1st September. There was one entry, written in neatly-formed, minuscule letters: 42 Southampton Terrace. That was all. The blood tingled, and with a flash of utter certitude Morse knew that he hardly needed to look up the postal district of 42 Southampton Terrace. He *would* check it, naturally; he would look it up immediately he got home.

But without the slightest shadow of doubt he knew it already. It would be E.C.4.

He was back in his North Oxford bachelor home by a quarter to eleven, and finally discovered the street map of London, tucked neatly away behind *The Collected Works of Swinburne* and *Extracts from Victorian Pornography*. (He must put that book somewhere less conspicuous.) Impatiently he consulted the alphabetical index and frowned as he found Southampton Terrace. His frown deepened as he traced the given co-ordinates and studied the grid square. Southampton Terrace was one of the many side-streets off the Upper Richmond Road, south of the river, beyond Fulham Bridge. The postal district was S.W.12. He suddenly decided he had done enough for one day.

He left the map and the diary on top of the bookshelf, made himself a cup of instant coffee and selected from his precious Wagner shelf the Solti recording of *Die Walküre*. No fat man, no thin-lipped woman, no raucous tenor, no sweaty soprano distracted his mind as Sieg-mund and Sieglinde poured forth their souls in an ecstasy of recognition. The coffee remained untouched and gradually grew cold.

But even before the first side was played through, a fanciful notion was forming in his restless brain. There was surely a very simple reason for Ainley's visit to London. He should have thought of it before. Day off; busy, preoccupied, uncommunicative. He'd bet that was it! No. 42 Southampton Terrace. Well, well! *Old Ainley had been seeing another woman, perhaps.*

Chapter Four

As far as I could see there was no connection between them beyond the tenuous nexus of succession.

PETER CHAMPKIN

In different parts of the country on the Monday following Morse's interview with Strange, four fairly normal people were going about their disparate business. What each was doing was, in its own way, ordinary enough— in some cases ordinary to the point of tediousness. Each of them, with varied degrees of intimacy, knew the others, although one or two of them were hardly worthy of any intimate acquaintanceship. They shared one common bond, however, which in the ensuing weeks would inexorably draw each of them towards the centre of a criminal investigation. For each of them had known, again with varied degrees of intimacy, the girl called Valerie Taylor.

Mr. Baines had been second master in Kidlington's Roger Bacon Comprehensive School since its opening three years previously. Before that time he had also been second master, in the very same buildings, although then they had housed a secondary modern school, now incorporated into the upper part of a three-tier comprehensive system—a system which in their wisdom or unwisdom (Baines wasn't sure) the Oxfordshire Education Committee had adopted as its answer to the problems besetting the educational world in general and the children of

Kidlington in particular. The pupils would be returning the following day, Tuesday, 16th September, after a break of six and a half weeks, for much of which time, whilst some of his colleagues had motored off to Continental resorts, Baines had been wrestling with the overwhelmingly-complex problems of the timetable. Such a task traditionally falls upon the second master, and in the past Baines had welcomed it. There was a certain intellectual challenge in dovetailing the myriad options and combinations of the curriculum to match the inclinations and capacities of the staff available; and, at the same time (for Baines) a vicarious sense of power. Sadly, Baines had begun to think of himself as a good loser, a best man but never the groom. He was now fifty-five, unmarried, a mathematician. He had applied for many headships over the years, and on two occasions had been the runner-up. His last application had been made three and a half years ago, for the headship of his present school, and he thought he'd had a fairly good chance; but even then, deep down, he knew that he was getting past it. Not that he had been much impressed by the man they appointed, Phillipson. Not at the time, anyway. Only thirty-four, full of new ideas. Keen on changing everything—as if change inevitably meant a change for the better. But over the last year or so he had learned to respect Phillipson a good deal more. Especially after that glorious showdown with the odious caretaker.

Baines was sitting in the small office which served as a joint H.Q. for himself and for Mrs. Webb, the headmaster's secretary—a decent old soul who like himself had served in the old secondary modern school. It was mid-morning and he had just put the finishing touches to the staff dinner-duty roster. Everyone was neatly fitted in, except the headmaster, of course. And himself. He had to pick up his perks from somewhere. He walked across the cluttered office clutching the hand-written sheet.

"Three copies, my old sugar."

"Immediately, I suppose," said Mrs. Webb good-naturedly, picking up another sealed envelope and looking at the addressee before deftly slitting it along the top with a paperknife.

"What about a cup of coffee?" suggested Baines.

"What about your roster?"

"O.K. I'll make the coffee."

"No you won't." She got up from her seat, picked up the kettle and walked out to the adjacent cloakroom. Baines looked ruefully at the pile of letters. The usual sort of thing, no doubt. Parents, builders, meetings, insurance, examinations. *He* would have been dealing with all that if . . . He poked haphazardly among the remaining letters, and suddenly a flicker of interest showed in his shrewd eyes. The letter was lying face down and on the sealed flap he read the legend "Thames Valley Police." He picked it up and turned it over. It was addressed to the headmaster with the words PRIVATE AND CONFIDENTIAL typed across the top in bold red capitals.

"What are you doing going through my mail?" Mrs. Webb plugged in the kettle and with mock annoyance snatched the letter from him.

"See that?" asked Baines.

Mrs. Webb looked down at the letter. "None of our business, is it?"

"Do you think he's been fiddling his tax returns?" Baines chuckled deeply.

"Don't be silly."

"Shall we open it?"

"We shall *not*," said Mrs. Webb.

Baines returned to his cramped desk and started on the prefects' roster. Phillipson would have to appoint half a dozen new prefects this term. Or, to be more precise, he would ask Baines to give him a list of possible names. In some ways the head wasn't such a bad chap.

Phillipson himself came in just after eleven. "Morning, Baines. Morning, Mrs. Webb." He sounded far too cheerful. Had he forgotten that school was starting tomorrow?

"Morning, headmaster." Baines always called him "headmaster"; the rest of the staff called him "sir." It was only a little thing, but it was something.

Phillipson walked across to his study door and paused by his secretary's desk. "Anything important, Mrs. Webb?"

"I don't think so, sir. There's this, though." She handed him the letter marked "Private and Confidential," and Phillipson, with a slightly puzzled frown upon his face, entered his study and closed the door behind him.

In the newly-appointed county of Gwynedd, in a small semi-detached house on the outskirts of Caernarfon, another schoolmaster was acutely conscious that school restarted on the morrow. They had returned home only the previous day from a travesty of a holiday in Scotland—rain, two punctures, a lost Barclaycard and more rain—and there was a host of things to be done. The lawn, for a start. Benefiting (where he had suffered) from a series of torrential downpours, it had sprouted to alarming proportions during their absence, and was in urgent need of an instant crop. At 9:30 A.M. he discovered that the extension for the electric mower was not functioning, and he sat himself down on the back-door step with a heavy heart and a small screwdriver.

Life seldom seemed to run particularly smoothly for David Acum, until two years ago assistant French master at the Roger Bacon Comprehensive School in Kidlington, and now, still an assistant French master, at the City of Caernarfon School.

He could find no fault with the fittings at either end of the extension wire, and finally went inside again. No sign of life. He walked to the bottom of the stairs and yelled, his voice betraying ill-temper and exasperation. "Hey! Don't you think it's about time you got out of that bloody bed?"

He left it at that and, back in the kitchen, sat down cheerlessly at the table where half an hour earlier he had made his own breakfast, and dutifully taken a tray of tea and toast upstairs. Ineffectually he tinkered once more with one of the wretched plugs. She joined him ten minutes later, dressing-gowned and beslippered.

"What's eating you?"

"Christ! Can't you see? I suppose you beggered this up the last time you hoovered—not that I can remember when that was!"

She ignored the insult and took the extension from him. He watched her as she tossed her long blonde hair from her face and deftly unscrewed and examined the troublous plugs. Younger than he was—a good deal younger, it seemed—he found her enormously attractive still. He wondered, as he often wondered, whether he had made the right decision, and once more he told himself he had.

The fault was discovered and corrected, and David felt better.

"Cup of coffee, darling?" All sweetness and light.

"Not just yet. I've got to get cracking." He looked out at the overgrown lawn and swore softly as faintly-dotted lines of slanting drizzle formed upon the window pane.

A middle-aged woman, blowzy, unkempt, her hair in cylindrical curlers, materialised from a side door on the ground floor; her quarry was bounding clumsily down the stairs.

"I want to speak to yer."

"Not now, sweetheart. Not now. I'm late."

"If yer can't wait now yer needn't come back. Yer things'll be in the street."

"Now just a minute, sweetheart." He came close to her, leaned his head to one side and laid a hand on each of her shoulders. "What's the trouble? You know I wouldn't do anything to upset you." He smiled pleasantly enough and there was something approaching an engaging frankness in his dark eyes. But she knew him better.

"Yer've got a woman in yer room, 'aven't yer?"

"Now there's no need for you to get jealous, you know that."

She found him repulsive now, and regretted those early days. "Get 'er out and keep 'er out—there's to be no more women 'ere." She slapped his hands from her shoulders.

"She'll be going, she'll be going—don't worry. She's only a young chick. Nowhere to kip down—you know how it is."

"Now!"

"What do you mean, 'now'?"

"Now!"

"Don't be daft. I'm late already, and I'll lose the job if I ain't careful. Be reasonable."

"Yer'll lose yer bed an' all if yer don't do as I tell yer."

The youth took a dirty five-pound note from his hip pocket. "I suppose that'll satisfy you for a day or two, you old bitch."

The woman took the money, but continued to watch him. "It's got to stop."

"Yeah. Yeah."

"How long's she been 'ere?"

"A day or two."

"Fortnight, nearer, yer bleedin' liar."

The youth slammed the door after him, ran down to the bottom of the road, and turned right into the Upper Richmond Road.

Even by his own modest standards, Mr. George Taylor had not made much of a success of his life. Five years previously, an unskilled manual worker, he had accepted "voluntary redundancy" money after the shake-up that followed the reorganisation of the Cowley Steel plant, had then worked for almost a year driving a bulldozer on the M40 construction programme, and spent the next year doing little but casual jobs, and drinking rather too much and gambling rather too much. And then that terrible row and, as a result of it, his present employment. Each morning at 7:15 A.M. he drove his rusting, green Morris Oxford from his Kidlington council house into the city of Oxford, down past Aristotle Lane into Walton Street, and over the concreted track that led through the open fields, between the canal and the railway line, where lay the main city rubbish-dump. Each morning of the working week for the past three years—including the day when Valerie had disappeared—he had made the same journey, with his lunch-time sandwiches and his working overalls beside him on the passenger seat.

Mr. Taylor was an inarticulate man, utterly unable to rationalise into words his favourable attitude towards his present job. It would have been difficult for anyone. The foul detritus of the city was all around him, rotten food and potato-peelings, old mattresses, sheer filth, rats and always (from somewhere) the scavenger gulls. And yet he liked it.

At lunchtime on Monday, 15th, he was sitting with his permanent colleague on the site, a man with a miry face ingrained with dirt, in the wooden hut which formed the only semi-hygienic haven in this wilderness of waste. They were eating their sandwiches and swilling down the thick bread with a dirty-brown brew of ugly-looking tea. Whilst his companion mused over the racing columns of the *Sun*, George Taylor sat silent, a weary expression on his stolid face. The letter had brought the whole thing back to the forefront of his mind and he was thinking again of Valerie. Had he been right to persuade the wife to take it to the police? He didn't know. They would soon be round again; in fact he was surprised they hadn't been round already. It would upset the wife again—and she'd been nothing but a bag of nerves from the beginning. Funny that the letter had come just after Inspector Ainley was killed. Clever man, Ainley. He'd been round to see them only three weeks ago. Not official, like, but he was the sort of bloke who never let anything go. Like a dog with a bone.

Valerie . . . He'd thought a lot of Valerie.

A corporation vehicle lumbered to a halt outside the hut, and George Taylor poked his head through the door. "On the top side, Jack. Shan't be a minute." He pointed vaguely away to the far corner of the tip, swallowed the last few mouthfuls of his tea and prepared for the afternoon's work.

At the far edge of the tip the hydraulic piston whirred into life and the back of the lorry tilted slowly down and its contents were deposited upon the sea of stinking refuse.

For Morse, this same Monday was the first day of a frustrating week. Another series of incendiary devices had been set off over the weekend in clubs and cinemas, and the whole of the top brass, including himself, had been summoned into urgent conclave. It was imperative that all available police personnel should be mobilised. All known suspects from Irish republicans to international anarchists were to be visited and questioned. The Chief Constable wanted quick results.

On Friday morning a series of arrests were made in a dawn swoop, and later that day eight persons were charged with conspiracy to cause explosions in public places. Morse's own contribution to the successful outcome of the week's enquiries had been virtually nil.

Chapter Five

She turned away, but with the autumn weather
Compelled my imagination many days,
Many days and many hours.
T. S. ELIOT, *La Figlia Che Piange*

As he lay abed on Sunday, 21st September, Morse was beset by the nagging feeling that there was so much to be done if only he could summon up the mental resolve to begin. It was like deferring a long-promised letter; the intention lay on the mind so heavily that the simple task seemed progressively to assume almost gigantic proportions. True, he had written to the headmaster of the Roger Bacon Comprehensive School—and had received an immediate and helpful reply. But that was all; and he felt reluctant to follow it up. Most of his fanciful notions about the Taylor girl had evaporated during the past week of sober, tedious routine, and he had begun to suspect that further investigation into Valerie's disappearance would involve little more than an unwelcome continuation of similar sober and tedious routine. But he was in charge now. It was up to him.

Half-past nine already. His head ached and he resolved on a day of total abstinence. He turned over, buried his head in the pillow, and tried to think of nothing. But for Morse such a blessed state of nihilism was utterly impossible. He finally arose at ten, washed and shaved and set off briskly down the road for a Sunday morning newspaper. It was no more than twenty minutes' walk and

Morse enjoyed the stroll. His head felt clearer already and he swung along almost merrily, mentally debating whether to buy the *News of the World* or the *Sunday Times*. It was the regular hebdomadal debate which paralleled the struggle in Morse's character between the Coarse and the Cultured. Sometimes he bought one; sometimes he bought the other. Today he bought both.

At half-past eleven he switched on his portable to listen to Record Review on Radio Three, and sank back in his favourite armchair, a cup of hot, strong coffee at his elbow. Life was good sometimes. He picked up the *News of the World*, and for ten minutes wallowed in the Shocking Revelations and Startling Exposures which the researchers of that newspaper had somehow managed to rake together during the past seven days. There were several juicy articles and Morse started on the secret sex-life of a glamorous Hollywood pussycat. But it began to pall after the first few paragraphs. Ill-written and (more to the point) not even mildly titillating; it was always the same. Morse firmly believed that there was nothing so unsatisfactory as this kind of half-way-house pornography; he liked it hot or not at all. He wouldn't buy the wretched paper again. Yet he had made the same decision so many times before, and knew that next week again he would fall the same silly sucker for the same salacious front-page promises. But for this morning he'd had enough. So much so that he gave no more than a passing glance to a provocative photograph of a seductive starlet exposing one half of her million-dollar breasts.

After relegating (as always) the Business News Section to the waste-paper basket, he graduated to the *Sunday Times*. He winced to see that Oxford United had been comprehensively trounced, read the leading articles and most of the literary reviews, tried unsuccessfully to solve the bridge problem, and finally turned to the Letters. Pensions, Pollution, Private Medicine—same old topics; but a good deal of sound commonsense. And then his eye caught a letter which made him sit bolt upright. He read it and a puzzled look came to his face. August 24th? He couldn't have bought the *Sunday Times* that week. He read the short letter again.

> *To the Editor. Dear Sir,*
>   *My wife and I wish to express our deep gratitude to your newspaper for the feature "Girls Who Run Away from Home" (Colour Suppt. August 24th). As a direct result of reading the article, our only daughter, Christine, returned home last week after being away for over a year. We thank you most sincerely.*
> *Mr. and Mrs. J. Richardson (Kidderminster).*

Morse got up and went to a large pile of newspapers neatly bundled in string that lay in the hallway beside the front door. The Boy Scouts collected them once a month, and although Morse had never been a tenderfoot himself he gave the movement his qualified approval. Impatiently he tore at the string and delved into the pile. 31st August. 14th September. But no 24th August. It may have gone with the last pile. Blast. He looked through again, but it wasn't there. Now who might have a copy? He tried his next-door neighbour, but on reflection he might have saved himself the bother. What about Lewis? Unlikely, yet worth a try. He telephoned his number.

"Lewis? Morse here."

"Ah. Morning, sir."

"Lewis, do you take the *Sunday Times*?"

" 'Fraid not, sir. We have the *Sunday Mirror*." He sounded somewhat apologetic about his Sabbath-day reading.

"Oh."

"I could get you a copy, I suppose."

"I've got today's. I want the copy for August 24th."

It was Sergeant Lewis's turn to say, "Oh."

"I can't really understand an intelligent man like you, Lewis, not taking a decent Sunday newspaper."

"The sport's pretty good in the *Sunday Mirror*, sir."

"Is it? You'd better bring it along with you in the morning, then."

Lewis brightened. "I won't forget."

Morse thanked him and rang off. He had almost said he would swop it for his own copy of the *News of the World*, but considered it not improper to conceal from his subordinates certain aspects of his own depravity.

He could always get a back copy from the Reference Library. It could wait, he told himself. And yet it couldn't wait. Again he read the letter from the parents of the prodigal daughter. They would be extra-pleased now, with a letter in the newspaper, to boot. Dad would probably cut it out and keep it in his wallet—now that the family unit was functioning once more. We were all so vain. Cuttings, clippings and that sort of thing. Morse still kept his batting averages somewhere . . .

And suddenly it hit him. It all fitted. Four or five weeks ago Ainley had resurrected the Taylor case of his own accord and pursued it in his own spare time. Some reporter had been along to Thames Valley Police and got Ainley to spill the beans on the Taylor girl. Ainley had given him the facts (no fancies with Ainley!) and somehow, as a result of seeing the facts again, he had spotted something that he had missed before. It was just like doing a crossword puzzle. Get stuck. Leave it for ten minutes. Try again—and eureka! It happened to everyone like that. And, he repeated to himself, *Ainley had seen something new*. That must be it.

As a corollary to this, it occurred to Morse that if Ainley had taken a hand in the article, not only would Valerie Taylor have been one of the missing girls featured, but Ainley himself would almost certainly have kept the printed article—just as surely as Mr. J. Richardson would be sticking his own printed letter into his Kidderminster wallet.

He rang Mrs. Ainley. "Eileen?" (Right this time.) "Morse here. Look, do you happen to have kept that bit of the *Sunday Times*—you know, that bit about missing girls?"

"You mean the one they saw Richard about?" He *had* been right.

"That's the one."

"Yes. I kept it, of course. It mentioned Richard several times."

"Can I, er, can I come round and have a look at it?"

"You can have it with pleasure. I don't want it any more."

Some half an hour later, forgetful of his earlier pledge, Morse was seated with a pint of flat beer and a soggy steak-and-mushroom pie. He read the article through with a feeling of anti-climax. Six girls were featured—after the preliminary sociological blurb about the problems of adolescence—with a couple of columns on each of them. But the central slant was on the parents the girls had left behind them. "The light in the hall has been left on every night since she went," as one of the anguished mothers was reported. It was pathetic and it was distressing. There were pictures, too. First, pictures of the girls, although (of necessity) none of the photographs was of a very recent vintage, and two or three (including that of Valerie herself) were of less than definitive clarity. And thus it was for the first time that Chief Inspector Morse looked down upon the face of Valerie Taylor. Of the six she would certainly be in the running for the beauty crown—though run close by a honey of a girl from Brighton. Attractive face, full mouth, come-hither eyes, nice eyebrows (plucked, thought Morse) and long dark-brown hair. Just the face—no figure to admire. And then, over the page, the pictures of the parents. Mr. and Mrs. Taylor seemed an unremarkable pair, seated unnaturally forward on the shabby sofa: Mr. wearing a cheap Woolworth tie, with his rolled-up sleeves revealing a large purple tattoo on his broad right forearm; Mrs. wearing a plain cotton dress with a cameo brooch somewhat ostentatiously pinned to the collar. And on a low table beside them, carefully brought into the focus of the photograph, a cohort of congratulatory cards for their 18th wedding anniversary. It was predictable and posed, and Morse felt that a few tears might well have been nearer the truth.

He ordered another pint and sat down to read the commentary on Valerie's disappearance.

Two years ago, the month of June enjoyed a long, unbroken spell of sunny weather, and Tuesday 10th June was a particularly sweltering day at the village of Kidlington in the county of Oxfordshire. At 12:30 P.M. Valerie Taylor left the Roger Bacon Comprehensive

School to walk to her home in Hatfield Way on the council estate nearby, no more than six or seven hundred yards from the school. Like many of her friends Valerie disliked school dinners and for the previous year had returned home each lunchtime. On the day of her daughter's disappearance Valerie's mother, Mrs. Grace Taylor, had prepared a ham salad, with blackcurrant tart and custard for sweet, and together mother and daughter ate the meal at the kitchen table. Afternoon lessons began again at 1:45, and Valerie usually left the house at about 1:25. She did so on 10th June. Nothing seemed amiss that cloudless Tuesday afternoon. Valerie walked down the short front path, turned in the direction of the school, and waved a cheery farewell to her mother. She has never been seen again.

Mr. George Taylor, an employee of the Oxford City Corporation, returned from work at 6:10 P.M. to find his wife in a state of considerable anxiety. It was quite unlike Valerie not to tell her mother if she was likely to be late, yet at that point there seemed little cause for immediate concern. The minutes ticked by; the quarters chimed on the Taylors' grandfather clock, and then the hours. At 8:00 P.M. Mr. Taylor got into his car and drove to the school. Only the caretaker was still on the premises and he could be of no help. Mr. Taylor then called at the homes of several of Valerie's friends, but they likewise could tell him nothing. None of them could remember seeing Valerie that afternoon, but it had been "games" and it was nothing unusual for pupils to slip away quietly from the sports field.

When Mr. Taylor returned home it was 9:00 P.M. "There must be some simple explanation," he told his wife; but if there was, it was not forthcoming, and the time pressed slowly on. 10:00 P.M. 11:00 P.M. Still nothing. George Taylor suggested they should notify the police, but his wife was terrified of taking such a step.

When I interviewed them this week both Mr. and Mrs. Taylor were reluctant (and understandably so) to talk about the agonies they suffered that night. Throughout the long vigil it was Grace Taylor who feared the worst and suffered the most, for her husband felt sure that Valerie had gone off with some boyfriend and would be back the next morning. At 4:00 A.M. he managed to persuade his wife to take two sleeping tablets and he took her upstairs to bed.

She was still sleeping when he left the house at 7:30 A.M., leaving a note saying that he would be back at lunchtime, and that if Valerie still had not returned they would have to call the police. In fact the police were notified earlier than that. Mrs. Taylor had awoken at about nine and, in a distraught state, had rung them from a neighbour's telephone.

Detective Chief Inspector Ainley of the Thames Valley Police was put in charge of the case, and intensive enquiries were immediately begun. During the course of the next week the whole of the area in the vicinity of Valerie's home and the area of woodland behind the school were searched with painstaking care and patience; the river and the reservoir were dragged ... But no trace was found of Valerie Taylor.

Inspector Ainley himself was frankly critical of the delay. At least twelve hours had been lost; fifteen, if the police had been notified as soon as the Taylors' anxiety had begun to deepen into genuine alarm.

Such delay is a common feature of the cases assembled here. Vital time lost; perhaps vital clues thrown to the wind—and all because parents think they will be wasting the time of the police and would seem to look foolish if the wayward offspring should suddenly turn up whilst the police were busy taking statements. It is a common human weakness, and it is only too easy to blame parents like the Taylors. But would we ourselves have acted all that differently? I knew exactly what Mrs. Taylor meant when she said to me, "I felt all the time that if we called the police something dreadful must have happened." Illogical, you may say, but so very understandable.

Mr. and Mrs. Taylor still live on the council estate in Hatfield Way. For over two years now they have waited and prayed for their daughter to return. As in the five other cases discussed here, the police files remain open. "No," said Inspector Ainley, "we shan't be closing them until we find her."

Not bad reporting, thought Morse. There were several things in the article that puzzled him slightly, but he deliberately suppressed the fanciful notions that began to flood his mind. He had been right earlier. When Ainley had got the hard facts down on paper, he had spotted something that for over two years had lurked in the darkness and eluded his grasp. Some clue or other which had monopolised his attention and filled his spare time, and eventually, if indirectly, led to his death.

Just stick to the facts, Morse, stick to the facts! It would be difficult, but he would try. And tomorrow he and Lewis would start on the files wherein lay the facts as Ainley had gleaned them. Anyway, Christine was back in Kidderminster and, like as not, Valerie would be back in Kidlington before the end of the month. The naughty girls were all coming home and would soon be having the same sort of rows they'd had with mum and dad before they left. Life, alas, was like that.

Over his third pint of beer Morse could stem the flood of fancy no longer. He read the article through quickly once again. Yes, there was something wrong there. Only a small thing, but he wondered if it was the same small thing that had set Ainley on a new track ... And the strangest notion began to formulate in the mind so recently dedicated to the pursuit of unembellished fact.

Chapter Six

> He certainly has a great deal of fancy, and a very good
> memory; but, with a perverse ingenuity, he employs these
> qualities as no other person does.
>
> RICHARD BRINSLEY SHERIDAN

As he knocked at the door of Morse's office Sergeant
Lewis, who had thoroughly enjoyed the police routine of
the previous week, wondered just what was in store for
him now. He had worked with the unpredictable
inspector before and got on fairly well with him; but he
had his reservations.

Morse was seated in his black leather chair and before
him on his untidy desk lay a green box-file.

"Ah. Come in, Lewis. I didn't want to start without
you. Wouldn't be fair, would it?" He patted the box-file
with a gesture of deep affection. "It's all there, Lewis,
my boy. All the facts. Ainley was a fact man—no day-
dreaming theorist was Ainley. And we shall follow
where the great man trod. What do you say?" And
without giving his sergeant the slightest opportunity to
say anything, he emptied the contents of the file face
downwards upon the desk. "Shall we start at the top or
the bottom?"

"Might be a good idea to start at the beginning, don't
you think, sir?"

"I think we could make out a good case for starting
at either end—but we shall do as you say." With some

difficulty Morse turned the bulky sheaf of papers the right way up.

"What exactly are we going to do?" asked Lewis blankly.

Morse proceeded to recount his interview with Strange, and then passed across to Lewis the letter received from Valerie Taylor. "And we're taking over, Lewis—you happy about that?" Lewis nodded half-heartedly. "Did you remember the *Sunday Mirror?*"

Lewis dutifully took the paper from his coat pocket and handed it to Morse, who took out his wallet, found his football coupon and with high seriousness began to check his entry. Lewis watched him as his eyes alternately lit up and switched off, before the coupon was comprehensively shredded and hurled in the general direction of the waste-paper basket.

"I shan't be spending next week in the Bahamas, Lewis. What about you?"

"Nor me, sir."

"Do you ever win anything?"

"Few quid last year, sir. But it's a million to one chance—getting a big win."

"Like this bloody business," mumbled Morse, distastefully surveying the fruits of Ainley's labours.

For the next two and a half hours they sat over the Taylor documents, occasionally conferring over an obscure or an interesting point—but for the most part in silence. It would have been clear to an independent witness of these proceedings that Morse read approximately five times as quickly as his sergeant; but whether he remembered five times as much of what he read would have been a much more questionable inference. For Morse found it difficult to concentrate his mind upon the

documents before him. As he saw it, the facts, the bare
unadulterated facts, boiled down to little more than he
had read in the pub the previous day. The statements
before him, checked and signed, appeared merely to confirm the bald, simple truth: after leaving home to return
to school Valerie Taylor had completely vanished. If
Morse wanted a fact, well, he'd got one. Parents, neighbours, teachers, classmates—all had been questioned at
length. And amidst all their well-meaning verbosity they
all had the same thing to say—nothing. Next, reports of
Ainley's own interviews with Mr. and Mrs. Taylor, with
the headmaster, with Valerie's form tutor, with her
games mistress and with two of her boyfriends. (Ainley
had clearly liked the headmaster, and equally clearly had
disapproved of one of the boyfriends.) All nicely, neatly
written in the small, rounded hand that Morse had
already seen. But—nothing. Next, reports of general
police enquiries and searches, and reports of the missing
girl being spotted in Birmingham, Clacton, London,
Reading, Southend, and a remote village in Morayshire.
All wild goose chases. All false alarms. Next, personal
and medical reports on Valerie herself. She did not
appear academically gifted in any way; or if she was, she
had so far successfully concealed her scholastic potential
from her teachers. School reports suggested a failure,
except in practical subjects, to make the best of her
limited abilities (familiar phrases!), but she seemed a
personable enough young lady, well-liked (Morse drew
his own conclusions) by her fellow pupils of either sex.
On the day of her disappearance she was attested by
school records to be seventeen years and five months old,
and 5′ 6″ in height. In her previous academic year she
had taken four C.S.E. subjects, without signal success,

and she was at that time sitting three G.C.E. O-level subjects—English, French and Applied Science. From the medical report it appeared that Valerie was quite remarkably healthy. There were no entries on her National Health medical card for the last three years, and before that only measles and a bad cut on the index finger of her left hand. Next, a report, over which Ainley had obviously (and properly) taken considerable pains, on the possibility of any trouble on the domestic front which may have caused friction between Valerie and her parents, and led to her running away from home. On this most important point Ainley had gone to the trouble of writing out two sheets of foolscap in his own fair hand; but the conclusions were negative. On the evidence of Valerie's form tutor (among whose manifold duties something designated "pastoral care" appeared a high priority), on the evidence of the parents themselves, of the neighbours and of Valerie's own friends, there seemed little reason to assume anything but the perfectly normal ups-and-downs in the relationship between the members of the Taylor clan. Rows, of course. Valerie had been home very late once or twice from dances and discos, and Mrs. Taylor could use a sharp tongue. (Who couldn't?) Ainley's own conclusion was that he could find no immediate cause within the family circle to account for a minor squabble—let alone the inexplicable departure of an only daughter. In short—nothing. Morse thought of the old Latin proverb. *Ex nihilo nihil fit.* Out of nothing you'll get nothing. Not that it helped in any way.

Apart from the typed and handwritten documents, there were three maps: an ordnance-survey map of the Oxford district showing the areas covered by the search

parties; a larger map of the Oxfordshire region on which
the major road and rail routes were marked with cryptic
symbols; and finally a sketch-map of the streets between
the Roger Bacon School and the Taylors' house, with
Valerie's route to and from her school carefully and
neatly drawn in in red Biro by the late chief inspector.
Whilst Lewis was plodding along, several miles behind
his master, the master himself appeared to be finding
something of extraordinary interest in this last item: his
right hand shaded his forehead and he seemed to Lewis
in throes of the deepest contemplation.

"Found something, sir?"

"Uh? What?" Morse's head jerked back and the idle
day-dream was over.

"The sketch-map, sir."

"Ah, yes. The map. Very interesting. Yes." He looked
at it again, decided that he was unable to recapture whatever interest may have previously lain therein and picked
up the *Sunday Mirror* once more. He read his horoscope:

> *You're doing better than you realise, so there could
> be a major breakthrough as far as romance is con-
> cerned. This week will certainly blossom if you spend
> it with someone witty and bright.*

He looked glumly across at Lewis, who for the
moment at least appeared neither very witty nor very
bright.

"Well, Lewis. What do you think?"

"I've not quite finished yet, sir."

"But you must have some ideas, surely."

"Not yet."

"Oh, come on. What do you think happened to her?"

Lewis thought hard, and finally gave expression to a conviction which had grown steadily stronger the more he had read. "I think she got a lift and ended up in London. That's where they all end up."

"You think she's still alive, then?"

Lewis looked at his chief in some surprise. "Don't you?"

"Let's go for a drink," said Morse.

They walked out of the Thames Valley H.Q. and at the Belisha crossing negotiated the busy main road that linked Oxford with Banbury.

"Where are we going, sir?"

Morse took Ainley's hand-drawn map from his pocket. "I thought we ought to take a gentle stroll over the ground, Lewis. You never know."

The council estate was situated off the main road, to their left as they walked away from Oxford, and very soon they stood in Hatfield Way.

"We going to call?"

"Got to make a start somewhere, I suppose," said Morse.

The house was a neat, well-built property, with a circular rose-bed cut into the centre of the well-tended front lawn. Morse rang the bell, and rang again. It seemed that Mrs. Taylor was out. Inquisitively Morse peered through the front window, but could see little more than a large, red settee and a diagonal line of ducks winging their inevitable way towards the ceiling. The two men walked away, carefully closing the gate behind them.

"If I remember rightly, Lewis, there's a pub just around the corner."

They ordered a cheese cob and a pint apiece and

Morse handed to Lewis the Colour Supplement of 24th August.

"Have a quick look at that."

Ten minutes later, with Morse's glass empty and Lewis's barely touched, it was clear that the quick look was becoming a rather long look, and Morse replenished his own glass with some impatience.

"Well? What's troubling you?"

"They haven't got it quite right, though, have they?"

Morse looked at him sharply. "What's that supposed to mean?"

"Well. It says here that she was never seen again after leaving the house."

"She wasn't."

"What about the lollipop-man?"

"The *what*?"

"The lollipop-man. It was in the file."

"Oh, was it?"

"You did seem a bit tired, I thought, sir."

"Tired? Nonsense. You need another pint." He drained what was left in his own glass, picked up Lewis's and walked across to the bar.

An elegantly-dressed woman with a full figure and pleasingly slim legs had just bought a double whisky and was pouring a modicum of water into it, the heavy diamond rings on the fingers of her left hand sparkling wickedly and bright.

"Oh, and Bert, twenty Embassy, please." The landlord reached behind him, handed over the cigarettes, squinted his eyes as he calculated the tariff, gave her the change, said "Ta, luv," and turned his attention to Morse.

"Same again, sir?"

As the woman turned from the counter, Morse felt sure

he had seen her somewhere before. He seldom forgot a face. Still, if she lived in Kidlington, he could have seen her anywhere. But he kept looking at her; so much so that Lewis began to suspect the inspector's intentions. She was all right—quite nice, in fact. Mid-thirties, perhaps, nice face. But the old boy must be hard up if . . .

Two dusty-looking builders came in, bought their ale and sat down to play dominoes. As they walked to the table one of them called over to the woman: "Hallo, Grace. All right?" Morse showed little surprise. Hell of a sight better-looking than her photograph suggested, though.

At 1:20 Morse decided it was time to go. They walked back the way they had come, past the Taylors' house and down to the main road, busy at this time with a virtually continuous stream of traffic either way. Here they turned right and came up to the Belisha crossing.

"Do you think that's our lollipop-man?" asked Morse. In the middle of the road stood a white-coated attendant in a peak cap, wielding the sceptre of his authority like an arthritic bishop with a crook. Several pupils of the Roger Bacon School were crossing under the aegis of the standard-bearer, the girls in white blouses, grey skirts and red knee-length socks, the boys (it seemed to Morse) in assorted combinations of any old garments. When the attendant returned from mid-stream, Morse spoke to him in what he liked to think of as his intimate, avuncular manner.

"Been doing this long?"

"Just over a year." He was a small, red-faced man with gnarled hands.

"Know the chap who did it before?"

"You mean old Joe. 'Course I did. 'E did it for—oh, five or six year."

"Retired now, has he?"

"Ah. S'pose you could say so. Poor old Joe. Got knocked ovver—feller on a motorbike. Mind you, old Joe were gettin' a bit slow. Seventy-two he were when he were knocked ovver. Broke 'is 'ip. Poor old Joe."

"Not still in hospital, I hope?" Morse fervently prayed that poor old Joe was still limping along somewhere in the land of the living.

"No. Not 'im. Down at the old folkses place at Cowley."

"Well, you be careful," said Morse, as he and Lewis crossed over with another group of schoolchildren, and stood and watched them as they dawdled past the line of shops and the public lavatories, and reluctantly turned into the main drive leading to the school.

Back in the office, Morse read aloud the relevant part of the testimony of Mr. Joseph Godberry, Oxford Road, Kidlington:

"I almost always saw Valerie Taylor at dinner times, and I saw her on 10th June. She didn't cross by my Belisha because when I saw her she was on the other side of the road. She was running fairly quickly as if she was in a dickens of a hurry to meet somebody. But I remember she waved to me. I am quite sure it was Valerie. She would often stop and have a quick word with me. 'Joe' she called me, like most of them. She was a very nice girl and always cheery. I don't know what she did after I saw her. I thought she was going back to school."

Morse looked thoughtful. "I wonder, now," he said.

"Wonder what, sir?"

Morse was looking into the far distance, through the office window, and into the filmy blue beyond, excitement glowing in his eyes. "I was just wondering if she was carrying a bag of some sort when old Joe Godberry saw her."

Lewis looked as mystified as he felt, but received no further elucidation. "You see," said Morse, his eyes gradually refocusing on his sergeant, "you see, if she *was*, I'm beginning to think that you're wrong."

"Wrong, sir?"

"Yes, wrong. You said you thought Valerie Taylor was still alive, didn't you?"

"Well, yes. I think she is."

"And I think, *think*, mind you, that you're wrong, Lewis. *I think that Valerie Taylor is almost certainly dead.*"

Chapter Seven

> And French she spak ful faire and fetisly,
> After the scole of Stratford atte Bowe,
> For French of Paris was to hir unknowe.
> GEOFFREY CHAUCER, *Canterbury Tales*

Donald Phillipson arrived in school at 8:00 A.M. on Tuesday morning. The Michaelmas term had been under way for one full week now and things were going well. The anti-litter campaign was proving moderately successful, the new caretaker seemed an amenable sort of fellow, and the Parent-Teacher Association had (somewhat surprisingly, he thought) backed him up to the hilt in his plea for a more rigid ruling on school uniforms. On the academic side, only four members of staff had left in the summer (one quarter the previous year's total), the G.C.E. and C.S.E. results had been markedly better than before, and the present term saw the first full intake of thirteen-plus pupils, among whom (if junior-school headmasters could be believed) were some real high-flyers. Perhaps in a few years' time there would be one or two Open Awards at Oxbridge ... Yes, he felt more than a little pleased with himself and with life this Tuesday morning. The only thing that marred the immediate prospect was a cloud, rather larger than a man's hand, on the not-so-distant horizon. But he felt confident that he would be able to weather whatever storm might break from that quarter, although he must think things through rather more carefully than he had done hitherto.

At 8:20 the head boy and the head girl would be coming to his study, as they did each morning, and there were several matters requiring his prompt attention. He heard Mrs. Webb come in at 8:15, and Baines at 8:30. Punctuality was sharper, too. He did a small amount of teaching with the sixth form (he was an historian), but he kept Tuesdays completely free. It had been his practice since he was appointed to take off Tuesday afternoons completely and he looked forward to a fairly gentle day.

The morning's activities went off well enough—even the singing of the hymns in assembly was improving—until 11:15 when Mrs. Webb received the telephone call.

"Is the headmaster there?"

"Who shall I say is calling, please?"

"Morse. Inspector Morse."

"Oh, just a minute, sir. I'll see if the headmaster's free." She dialled the head's extension. "Inspector Morse would like a word with you, sir. Shall I put him through?"

"Oh. Er. Yes, of course."

Mrs. Webb switched the outside call to the headmaster's study, hesitated a moment, and then quickly lifted the receiver to her ear again.

". . . hear from you. Can I help?"

"I hope you can, sir. It's about the Taylor girl. There are one or two things I'd like to ask you about."

"Look, inspector. It's not really very convenient to talk at the minute—I'm interviewing some of the new pupils this morning. Don't you think it would be . . ." Mrs. Webb put the phone down quickly and quietly, and when Phillipson came out her typewriter was chattering along merrily. "Mrs. Webb, Inspector Morse will be coming in this afternoon at three o'clock, so I shall have to be here. Can you arrange some tea and biscuits for us?"

"Of course." She made a note in her shorthand book. "Just the two of you?"

"No. Three. He's bringing a sergeant along—I forgot his name."

The anonymous sergeant himself was spending the same morning at the old people's home in Cowley, and finding Mr. Joseph Godberry (in small doses) an interesting sort of fellow. He had fought at Mons in the '14–'18 War, had slept, by his own account, with all the tarts within a ten mile radius of Rouen, and been invalided out of the army in 1917 (probably from sexual fatigue, thought Lewis). He reminisced at considerable length as he sat by his bed in D ward, accepting his present confinement with a certain dignity and good humour. He explained that he could hardly walk now and recounted to Lewis in great detail the circumstances and consequences of his memorable accident. In fact the "accident," together with Mons and Rouen, had become one of the major incidents of his life and times; and it was with some difficulty that Lewis managed to steer Joe's thoughts to the disappearance of Valerie Taylor. Oh, he remembered her, of course. Very nice girl, Valerie. In London, bet your bottom dollar. Very nice girl, Valerie.

But could Joe remember the day she disappeared? Lewis listened carefully as he rambled on, repeating with surprising coherence and accuracy most of what he had said in his statement to the police. In Lewis's opinion, he was a good witness, but he was becoming tired and Lewis felt the moment had come to put the one question which Morse had been so eager for him to ask.

"Do you remember by any chance if Valerie was carrying anything when you saw her that day—the day she disappeared?"

Joe moved uneasily in his chair and slowly turned his rheumy old eyes on Lewis. Something seemed to be stirring there and Lewis pressed home the point.

"You know what I mean, a carrier bag, or a case, or anything like that?"

"Funny you should say that," he said at last. "I never thought about it afore." He looked as though he were about to haul out some hazy memory on to the shores of light, and Lewis held his breath and waited. "I reckon as you're right, you know. She were carryin' something. That's it. She were carryin' a bag of some sort; carryin' it in 'er left hand, if me memory serves me correck."

In Phillipson's study formalities were exchanged in friendly fashion. Morse asked polite questions about the school—quite at his best, thought Lewis. But the mood was to change swiftly.

Morse informed the headmaster that he had taken over the Taylor case from Chief Inspector Ainley, and the ceasefire was duly observed for a further few minutes whilst the proper commiserations were expressed. It was only when he produced the letter from Valerie that Morse's manner appeared to Lewis to become strangely abrasive.

Phillipson read through the letter quickly.

"Well?" said Morse.

Lewis felt that the headmaster was more surprised by the sharp tone in the inspector's voice than by the arrival of a letter from his troublesome, long-lost ex-pupil.

"Well what?" Phillipson clearly was not a man easily bullied.

"Is it her writing?"

"I can't tell. Don't her parents know?"

Morse ignored the question. "You can't tell me." The statement was flat and final, with the tacit implication that he had expected something better.

"No."

"Have you got some of her old exercise books we could look at?"

"I don't really know, inspector."

"Who would know?" Again the astringent impatience in his voice.

"Perhaps Baines would."

"Ask him in, please," snapped Morse.

"I'm sorry, inspector, but Baines has this afternoon off. Tuesday is games afternoon and . . ."

"I know, yes. So Baines can't help us either. Who can?"

Phillipson got up and opened the study door. "Mrs. Webb? Will you come in here a minute, please."

Was Lewis mistaken, or did she throw a rather frightened glance in Morse's direction?

"Mrs. Webb, the inspector here wonders if any of Valerie Taylor's old exercise books may have been kept somewhere in the school. What do you think?"

"They may be in the store-room, I suppose, sir."

"Would it be the usual practice for pupils themselves to keep them?" Morse addressed himself directly to the secretary.

"Yes, it would. But in this case I should think her desk would have been turned out at the end of term and the books would be . . ." She was getting lost and looked helplessly towards the headmaster.

"I'm sure Mrs. Webb is right, inspector. If the books are anywhere, they will be in the store-room."

Mrs. Webb nodded, swallowed hard and was given leave to withdraw.

"We'd better have a look in the store-room, then. You've no objections?"

"Of course not. But it's in a bit of a mess, I should think. You know how things are at the beginning of term."

Morse smiled weakly and neither confirmed nor refuted his knowledge of such matters.

They walked along the corridor, down some steps, and turned off right through a classroom, wherein all the chairs were neatly placed upon the tops of the desks. The school was virtually deserted, but intermittent shrieks of joyous laughter from the direction of the sports field seemed to belie the view that games were too unpopular with the majority of pupils.

The headmaster unlocked the door to the large unwindowed, unventilated store-room, and when the three men entered Lewis found himself facing with some foreboding the piles of dusty textbooks, files and stationery.

"I'm afraid it may be a longish job," said Phillipson, with some irritation in his voice. "If you like, I could get some of the staff to go through all the old exercise books here." He pointed vaguely to great piles of books stacked on wooden shelves along the far wall.

"That's very kind of you, headmaster, but we can deal with this all right. No problem. If we can call back to your office when we've finished here?" It was an unmistakable hint that the presence of the headmaster would not profit the present stage of the investigation, and Morse listened carefully as Phillipson retraced his steps to his study. "He's a bit worried, wouldn't you say, Lewis?"

"I don't blame him, sir. You've been pretty sharp with him."

"Serve him right," said Morse.

"What's he done wrong?"

"I spoke to him on the phone this morning and he said he was interviewing some new pupils."

"Perhaps he was," suggested the honest Lewis.

"I had the feeling he didn't want to talk just then, and I was right." Lewis looked at him quizzically. "I heard a click on the line while we were talking. You can guess who was listening in."

"Mrs. Webb?"

"Mrs. Webb. I rang again later and asked her why she'd been eavesdropping. She denied it, of course; but I told her I'd forget all about it if she told me the truth about who had been in the headmaster's study. She was scared—for her job, I suppose. Anyway, she said that nobody had been in with Phillipson when I rang."

Lewis opened his mouth to say something but Morse was already pouncing on the piles of textbooks.

"Ah, Keats. Fine poet, Keats. You should read him, Lewis . . . Well, well, well. *Travels with a Donkey*." He picked up a copy and began to read under the cobwebbed central lightbulb.

Lewis made for the far wall of the room, where whole stacks of exercise books, used and unused, mauve, green, blue and orange, were heaped upon the shelves, some bundled neatly, but the majority in loose disarray. Lewis, as always, tackled his task with systematic thoroughness, although he doubted whether he would find anything. Fortunately, it was a good deal easier going than he had thought.

Half an hour later he found them. A pile of loose books, eight of them, each with the name Valerie Taylor inscribed in capitals on the front cover. He blew the dust off the edges and savoured his brief moment of triumph.

"I've found them, sir."

"Well done. Leave them where they are—don't touch them."

"I already have, I'm afraid, sir."

"Was there any dust on the top book?"

The sweet taste of success had already turned sour. "I don't know."

"Give 'em here." Morse was clearly very cross and muttered angrily under his breath.

"Pardon, sir?"

"I said I think someone else may well have been looking at these books recently. That's what I said!"

"I don't think the top book *was* dusty, sir. Just the edges."

"And where's the dust on the edges?"

"I blew it off."

"You blew it off! Christ, man. We've got a murder on our hands here, and we're supposed to be investigating it—not blowing all the bloody clues away!"

He gradually calmed down, and with a silent Lewis returned to Phillipson's study. It was now 4:30 and apart from the headmaster and Mrs. Webb the school was empty.

"I see you found the books."

Morse nodded curtly, and the three men sat down once

more. "Bit of luck, really," continued Phillipson. "It's a wonder they weren't thrown away."

"Where *do* you throw old books away?" It seemed an odd question.

"Funnily enough they get buried—down on the rubbish dump. It's a difficult job burning a whole lot of books, you know."

"Unless you've got a fiery furnace," said Morse slowly.

"Well, yes. But even . . ."

"You've got a furnace here?"

"Yes, we have. But . . ."

"And that would burn just about anything, would it?"

"Yes. But as I was going . . ." Again Morse cut him short.

"Would it burn a body all right?" His words hung in the air, and Lewis shivered involuntarily. Phillipson's eyes were steady as he looked directly at Morse.

"Yes. It would burn a body, and it wouldn't leave much trace, either."

Morse appeared to accept the remark without the slightest surprise or interest. "Let's get back to these books a minute, sir, if we may. Are there any missing?"

Phillipson hadn't the remotest idea and breathed an inner sigh of relief as Baines (answering an earlier urgent summons) knocked on the study door, was ushered in and introduced.

It was immediately clear that the second master was a mine of information on all curricular queries, and within ten minutes Morse had copies of the information he required: Valerie's timetable for the summer term in which she disappeared, her homework schedule for the same period, and a list of her subject teachers. No books, it seemed, were missing. He made some complimentary remarks on Baines's efficiency, and the second master's shrewd eyes blinked with gratification.

After they had all gone Phillipson sat behind his desk and groaned inwardly. In the space of one short afternoon the cloud on the horizon had grown to menacing proportions. What a bloody fool he had been!

As a husband and a father, Sergeant Lewis experienced the delights and despondencies, the difficulties and the duties of family life, and with Morse's blessing returned home at 5:45 P.M.

At the same time Morse himself, with no such responsibilities, returned to his office at police H.Q. He was quite looking forward to his evening's work.

First he studied Valerie's timetable for each of her Tuesday mornings during that last summer term.

9:15–10:00	Environmental Studies
10:00–10:45	Applied Science
10:45–11:00	Break
11:00–11:45	Sociology
11:45–12:30	French

He contemplated with supercilious disdain the academic disciplines (sub-disciplines, he would call them) which were now monopolising the secondary school curricula. "Environmental Studies," he doubted, was little more than a euphemism for occasional visits to the gas-works, the fire-station and the sewage installations; whilst for Sociology and Sociologists he had nothing but sour contempt, and could never discover either what was entailed in its subject-matter or how its practitioners deployed their dubious talents. With such a plethora of non-subjects crowding the timetable there was no room for the traditional disciplines taught in his own day . . . But French now. At least that had a bit of backbone, although he had always felt that a language which sanctioned the pronunciation of *donne*, *donnes* and *donnent* without the slightest differentiation could hardly deserve to be taken seriously. Anyway, she was studying French and it was French which won the day. He consulted the homework schedule and found that French was set on Friday evenings and (he guessed) it might be collected in and marked on the following Monday. He checked to see that French appeared on Monday's timetable. It did. And then handed back to the pupils on the Tuesday, perhaps? That is, if the teacher had remembered to set the home-work and if the teacher had been conscientious enough to mark it straightaway. Who was the teacher, anyway? He looked at the list. Mr. D. Acum. Well, a little inspection of Mr. Acum's discharge of duty was called for, and Morse flicked through the orange exercise book until he came to the last entry. He found the date, Friday, 6th June, carefully filled in and neatly underlined. He then turned his attention to Valerie's efforts, which had entailed the translation from English into French of ten short sentences. Judging, however, from the enormous quantity of red ink the despairing D. Acum had seen fit to squander upon her versions, judging from the treble underlinings, and the pathetic "Oh dear" written beside one particularly heinous blunder, Valerie's linguistic prowess seemed extraordinarily limited. But Morse's eye was not on the exercise itself. He had spotted it as soon as he turned to the page. Beneath the exercise Acum had written: "See me immediately after the lesson." Morse felt a shiver of excitement. "After the lesson." 12:30 P.M. Acum must have been one of the very last people to have seen Valerie before she . . . Before she what? He looked through his office window at the pale blue sky gradually edging into dusk—and he wondered. Had Ainley got on to Acum? Why had Acum wished to see Valerie Taylor that far-off Tuesday morning? The most likely answer, he supposed, was that Valerie would be ticked off good and proper for such disgusting work. But the simple fact remained: Acum had been one of the very last people to see Valerie alive.

Before leaving for home Morse looked once again at the short letter from Valerie and compared its handwriting with that of the exercise books. On the face of it, certainly, there seemed an undeniable similarity. But for a definitive opinion he would have to wait until the forensic experts had considered the specimens; and that would mean waiting until fairly late tomorrow evening, for he and Lewis had a trip to London in the morning. Would he believe them if their report stated categorically that the letter was written by Valerie Taylor? Yes. He would have no choice but to accept such a conclusion. But he thought he need have little worry on that score: for it was now his firm conviction that the letter had not been written by Valerie at all, but by someone who had carefully copied her writing—copied it rather *too* well, in fact. Further, Morse felt he knew who had copied it, although the reasons for the deception he could, at this stage, only dimly descry. Quite indubitably now, in his own mind, the case was one of wilful murder.

Chapter Eight

Gypsy Rose Lee, the strip-tease artist, has arrived in Holly-wood with twelve empty trunks.
                        HARRY V. WADE, American Columnist

Doubtless in its hey-day a fine example of neo-Georgian elegance, the sturdily and attractively built house was now fallen on seedier times, the stuccoed front dirty and chipped. Stuck to one of the stout pillars which flanked the peeling front door was an outdated poster announcing the arrival of Maharaj Ji, and on the other, in black figures, the number 42.

The door was opened by a blowzy, middle-aged woman, a cigarette drooping from her lips and a head-scarf half hiding the hair-curlers—like a caricature of the screen charlady. She seemed to eye them shrewdly, but it may have been nothing more than the effect of avoiding the smoke from her cigarette.

"Police. It's Mrs., er?"

"Gibbs. What can I do for yer?"

"Can we come in?"

She hesitated, then moved aside. The door was closed and the two men stood awkwardly in the entrance hall, where they saw neither seats nor chairs of any description, only a grandfather clock showing the correct time (10:30), an overloaded coat-rack and an umbrella stand incongruously housing a set of ancient golf-clubs. It became clear that they were not to be invited into the cosiness of any inner sanctum.

"About three weeks ago, you had a call I think from one of my colleagues—Inspector Ainley." She considered the statement guardedly, nodded and said nothing. "You may have read in the papers that after he left here he was killed in a road accident."

Mrs. Gibbs hadn't, and the lady's latent humanity stirred to the extent of a mumbled phrase of commiseration if not to the removal of the cigarette from her lips, and Morse knew that he would have to chance his arm a bit.

"He wrote, of course, a full report of his visit here and, er, I think you will have a good idea why we've called again today."

"Nothing to do with me, is it?"

Morse seized his opportunity. "Oh, no, Mrs. Gibbs. Nothing at all. That was quite clear from the report. But naturally we need your help, if you'll be kind enough . . ."

" 'E's not 'ere. 'E's at work—if yer can call it work. Not that 'e'll be 'ere much longer, anyway. Caused me quite enough trouble, 'e 'as."

"Can we see his room?"

She hesitated. "Yer got the authority?"

It was Morse's turn to hesitate, before suddenly producing an official-looking document from his breast pocket.

Mrs. Gibbs fiddled in her apron pocket for her spectacles. "That other policeman—'e told me all about the legal position. Said as 'ow I shouldn't let anyone in 'ere as 'adn't got the proper authority."

Trust Ainley, thought Morse. "He was quite right of course." Morse directed the now bespectacled lady's attention to an impressive-looking signature and beneath it, in printed capitals, CHIEF CONSTABLE (OXON). It was enough, and Morse quickly repocketed the cyclostyled letter about the retirement pensions of police officers at and above the rank of Chief Inspector.

They made their way up three flights of dusty stairs, where Mrs. Gibbs produced a key from her multi-purpose apron pocket and opened a dingy, brown-painted door.

"I'll be downstairs when yer've finished."

Morse contented himself with a mild "phew" as the door closed, and the two men looked around them. "So this was where Ainley came." They stood in a bed-sitting room, containing a single (unmade) bed, the sheets dirty and creased, a threadbare settee, an armchair of more recent manufacture, a huge, ugly wardrobe, a black-and-white T.V. set and a small underpopulated bookcase. They passed through a door in the far wall, and found themselves in a small, squalid kitchen, with a greasy-looking gas cooker, a Formica-topped table and two kitchen stools.

"Hardly an opulent occupant?" suggested Morse. Lewis sniffed and sniffed again. "Smell something?"

"Pot, I reckon, sir."

"Really?" Morse beamed at his sergeant with delight, and Lewis felt pleased with himself.

"Think it's important, sir?"

"Doubt it," said Morse. "But let's have a closer look round. You stay here and sniff around—I'll take the other room."

Morse walked straight to the bookcase. A copy of the *Goon Show Scripts* appeared to be the high-water mark of any civilised taste in the occupant's reading habits. For the rest there was little more than a stack of Dracula

comics and half a dozen supremely pornographic magazines, imported from Denmark. The latter Morse decided
to investigate forthwith, and seated in the armchair he
was contentedly sampling their contents when Lewis
called from the kitchen.

"I've found something, sir."

"Shan't be a minute." He thought guiltily of sticking
one of the magazines in his pocket, but for once his
police training got the better of him. And with the air of
an Abraham prepared to sacrifice an Isaac upon the altar,
he replaced the magazines in the bookcase and went
through to his over-zealous sergeant.

"What about that, sir?" Morse nodded unenthusiasti-
cally at the unmistakable paraphernalia of the pot-
smoker's paradise. "Shall we pack this little lot up, sir?"

Morse thought for a while. "No, we'll leave it, I
think." Lewis's eagerness wilted, but he knew better than
to argue. "All we need to find out now is who he is,
Lewis."

"I've got that, too, sir." He handed the inspector an
unopened letter from Granada T.V. Rental Service,
addressed to Mr. J. Maguire.

Morse's eyes lit up. "Well, well. We might have
known it. One of the boyfriends, if I remember rightly.
Well done, Lewis! You've done a good job."

"You find anything, sir?"

"Me? Oh, no. Nothing, really."

Mrs. Gibbs, who was waiting for them as they reached
the bottom of the stairs, expressed the hope that the visit
was now satisfactorily terminated, and Morse said he
hoped so, too.

"As I told yer, 'e won't be 'ere much longer, the trouble 'e's caused me."

Sensing that she was becoming fractionally more communicative Morse kept the exchanges going. He had to, anyway.

"Great pity, you know, that Inspector Ainley was killed. You'd have finished with this business by now. It must be a bit of a nuisance . . ."

"Yes. He said as 'ow 'e 'oped he needn't come bothering me again."

"Was, er, Mr. Maguire here when he called?"

"No. 'E called about the same time as you gentlemen. 'Im" (pointing aloft) "—'e were off to work. Well, some people'd call it work, I s'pose."

"Where does he work now?" Morse asked the question lightly enough, but the guarded look came back to her eyes.

"Same place."

"I see. Well, we shall have to have a word with him, of course. What's the best way to get there from here?"

"Tube from Fulham Bridge to Piccadilly Circus—least, that's the way 'e goes."

"Could we park the car there?"

"In Brewer Street? Yer must be joking!"

Morse turned to Lewis. "We'd better do as Mrs. Gibbs says, sergeant, and get the tube."

On the steps outside Morse thanked the good lady profusely and, almost as an afterthought it seemed, turned to speak to her once more.

"Just one more thing, Mrs. Gibbs. It may be lunchtime before we get up there. Have you any idea where Mr. Maguire will be if he's not at work?"

"Like as not The Angel—I know 'e often 'as a drink in there."

As they walked to the car Lewis decided to get it off his chest. "Couldn't you just have asked her straight out where he worked?"

"I didn't want her to think I was fishing," replied Morse. Lewis thought she must be educationally subnormal if she hadn't realised that by now. But he let it go. They drove down to Fulham Bridge, parked the car on a TAXIS ONLY plot and caught the tube to Piccadilly Circus.

Somewhat to Lewis's surprise, Morse appeared to be fairly intimately conversant with the geography of Soho, and two minutes after emerging from the tube in Shaftesbury Avenue they found themselves standing in Brewer Street.

"There we are then," said Morse, pointing to The Angel, Bass House, only thirty yards away to their left. "Might as well combine business with a little pleasure, don't you think?"

"As you wish, sir."

Over their beer, Morse asked the barman if the manager was around, and learned that the barman was the manager. Morse introduced himself, and said he was looking for a Mr. J. Maguire.

"Not in any trouble, is he?" asked the barman.

"Nothing serious."

"Johnny Maguire, you say. He works over the way at the strip club—The Penthouse. On the door, mostly."

Morse thanked him, and he and Lewis walked over to the window and looked outside. The Penthouse was almost directly opposite.

"Ever been to a strip club, Lewis?"

"No. But I've read about 'em, of course."

"Nothing like first-hand experience, you know. C'mon, drink up."

Outside the club Morse surveyed the pictorial preview of the erotic delights to be savoured within. 18 GORGEOUS GIRLS. THE SEXIEST SHOW IN LONDON. 95P ONLY. NO OTHER ADMISSION CHARGE.

"The real thing this is, gentlemen. Continuous performance. No G-strings." The speaker was a ginger-haired youth, dressed in a dark green blazer and grey slacks, who sat in a small booth at the entrance lobby.

"Bit expensive, isn't it?" asked Morse.

"When you've seen the show, sir, you'll think it's cheap at the price."

Morse looked at him carefully, and thought there was something approaching honesty in the dark eyes. Maguire—almost certainly; but he wouldn't run away. Morse handed over two pound-notes and took the tickets. To the young tout the policemen were just another couple of frustrated middle-aged voyeurs, and he had already spotted another potential customer studying the stills outside.

"The real thing this is, sir. Continuous performance. No G-strings."

"You owe me 10p," said Morse.

They walked through a gloomy passage-way and heard the music blaring from behind a screened partition, where sat a smallish, swarthy gentleman (Maltese, thought Morse) with a huge chest and bulging forearms.

He took the tickets and tore them across. "Can I see membership cards, please?"

"What membership cards?"

"You must be members of the club, sir." He reached for a small pad, and tore off two forms. "Fill in, please."

"Just a minute," protested Morse. "It says outside that there's no other admission charge and . . ."

"One pown each, please."

". . . We've paid our 95p and that's all we're paying."

The small man looked mean and dangerous. He rose to his meagre height and moved a thick arm to Morse's jacket. "Fill in, please. That will be one pown each."

"Will it buggery!" said Morse.

The Maltese advanced slightly and his hands glided towards Morse's wallet-pocket.

Neither Morse nor Lewis were big men, and the last thing that Morse wanted at this juncture was a rough house. He wasn't in very good condition anyway . . . But he knew the type well. Courage, Morse! He brushed the man's hand forcibly from his jacket and stepped a menacing pace forward.

"Look, you miserable wog. You want a fight? That's fine. I wouldn't want to bruise my fist against your ugly chops, myself, but this pal of mine here will do it with the greatest pleasure. Just up his street. Army middleweight champion till a year ago. Where shall we go, you dirty little squit?"

The little man sat back and sagged in his chair like a wilting balloon, and his voice was a punctured whine.

"You got to be members of the club. If you not I get prosecuted by police."

"F——off," said Morse, and with the ex–boxing champion behind him walked through the screen partition.

In the small auditorium beyond sat a sprinkling of males, dotted around on the three rows of seats facing the small, raised stage, on which a buxom blonde stripper had just, climactically, removed her G-string. At least one of the management's promises was being honoured.

The curtains closed and there was a polite smatter of half-hearted applause.

"How did you know I was a boxing champion?" whispered Lewis.

"I didn't," said Morse, with genuine surprise.

"You might get it right, though, sir. *Light* middleweight."

Morse grinned happily, and a disembodied voice from the wings announced the advent of The Fabulous Fiona. The curtains opened jerkily to reveal a fully-clothed Fiona; but it was immediately apparent that her fabulous body, whatever delights were soon to be unveiled, was signally bereft of any rhythmic suppleness as she struggled amateurishly to synchronise a few elementary dance-steps with the languorously-suggestive music.

After The Sexy Susan and The Sensational Sandra even Morse was feeling a trifle blasé; but, as he explained to an unenthusiastic Lewis, there might be better things to come. And indeed The Voluptuous Vera and The Kinky Kate certainly did something to raise the general standard of the entertainment. There were gimmicks aplenty: fans, whips, bananas and rubber spiders; and Morse dug Lewis in the ribs as an extraordinarily-shapely girl, dressed for a fancy-dress ball, titillatingly and tantalisingly divested herself of all but an incongruously-ugly mask.

"Bit of class there, Lewis."

But Lewis remained unimpressed; and when the turn came round for the reappearance of The Fabulous Fiona Morse reluctantly decided they had better go. The little gorilla was fleecing a thin, spotty-faced young man of his one pown membership fee as they walked out of the club into the dazzling sunshine of the London street. After a few breaths of comparatively clean air, Morse returned to the entrance and stood by the young man.

"What's your name, lad?"

"William Shakespeare. What's yours?" He looked at Morse with considerable surprise. Who the hell did he think he was? It was over two years ago since anyone had spoken to him in that tone of voice. At school, in Kidlington.

"Can we go and talk somewhere?"

"What *is* this?"

"John Maguire, if I'm not mistaken? I want to talk to you about Miss Valerie Taylor—I think you may have heard of her. Now we can do it quietly and sensibly, or you can come along with me and the sergeant here to the nearest police station. Up to you."

Maguire was obviously worried. "Look. Not here, please. I've got half an hour off at four o'clock. I'll meet you then. I'll be in there." He pointed anxiously to a sleazy-looking snack bar across the road next to The Angel.

Morse pondered what to do.

"Please," urged Maguire. "I'll be there. Honest, I will."

It was a difficult decision, but Morse finally agreed. He thought it would be foolish to antagonise Maguire before he'd even started on him.

. Morse gave quick instructions to Lewis as they walked away. He was to take a taxi back to Southampton Terrace and wait until Morse returned. If Maguire did decide to scuttle (it seemed unlikely, though) he would almost certainly go back there for some of his things.

At the end of the street Lewis found a cab almost immediately, and Morse guiltily strolled back to The Penthouse.

"You'd better give me another ticket," demanded

Morse brusquely. He walked once more down the murkily-lit passage, gave his ticket to a surprised and silent dwarf, and without further trouble re-entered the auditorium. He recognised The Voluptuous Vera without difficulty and decided that it would be no more than a minimal hardship thus to while away the next hour and a half. He just hoped the masked young lady was still on the bill . . .

At 4:00 P.M. they sat opposite each other in the snack bar.

"You knew Valerie Taylor then?"

"I was at school with her."

"Her boyfriend, weren't you?"

"One of 'em."

"Like that, was it?" Maguire was non-committal. "Why did Inspector Ainley come to see you?"

"You know why."

"Did you know he was killed in a road accident the day he saw you?"

"No, I didn't."

"I asked you why he came to see you."

"Same reason as you, I suppose."

"He asked you about Valerie?"

Maguire nodded, and Morse had the feeling that the boy was suddenly feeling more relaxed. Had Morse missed the turning?

"What did you tell him?"

"What could I tell him? Nothing more to tell, is there? They got me to write out a statement when I was at school, and I told them the truth. Couldn't do much more than that, could I?"

"You told the truth?"

"Course, I did. I couldn't have had anything to do with it. I was in school all day, remember?"

Morse did remember, although he cursed himself for not bringing the boy's statement with him. Maguire had stayed at school for dinner and had been playing cricket the whole afternoon. At the time he must have seemed a peripheral figure in the investigation. Still was, perhaps. But why, then, *why* had Ainley come to London just to see him again—after all that time? There must have been *something*, something big. Morse finished the last dregs of his cold coffee and felt a bit lost. His devious manoeuvrings of the day began to look unnecessarily theatrical. Why couldn't he be a straight policeman for once in his life? Still, he had a couple of trump cards, and one never knew. He prepared to play the first.

"I'll give you one more chance, Maguire, but this time I want the truth—all of it."

"I've just told you . . ."

"Let's get one thing straight," said Morse. "I'm interested in Valerie Taylor—that's all. I'm not worried about any of those other things . . ." He left the words in the air, and a flash of alarm glinted in the boy's eyes.

"What other things? I don't know what you're talking about."

"We've been to your flat today, lad."

"So?"

"Mrs. Gibbs doesn't seem too happy, does she, about one or two things . . . ?"

"Old cow."

"She didn't have to *tell* us anything, you know."

"What am I supposed to have done? Come on—let's have it."

"How long have you been on drugs, lad?"

It hit him solidly between the eyes, and his effort at recovering was short of convincing. "What drugs?"

"I just told you, lad. We've been to your flat today."

"And I suppose you found some pot. So what? Just about everybody smokes pot here."

"I'm not talking about everybody." Morse leaned forward and let him have it. "I'm talking about you, lad. Smoking pot's illegal, you know that, and I could frogmarch you out of here and ship you to the nearest police station—remember that! But I've just told you, lad, I'm quite prepared to let it ride. Christ, why do you have to make it so hard for yourself? You can go back to your bloody flat and pump yourself with heroin for all I care. I'm just not bothered, lad—not if you co-operate with me. Can't you get that into your thick skull?"

Morse let it sink in a minute before continuing. "I want to know just one thing—what you told Inspector Ainley, that's all. And if I can't get it out of you here, I'll take you in and I'll get it out of you somewhere else. Please yourself, lad."

Morse picked up his overcoat from the seat beside him and draped it across his knees. Maguire stared dejectedly at the table-top and played nervously with a bottle of tomato ketchup. There was indecision in his eyes, and Morse timed what he hoped was his second trump card perfectly.

"How long had you known that Valerie was pregnant?" he asked quietly.

Bull's eye. Morse replaced his coat on the seat beside him, and Maguire spoke more freely. "About three weeks before."

"Did she tell anyone else?"

Maguire shrugged his shoulders. "She was a real sexy kid—everyone was after her."

"How often did you go to bed with her?"

"Ten—dozen times, I suppose."

"The truth, please, lad."

"Well, three or four times, maybe. I don't know."

"Where was this?"

"My place."

"Your parents know?"

"No. They were out working."

"And she said you were the father?"

"No. She wasn't like that. Said I could have been, of course."

"Did you feel jealous?" Morse had a suspicion that he did, but Maguire made no answer. "Was she very upset?"

"Just scared."

"What of? Scandal?"

"More scared of her mum, I think."

"Not her dad?"

"She didn't say so."

"Did she talk about running away?"

"Not to me."

"Who else might she have spoken to?" Maguire hesitated. "She had another boyfriend, didn't she," persisted Morse, "apart from you?"

"Pete?" Maguire could relax again. "He didn't even touch her."

"But she might have spoken to him?" Maguire was amused, and Morse felt that his questioning had lost its impetus. "What about her form tutor? She might have gone to her, perhaps?"

Maguire laughed openly. "You don't understand."

But suddenly Morse realised that he was beginning to

understand, and as the dawn was slowly breaking in his mind, he leaned forward and fixed Maguire with grey eyes, hard and unblinking.

"She could have gone to the headmaster, though." He spoke the words with quiet, taut emphasis, and the impact upon Maguire was dramatic. Morse saw the sudden flash of burning jealousy and knew that gradually, inch by inch, he was moving nearer to the truth about Valerie Taylor.

Morse took a taxi to Southampton Terrace where he found a patient Lewis awaiting him. The car was ready and they were soon heading out along the M40 towards Oxford. Morse's mind was simultaneously veering in every direction, and he lapsed into uncommunicative introversion. It wasn't until they left the three-lane motorway that he broke the long silence.

"Sorry you had such a long wait, Lewis."

"That's all right, sir. You had a long wait, too."

"Yes," said Morse. He made no mention of his return to The Penthouse. He must have gone down a good deal already in his sergeant's estimation; he had certainly sunk quite low enough in his own.

It was five miles outside Oxford that Lewis exploded the minor bombshell.

"I was having a talk with Mrs. Gibbs, sir, while you were with Mr. Maguire."

"Well?"

"I asked her why he'd been such a nuisance."

"What did she say?"

"She told me that until recently he'd had a girl in the flat."

"She *what*?"

"Yes, sir. Almost a month, she said."

"But why the hell didn't you tell me before, man? You surely realise. . . ?" He glared at Lewis, incredulous and exasperated, and sank back in despair behind his safety-belt.

His stubborn conviction that Valerie was no longer alive would (one had thought) have been sorely tested when he looked back into his office at 8:00 P.M. Awaiting him was a report from the forensic laboratory, short and to the point.

"Sufficient similarities to warrant positive identification. Suggest that investigation proceed on firm assumption that letter was written by signatory, Miss Valerie Taylor. Please contact if detailed verification required."

But Morse seemed far from impressed. In fact, he looked up from the report and smiled serenely. Reaching for the telephone directory, he looked up Phillipson, D. There was only one Phillipson: "The Firs," Banbury Road, Oxford.

Chapter Nine

Sheila Phillipson was absolutely delighted with her Oxford home, a four-bedroomed detached house, just below the Banbury Road roundabout. Three fully-grown fir trees screened the spacious front garden from the busy main road, and the back garden, with its two old apple trees and its goldfish pond, its beautifully-conditioned lawn and its neatly-tended borders, was an unfailing joy. With unimaginative predictability she had christened it "The Firs."

Donald would be late home from school; he had a staff meeting. But it was only a cold salad, and the children had already eaten. She could relax. At a quarter to six she was sitting in a deck-chair in the back garden, her eyes closed contentedly. The evening air was warm and still ... She felt so proud of Donald; and of the children, Andrew and Alison, now contentedly watching the television. They were both doing so well at their primary school. And, of course, if they didn't really get the chances they deserved, they could always go to private schools; and Donald would probably send them there— in spite of what he'd told the parents at the last speech day. The Dragon, New College School, Oxford High, Headington—one heard such good reports. But that was

83

all in the future. For the moment everything in the garden was lovely. She lifted her face to catch the last rays of the sloping sun and breathed in the scent of thyme and honeysuckle. Lovely. Almost too lovely, perhaps. At half-past six she heard the crunch of Donald's Rover on the drive.

Later in the evening Sheila did not recognise the man at the door, a slimly-built man with a clean, sensitive mouth and wide light-grey eyes. He had a nice voice, she thought, for a police inspector.

In spite of Morse's protests that Tom and Jerry ranked as his very favourite T.V. programme, the children were immediately sent upstairs to bed. She was cross with herself for not having packed them off half an hour ago; toys littered the floor, and she fussily and apologetically gathered together the offending objects and took them out. On her return she found her visitor gazing with deep interest at a framed photograph of herself and her husband.

"Press photograph, isn't it?"

"Yes. We had a big party in Donald's, er, in my husband's first term here. All the staff, husbands and wives—you know the sort of thing. The *Oxford Mail* took that. Took a lot of photographs, in fact."

"Have you got the other photographs?"

"Yes. I think so. Would you like to look at them? My husband won't be long. He's just finishing his bath."

She rummaged about in a drawer of the bureau, and handed to Morse five glossy, black and white photographs. One of them, a group photograph, held his keen attention: the men in dinner-jackets and black bow-ties, the ladies in long dresses. Most of them looked happy enough.

"Do you know some of the staff?" she asked.

"Some of them."

He looked again at the group. "Beautifully clear photograph."

"Very good, isn't it?"

"Is Acum here?"

"Acum? Oh yes, I think so. Mr. Acum left two years ago. But I remember him quite well—and his wife." She pointed them out on the photograph; a young man with a lively, intelligent face and a small goatee beard; and, her arm linked through his, a slim, boyish-figured girl, with shoulder-length blonde hair, not unattractive perhaps, but with a face (at least on this evidence) a little severe and more than a little spotty.

"You knew his wife, you say?" asked Morse.

Sheila heard the gurgling death-rattle of the bath upstairs, and for some inexplicable reason felt a cold shudder creeping along her spine. She felt just as she did as a young girl when she had once answered the phone for her father. She recalled the strange, almost frightening questions . . .

A shiningly-fresh Phillipson came in. He apologised for keeping Morse waiting, and in turn Morse apologised for his own unheralded intrusion. Sheila breathed an inward sigh of relief, and asked if they'd prefer tea or coffee. With livelier brews apparently out of the question, Morse opted for coffee and, like a good host, the headmaster concurred.

"I've come to ask about Acum," said Morse, with brisk honesty. "What can you tell me about him?"

"Acum? Not much really. He left at the end of my first

year here. Taught French. Well-qualified chap. Exeter—took a second if I remember rightly."

"What about his wife?"

"She had a degree in Modern Languages, too. They met at Exeter University, I think. In fact she taught with us for a term when one of the staff was ill. Not too successfully, I'm afraid."

"Why was that?"

"Bit of a tough class—you know how it is. She wasn't really up to it."

"They gave her a rough ride, you mean?"

"They nearly took her pants down, I'm afraid."

"You're speaking metaphorically, I hope."

"I hope so, too. I heard some hair-raising rumours, though. Still, it was my fault for taking her on. Too much of a bluestocking for that sort of job."

"What did you do?"

Phillipson shrugged. "I had to get rid of her."

"What about Acum himself? Where did he go?"

"One of the schools in Caernarfon."

"He got a promotion, did he?"

"Well no, not really. He'd only been teaching the one year, but they could promise him some sixth-form work. I couldn't."

"Is he still there?"

"As far as I know."

"He taught Valerie Taylor—you know that?"

"Inspector, wouldn't it be fairer if you told me why you're so interested in him? I might be able to help more if I knew what you were getting at."

Morse pondered the question. "Trouble is, I don't really know myself."

Whether he believed him or not, Phillipson left it at

that. "Well, I know he taught Valerie, yes. Not one of his brightest pupils, I don't think."

"Did he ever talk to you about her?"

"No. Never."

"No rumours? No gossip?"

Phillipson took a deep breath, but managed to control his mounting irritation. "No."

Morse changed his tack. "Have you got a good memory, sir?"

"Good enough, I suppose."

"Good enough to remember what you were doing on Tuesday 2nd September this year?"

Phillipson cheated and consulted his diary. "I was at a Headmasters' Conference in London."

"Whereabouts in London?"

"It was at the Café Royal. And if you must know the conference started at . . ."

"All right. All right." Morse held up his right hand like a priest pronouncing the benediction, as a flush of anger rose in the headmaster's cheeks.

"Why did you ask me that?"

Morse smiled benignly. "That was the day Valerie wrote to her parents."

"What the hell are you getting at, inspector?"

"I shall be asking a lot of people the same question before I've finished, sir. And some of them will get terribly cross, I know that. But I'd rather hoped that you would understand."

Phillipson calmed down. "Yes, I see. You mean . . ."

"I don't mean anything, sir. All I know is that I have to ask a lot of awkward questions; it's what they pay me for. I suppose it's the same in your job."

"I'm sorry. Go ahead and ask what you like. I shan't mind."

"I shouldn't be too sure of that, sir." Phillipson looked at him sharply. "You see," continued Morse, "I want you to tell me, if you can, exactly what you were doing on the afternoon that Valerie Taylor disappeared."

Mrs. Phillipson brought in the coffee, and after she had retired once more to the kitchen the answer was neatly wrapped and tied.

"I had lunch at school that day, drove down into Oxford, and browsed around in Blackwells. Then I came home."

"Do you remember what time you got home?"

"About three."

"You seem to remember that afternoon pretty well, sir?"

"It *was* rather an important afternoon, wasn't it, inspector?"

"Did you buy any books?"

"I don't remember that much, I'm afraid."

"Do you have an account with Blackwells?"

Momentarily Phillipson hesitated. "Yes. But . . . but if I'd just bought a paperback or something I would have paid in cash."

"But you might have bought something more expensive?" Morse looked along the impressive rows of historical works that covered two walls of the lounge from floor to ceiling, and thought of Johnny Maguire's pathetic little collection.

"You could check up, I suppose," said Phillipson curtly.

"Yes. I suppose we shall." Morse felt suddenly very tired.

* * *

At half-past midnight Sheila Phillipson tiptoed quietly down the stairs and found the Codeine bottle. It kept coming back to her mind and she couldn't seem to push it away from her—that terrible night when Donald had been making love to her, and called her Valerie. She'd never mentioned it, of course. She just couldn't.

Suddenly she jumped, a look of blind terror in her eyes, before subsiding with relief upon a kitchen stool.

"Oh, it's only you, Donald. You frightened me."

"Couldn't you sleep either, darling?"

Chapter Ten

> Not a line of her writing have I,
> Not a thread of her hair.
> THOMAS HARDY, *Thoughts of Phena*

Morse seemed reluctant to begin any work when he arrived, late, in his office on Thursday morning. He handed Lewis the report on Valerie's letter and started on *The Times* crossword puzzle. He looked at his watch, marked the time exactly in the margin of the newspaper and was soon scribbling in letters at full speed. Ten minutes later he stopped. He allowed himself only ten minutes, and almost always completed it. But this morning one clue remained unsolved.

"What's this, Lewis? Six letters. Blank A—Blank S—Blank N. *Eyes had I—and saw not?*"

Lewis jotted down the letters and pretended to think. He just hadn't a crossword mind. "Could it be 'parson,' sir?"

"Why on earth should it be 'parson'?"

"Well, it fits."

"So do a hundred and one other words."

"Such as?" Morse struggled hard before producing "damson." "I'd rather have my parson, sir."

Morse put the paper aside. "Well. What do you think?"

"Seems to be her writing, doesn't it?"

There was a knock on the door and a pretty young office girl deposited the morning post into the in-tray.

Cursorily and distastefully Morse looked through the correspondence.

"Nothing urgent here, Lewis. Let's go along to the lab. I think old Peters must be getting senile."

Now in his early sixties, Peters had previously worked for twenty years as a Home Office pathologist, and somewhere along the line the juices of human fallibility had been squeezed from his cerebral processes. His manner was clinical and dry, and his words seemed to be dictated by a mini-computer installed somewhere inside his brain. His answers were slow, mechanical, definitive. He had never been known to argue with anyone. He just read the information-tapes.

"You think this is Valerie Taylor's writing, then?"

He paused and answered. "Yes."

"Can you ever be certain about things like handwriting, though?"

He paused and answered. "No."

"How certain are you?"

He paused and answered. "Ninety per cent."

"You'd be surprised then if it turned out that she didn't write it?"

He paused and the computer considered its reaction to the improbability. "Yes. Surprised."

"What makes you think she wrote it?"

He paused and lectured briefly and quietly on the evidence of loops and quirks and whorls. Morse battled on against the odds. "You can forge a letter, though, can't you?"

He paused and answered. "Of course."

"But you don't think this was forged?"

He paused and answered. "I think it was written by the girl."

"But a person's handwriting changes over the years, doesn't it? I mean the letter's written in almost exactly the same way as the exercise books."

He paused and answered. "There's a basic built-in style about all our handwriting. Slopes change, certainly, and other minor things. But whatever changes, there is still the distinctive style, carrying with it the essential features of our personal characteristics." He paused again, and Lewis had the impression he was reading it all out of a book. "In Greek, the word 'character' means handwriting, they tell me."

Lewis smiled. He was enjoying himself.

Morse put a penultimate problem to the computer. "You wouldn't go into the witness box and say it definitely *was* her writing, would you?"

He paused and answered. "I would tell a jury what I've told you—that the order of probability is somewhere in the region of ninety per cent."

Morse turned as he reached the door. "Could *you* forge her handwriting convincingly?"

The desiccated calculating-machine actually smiled and the hesitation this time was minimal. "I've a lot of experience in this field, you know."

"You *could* then?"

He paused and answered. "*I* could, yes."

Back in his office Morse brought Lewis up to date with his visit the previous evening to the Phillipson residence.

"You don't like him much, do you, sir?"

Morse looked aggrieved. "Oh, I don't dislike him. It's

just that I don't think he's completely above-board with me, that's all."

"We've all of us got things we'd like to hide, haven't we, sir?"

"Mm." Morse was staring through the window. *Eyes had I—and saw not.* Six letters. It still eluded him. Like the answer to this case. A whole orchestra of instruments and some of them playing just slightly out of tune.

"Did you know that 'orchestra' was an anagram of 'carthorse,' Lewis?"

Lewis didn't. He idly wrote down the letters and checked. "So it is. Perhaps the clue you can't get is an anagram, sir."

The light dawned in Morse's eyes. "You're a genius. SAW NOT." Sherlock Holmes picked up *The Times* again, wrote in the answer and beamed at his own Doctor Watson.

"Now let's consider the case so far." Lewis sat back and listened. Morse was away.

"We can say, can we not, that the letter was either written by Valerie herself or by another person. Agreed?"

"With odds of nine to one on Valerie."

"Yes, with strong odds on Valerie. Now if Valerie herself wrote the letter, we can reasonably assume that she is still alive, that she probably ran off to London, that she's still there, that she's quite happy where she is, doesn't want to come back to Kidlington—and that we're wasting our bloody time."

"Not if we find her."

"Of course we are. What do we do if we find her? Bring her back home to mummy and tell her what a naughty girl she's been? What's the point of that?"

"It would clear up the case, though."

"If she wrote the letter, there *is* no case."

Something had been troubling Lewis sorely since the previous evening and he got it off his conscience. "Do you think what Mrs. Gibbs told me was important, sir— you know, about the girl in Maguire's flat?"

"Doubt it," said Morse.

"You don't think it could have been Valerie?"

"I keep telling you, Lewis. *She's dead*—whatever that pettifogging Peters says, *she couldn't have written that letter*."

Lewis groaned inwardly. Once the chief got an idea stuck firmly in his brain, something cataclysmic was needed to dislodge it.

"Let's just assume for a minute that the letter was *not* written by Valerie. In that case it was written by someone who copied her writing, and copied it with enormous care and skill. Yes?"

"But why should anyone . . ."

"I'm coming to that. Why should anyone want to make us believe that Valerie was still alive *if in fact she was dead*? Well, as I see it, there is one simple and over-whelmingly convincing answer to that question. Some-one wants us to believe Valerie is still alive because he or she sees a very real danger that further police investiga-tion in the Taylor girl affair is likely to uncover the truth, Lewis—which is that Valerie is dead and that someone murdered her. I think that for some reason this someone began to get very scared, and wrote that letter to put us off the scent. Or more specifically, perhaps, to put Ainley off the scent."

Lewis felt he could make no worthwhile contribution to such a weird hypothesis, and Morse continued.

"There is another possibility, though, and we mustn't discount it. The letter could have been written by someone for *precisely the opposite reason*—to put the police back on the scent. And if you think about it, that's precisely what has happened. Ainley was still working on the case—but unofficially. And when he was killed, if it hadn't been for the letter, the case would have been left where it was—unsolved and gradually forgotten. But once the letter arrived, what happened? Strange called me in and told me to take over, to reinvestigate the case officially. Precisely what we're doing now. Now let's follow this line of reasoning a bit further. Who would want the police to reopen the case? Not the murderer—that's for sure. Who then? It could be the parents, of course. They might think that the police weren't really doing much about things . . ."

Lewis looked stupefied. "You don't honestly think the Taylors wrote the letter, do you?"

"Had the possibility not occurred to you?" asked Morse quietly.

"No."

"Well it should have done. After all, they're as likely as anyone to make a good job of forging a letter in their daughter's handwriting. But there's a much more interesting possibility, I think. The letter could have been sent by someone who knew that Valerie had been murdered, who had a jolly good idea of who murdered her and who wanted the murderer brought to justice."

"But why . . ."

"Just a minute. Let's assume that such a person knew that Ainley was getting perilously close to the truth, had perhaps even helped Ainley towards the truth. What happens then? Tragedy. Ainley is killed and everything is back at square one. Look at it this way. Let's assume that Ainley went to London on the Monday and actually found Valerie Taylor alive. You with me? All right—the cat's out of the bag; she's been found. The next day she writes to her parents. There's no point in covering up any longer. If she doesn't tell them, Ainley will."

"That seems to fit, sir."

"Ah. But there's another interpretation, isn't there? Let's now assume that Ainley *didn't* find Valerie—and I don't think he did. Let's suppose he found something rather more sinister than Valerie Taylor alive and well. Because remember, Lewis, *something* took Ainley to London that day. We shall perhaps never know what, but he was getting nearer and nearer the truth all the time. And when he was killed someone, Lewis, *someone* desperately wanted his work to be followed up. And so the day after Ainley's death, a letter is written. It was written precisely because *Valerie Taylor was dead*—not alive, and it had exactly the effect it was intended to have. The case was reopened."

The convolutions of Morse's theories were beginning to defeat Lewis's powers of logical analysis. "I don't quite follow some of that, sir, but . . . you're still basing it all on the assumption that she didn't write the letter, aren't you? I mean if what Peters says is . . ."

The pretty office girl came in again and handed to Morse a buff-coloured file.

"Superintendent Strange says you may be interested in this, sir. It's been tested for fingerprints—no good, he says."

Morse opened the file. Inside was a cheap brown envelope, already opened, posted the previous day in central

London and addressed to the Thames Valley Police. The letter inside was written on ruled, white note-paper.

> *Dear Sir,*
>   *I hear you are trying to find me, but I don't want you to because I don't want to go back home.*
>   *Yours truly, Valerie Taylor.*

He handed the letter to Lewis. "Not the most voluminous of correspondents, our Valerie, is she?"

He picked up the phone and dialled the lab, and from the slight pause at the other end of the line he knew he must be speaking to the computer itself.

Chapter Eleven

> All women become like their mothers.
> That is their tragedy.
>
> OSCAR WILDE

For the second time within twenty-four hours Morse found himself studying a photograph with more than usual interest. Lewis he had left in the office to make a variety of telephone calls, and he himself stood, arms akimbo, staring fixedly at the young girl who stared back at him, equally fixedly, from the wall of the lounge. Slim, with dark-brown hair and eyes that almost asked if you'd dare and a figure that clearly promised it would be wonderful if you found the daring. She was a very attractive girl and, like the elders in Troy who looked for the first time upon Helen, Morse felt no real surprise that she had been the cause of so much trouble.

"Lovely looking girl, your daughter."

Mrs. Taylor smiled diffidently at the photograph. "It's not Valerie," she said, "it's me."

Morse turned with undisguised astonishment in his eyes. "Really? I didn't realise you were so much alike. I didn't mean to, er . . ."

"I used to be nice-looking, I suppose, in those days. I was seventeen when that was taken—over twenty years ago. It seems a long time."

Morse watched her as she spoke. Her figure was a good deal thicker round the hips now, and her legs, though still slim, were faintly lined with varicose veins. But it was her face that had changed the most: a few wisps of greying hair trailed over the worn features, the teeth yellowing, the flesh around the throat no longer quite so firm. But she was still . . . Men were luckier, he thought; they seemed to age much less perceptibly than women. On a low cupboard against the right-hand wall behind her stood an elegant, delicately-proportioned porcelain vase. Somehow it seemed to Morse so incongruously tasteful and expensive in this drably-furnished room, and he found himself staring at it with a slightly puzzled frown.

They talked for half an hour or so, mostly about Valerie; but there was nothing she could add to what she had told so many people so many times before. She recalled the events of that far off day like a nervous well-rehearsed pupil in a history examination. But that was no surprise to Morse. After all, as Phillipson had reminded him the previous evening, it *was* rather an important day. He asked her about herself and learned she had recently taken a job, just mornings, at the Cash and Carry stores—stocking up the shelves mostly; tiring, on her feet most of the time, but it was better than staying at home all day, and nice to have some money of her own. Morse refrained from asking how much she spent on drink and cigarettes, but there was something that he had to ask.

"You won't be upset, Mrs. Taylor, if I ask you one or two rather personal questions, will you?"

"I shouldn't think so."

She leaned back on the crimson settee and lit another cigarette, her hand shaking slightly. Morse felt he ought to have realised it before. He could see it in the way she sat, legs slightly parted, the eyes still throwing a distant, muted invitation. There was an overt if faded sensuality about the woman. It was almost tangible. He took a deep breath.

"Did you know that Valerie was pregnant when she disappeared?"

Her eyes grew almost dangerous. "She wasn't pregnant. I'm her mother, remember? Whoever told you that was a bloody liar." The voice was harsher now, and cheaper. The façade was beginning to crack, and Morse found himself wondering about her. Husband away; long, lonely days and daughter home only at lunchtimes—and that only during Valerie's last year at school.

He hadn't meant to ask his next question. It was one of those things that wasn't really anyone else's business. It had struck him, of course, the first time he had glanced at the Colour Supplement: the cards for the eighteenth wedding anniversary, and Valerie at the time almost twenty—or would have been, had she still been alive. He took another deep breath.

"Was Valerie your husband's child, Mrs. Taylor?"

The question struck home and she looked away. "No. I had her before I knew George."

"I see," said Morse gently.

At the door she turned towards him. "Are you going to see him?" Morse nodded. "I don't mind what you ask him but . . . but please don't mention anything about . . . about what you just asked me. He was like a father to her always but he . . . he used to get teased a lot about Valerie when we were first married especially . . . especially since we didn't have any kids ourselves. You know what I mean. It hurt him, I know it did, and . . . and I don't want him hurt, inspector. He's been a good man to me; he's always been a good man to me."

She spoke with a surprising warmth of feeling and as she spoke Morse could see the lineaments of an erstwhile beauty in her face. He heard himself promise that he wouldn't. Yet he found himself wondering who Valerie's real father had been, and if it might be important for him to find out. If he *could* find out. If anyone knew—including Valerie's mother.

As he walked slowly away he wondered something else, too. There had been something, albeit hardly perceptible, something slightly off-key about Mrs. Taylor's nervousness; just a little more than the natural nervousness of meeting a strange man—even a strange policeman. It was more like the look he had several times witnessed on his secretary's face when he had burst unexpectedly into her office and found her hastily and guiltily covering up some personal little thing that she hoped he hadn't seen. Had there been someone else in the house during his interview with Mrs. Taylor? He thought so. In an instant he turned on his heel and spun round to face the house he had just left—and he saw it. The right-hand curtain of an upstairs window twitched slightly and a vague silhouette glided back against the wall. It was over in a flash. The curtain was still; all sign of life was gone. A cabbage-white butterfly stitched its way along the privet hedge—and then that, too, was gone.

Chapter Twelve

Even the dustbin lid is raised mechanically
   At the very last moment
You could dispose of a corpse like this
Without giving the least offence.
                    D. J. ENRIGHT, *No Offence: Berlin*

It occurred to Morse as he drove down the Woodstock Road into Oxford that although he had done most things in life he had never before had occasion to visit a rubbish tip. In fact, as he turned into Walton Street and slowed to negotiate the narrowing streets that led down to Jericho, he could not quite account for the fact that he knew exactly where to go. He passed Aristotle Lane and turned right into Walton Well Road, over the hump-backed bridge that spanned the canal and stopped the Lancia beside an open gate, where a notice informed him that unauthorised vehicles were not allowed to drive further and that offenders would be prosecuted by an official with (it seemed to Morse) the portentous title of Conservator and Sheriff of Port Meadow. He slipped the car into first gear and drove on, deciding that he would probably qualify in the "authorised" category, and rather hoping that someone would stop him. But no one did. He made his way slowly along the concreted pathway, a thin belt of trees on his right and the open green expanse of Port Meadow on his left. Twice when corporation lorries came towards him he was forced off the track on to the grass, before coming finally to the edge of the site, where a high wooden gate over a deep cattle-grid effectively barred all further progress. He left the car and proceeded on foot, noting, as he passed another sign, that members of the public would be ill-advised to touch any materials deposited on the tip, treated as they were with harmful insecticides. He had gone more than 200 yards before he caught his first sight of genuine rubbish. The compacted surface over which he walked was flat and clear, scored by the caterpillar tracks of bulldozers and levellers, with only the occasional partially-submerged piece of sacking to betray the burial of the thousands of tons of rubbish beneath. Doubtless grass and shrubs would soon be burgeoning there, and the animals would return to their old territories and scurry once more in the hedgerows amid the bracken and the wild flowers. And people would come and scatter their picnic litter around and the whole process would begin again. Sometimes *homo sapiens* was a thoroughly disgusting species.

He made his way towards the only observable sign of life—a corrugated-iron shack, once painted green but ramshackle now and rusty, where an indescribably grimy labourer directed him deeper into the network of filth. Two magpies and an ominous-looking crow reluctantly took to flight as he walked by, and flapped their slow way across the blighted wilderness. At last Morse came to the main area of the tip: Pepsi and Coca-Cola tins, perished household gloves, lengths of rusting wire, empty cartons of washing-up liquid and a disintegrating dart-board; biscuit tins, worn-out shoes, a hot water bottle, ancient car seats and a comprehensive collection of cardboard boxes. Morse swatted away the ugly flies that circled his head, and was glad to find he had one last cigarette left. He threw the empty packet away; it didn't seem to matter much here.

George Taylor was standing beside a yellow bull-dozer, shouting to its driver above the deep-throated growl of the engine, and pointing towards a great mound of earth and stones piled like a rampart along the side of the shallow tip. Morse idly conjured up the image of some archaeologist who, some thousand years hence, might seek to discover the lifestyle of twentieth-century man, and Morse commiserated with him on the dismal débris he would find.

George was a heavily-built, broad-shouldered man, not too intelligent, perhaps, but, as Morse saw him, honest and likeable enough. He sat down upon a ten-gallon paraffin tin, Morse himself having declined the offer of similar accommodation, supposing that by this time George's trousers were probably immune from the harmful effects of all insecticides. And so they talked, and Morse tried to picture the scene as it must have been each night in the Taylor household: George arriving home, dirty and tired, at 6:15 or thereabouts; Mrs. Taylor cooking the evening meal and washing up the pots; and Valerie—but what did he know of Valerie? Occasionally condescending to do a modicum of homework? He didn't know. Three isolated personalities, under the same roof, somehow brought and kept together by that statistical unit beloved by the sociologists—the family. Morse asked about Valerie—her life at home, her life at school, her friends, her likes and her dislikes; but he learned little that was new.

"Have you ever thought that Valerie may have run away because she was expecting a baby?"

George slowly lit a Woodbine and contemplated the broken glass that littered the ground at his feet. "You think of most things, don't you, when summat like that happens. I remember when she were a young gal she were a bit late sometimes—and I used to think all sorts of things had happened." Morse nodded. "You got a family, inspector?"

Morse shook his head and, like George, contemplated the ground about his feet.

" 'Sfunny, really. You think of the most terrible things. And then she'd come back and you'd feel all sort of happy and cross at the same time, if you know what I mean."

Morse thought he knew; and for the first time in the case he saw something of the heartache and the sorrow of it all, and he began to hope that Valerie Taylor was still alive.

"Was she often late coming home?"

George hesitated. "Not really. Well, not till she were about sixteen, anyway."

"And then she was?"

"Well, not too late. Anyway, I allus used to wait up for her."

Morse put it more bluntly. "Did she ever stay out all night?"

"Never." It was a firm and categorical answer, but Morse wondered if it were true.

"When was the latest she came in? After midnight?" George nodded rather sadly. "Much after?"

"Sometimes."

"Rows, were there?"

"The wife got cross, of course. Well, so did I, really."

"She often stayed out late, then?"

"Well, no. Not often. Just once every few weeks, like she'd say she was going to a party with her friends, or summat like that." He rubbed his hand across his stubbled chin and shook his head. "These days it's not like it was when we was boys. I don't know."

They brooded silently and George kicked a flattened Coca-Cola tin a few yards further away.

"Did you give her much pocket money?" asked Morse.

"Quid a week—sometimes a bit more. And at weekends she used to work on the till down the supermarket. Used to spend it on clothes mostly—shoes, that sort of thing. She was never short of money."

With a powerful snarl the bulldozer shovelled a few more cubic yards of earth across a stinking stretch of refuse, and then slowly retreated to manoeuvre diagonally into position behind the next heap, criss-crossing the ground with the patterned tracks that Morse had noticed earlier. And as the gleaming teeth of the scoop dug again into the crumbling soil, something stirred vaguely in the back of Morse's mind; but George was speaking again.

"That inspector what was killed, you know, he came to see me a few weeks back."

Morse stood very still and held his breath, as if the slightest movement might be fatal. His question would appear, he hoped, to spring from casual curiosity.

"What did he want to see you about, Mr. Taylor?"

" 'Sfunny really. He asked me the same as you. You know, about Valerie staying out at nights."

Morse's blood ran slightly cold, and his grey eyes looked into the past and seemed to catch a glimpse of what had happened all that time ago . . . Another corporation lorry rumbled up the slight incline, ready to stockpile the latest consignment of rubbish, and George stood up to direct proceedings.

"Not been much help, I'm afraid, inspector."

Morse shook George's dirty, calloused hand, and prepared to leave.

"Do you think she's alive, inspector?"

Morse looked at him curiously. "Do you?"

"Well, there's the letter, isn't there, inspector?"

For some strange, intuitive reason Morse felt the question had somehow been wrong, and he frowned slightly as he watched George Taylor walk over to the lorry. Yes, there was the letter, and he hoped now that Valerie had written it, but . . .

He stood where he was and looked around him.

How would you like to be stuck in a filthy hole like this, Morse—probably for the rest of your life? And when anyone calls to see you, all you can offer is an old ten-gallon paraffin tin sprayed with harmful insecticide. You've got your own black leather chair and the white carpet and the desk of polished Scandinavian oak. Some people are luckier than others.

As he walked away the yellow bulldozer nudged its nose into another pile of earth; and soon the leveller would come and gradually smooth over the clay surface, like a passable cook with the chocolate icing on a cake.

Chapter Thirteen

> Man kann den Wald nicht vor Baümen sehen.
> German proverb

Lewis had gone home when Morse returned to his office at 5:30, and he felt it would probably be sensible for him to do the same. Many pieces of the jigsaw were now to hand, some of them big ugly pieces that looked as if they wouldn't fit anywhere; but they would—if only he had the time to think it all out. For the moment he was too much on top of things. Some of the trees were clear enough, but not the configuration of the forest. To stand back a bit and take a more synoptic view of things— that's what he needed.

He fetched a cup of coffee from the canteen, and sat at his desk. The notes that Lewis had made, and left conspicuously beneath a paperweight, he deliberately put to one side. There were other things in life than the Taylor case, although for the moment he couldn't quite remember what they were. He went through his in-tray and read through reports on the recent spate of incendiary bombings, the rôle of the police at pop festivals, and the vicious hooliganism after Oxford United's last home game. There were some interesting points. He crossed through his initials and stuck the reports in his out-tray. The next man on the list would do exactly the same; quickly glance through, cross through his initials, and stick them in his out-tray. There were too many reports, and the more there were the more self-defeating the whole exercise became. He would vote for a moratorium on all reports for the next five years.

He consulted his diary. The following morning he would be in the courts, and he'd better get home and iron a clean shirt. It was 6:25 and he felt hungry. Ah well. He'd call at the Chinese restaurant and take-away . . . He was pulling on his overcoat and debating between King Prawns and Chicken Chop Suey when the phone went.

"Personal call from a Mr. Phillipson. Shall I put him through, sir?" The girl on the switchboard sounded weary too.

"You're working late tonight, inspector?"

"I was just off," said Morse with a yawn in his voice.

"You're lucky," said Phillipson. "We've got a Parents' Evening—shan't be home till ten myself."

Morse was unimpressed and the headmaster got to the point.

"I thought I'd just ring up to say that I checked up at Blackwells—you remember?—about buying a book."

Morse looked at Lewis's notes and completed the sentence for him.

". . . and you bought Momigliano's *Studies in Historiography* published by Weidenfeld and Nicolson at two pounds fifty."

"You checked, then?"

"Yep."

"Oh well. I thought, er, I'd just let you know."

"Thoughtful of you, sir. I appreciate it. Are you speaking from school?"

"From my study, yes."

"I wonder if you've got a phone number for Mr. Acum there?"

"Just a minute, inspector."

Morse kept the receiver to his ear and read through the rest of Lewis's notes. Nothing from Peters yet about that second letter; nothing much from anybody . . .

To anyone with less than extremely acute hearing it would have been quite imperceptible. But Morse heard it, and knew once again that someone had been eavesdropping on the headmaster's telephone conversations. Someone in the office outside the head's study; and Morse's brain slid easily along the shining grooves.

"Are you there, inspector? We've got two numbers for Acum—one at school, one at home."

"I'll take 'em both," said Morse.

After cradling the receiver, he sat and thought for a moment. If Phillipson wanted to use the phone in his study, he would first dial 9, get an outside line automatically, and then ring the code and the number he wanted. Morse had noticed the set-up when he had visited the school. But if he, Morse, wanted to ring Phillipson, he wouldn't be able to get him unless someone were sitting by the switchboard in the outer office; and he doubted that the faithful Mrs. Webb would be required that evening for the Parents' Evening.

He waited a couple of minutes and rang.

Brr. Brr. It was answered almost immediately.

"Roger Bacon School."

"That the headmaster?" enquired Morse innocently.

"No. Baines here. Second master. Can I help you?"

"Ah, Mr. Baines. Good evening, sir. As a matter of fact it was you I was hoping to get hold of. I, er, wonder if we might be able to meet again fairly soon. It's this

Taylor girl business again. There are one or two points I think you could help me with."

Baines would be free about a quarter to ten, and he could be in the White Horse soon after that. No time like the present.

Morse felt pleased with himself. He would have been even more pleased had he been able to see the deeply-worried look on Baines's face as he shrugged into his gown and walked down into the Great Hall to meet the parents.

There was little point in going home now and he walked over to the canteen and found a copy of the *Telegraph*. He ordered sausages and mash, wrote the precise time in the right-hand margin of the back page and turned to 1 across. *Has been known to split under a grilling* (7). He smiled to himself. It was too many letters for BAINES, so he wrote in SAUSAGE.

Back in the office he felt he was in good form. Cross-word finished in only seven and a half minutes. Still, it was a bit easier than *The Times*. Perhaps this case would be easy if only he could look at it in the right way, and as Baines had said there was no time like the present. A long, quiet, cool, detached look at the case. But it never worked quite like that. He sat back and closed his eyes and for more than an hour his brain seethed in ceaseless turmoil. Ideas, ideas galore, but still the firm outline of the pattern eluded him. One or two of the pieces fitted firmly into place, but so many wouldn't fit at all. It was like doing the light-blue sky at the top of a jigsaw, with no clouds, not even a solitary sea-gull to break the boundless monochrome.

By nine o'clock he had a headache. Leave it. Give it a

rest and go back later. Like crosswords. It would come; it would come.

He consulted the STD codes and found that he would have to get Caernarfon through the operator. It was Acum who answered.

As succinctly as he could Morse explained the reason for his call, and Acum politely interjected the proper noises of understanding and approval. Yes, of course. Yes, of course he remembered Valerie and the day she had disappeared. Yes, he remembered it all well.

"Did you realise that you were one of the very last people to see Valerie before she, er, before she disappeared?"

"I must have been, yes."

"In fact, you taught her the very last school lesson she ever had, I think?"

"Yes."

"I mention this, sir, because I have reason to believe that you asked Valerie to see you after the lesson."

"Ye-es. I think I did."

"Remember why, sir?" Acum took his time and Morse wished that he could see the schoolmaster's face.

"If I remember rightly, inspector, she was due to sit her O-level French the next week, and her work was, well, pretty dreadful, and I was going to have a word with her about it. Not that she had much chance in the exam, I'm afraid."

"You said, sir, you were *going* to see her."

"Yes, that's right. As it happened I didn't get a chance. She had to rush off, she said."

"Did she say why?"

The answer was ready this time, and it took the wind out of Morse's sails. "She said she'd got to see the head."

"Oh, I see." Another piece that didn't fit. "Well, thank you, Mr. Acum. You've been most helpful. I hope I've not interrupted anything important."

"No. No. Just marking a few books, that's all."

"Well, I'll leave you to it. Thanks very much."

"Not at all. If I can help in any other way, don't hesitate to ring me, will you?"

"Er, no. I won't. Thanks again."

Morse sat still for many minutes and began to wonder if he ought not to turn the jigsaw upside down and work the blue sky in at the bottom. There was no doubt about it: he ought to have gone home as he'd promised himself earlier. He was just walking blindly in the forest bumping into one wretched tree after another. But he couldn't go home yet; he had an appointment.

Baines was there already and got up to buy the inspector a drink. The lounge was quiet and they sat alone in a corner and wished each other good health.

Morse tried to size him up. Tweed jacket, grey slacks, balding on top and rather flabby in the middle, but obviously nobody's fool. His eyes were keen and Morse imagined the pupils would never take too many liberties with Baines. He spoke with a slight North Country accent and as he listened to Morse he picked away at his lower nostrils with his index finger. Irritating.

What was the routine on Tuesday afternoons? Why was there no register taken? Was there any likelihood that Valerie had, in fact, returned to school that afternoon, and only later disappeared? How did the pupils work the skiving that was obviously so widespread? Was there any sort of skivers' den where the reluctant athletes could safely hide themselves away? Have a smoke perhaps?

Baines seemed rather amused. He could give the boys and girls a few tips about getting off games! By jove, he could. But it was the staff's fault. The P.E. teachers were a bloody idle lot—worse than the kids. Hardly bothered to get changed, some of them. And anyway there were so many activities: fencing, judo, table-tennis, athletics, rounders, netball—all this self-expression nonsense. No one really knew who was expected when and where. Bloody stupid. Things had tightened up a bit with the new head, but—well. Baines gave the impression that for all his possible virtues Phillipson had a long way still to go. Where they went to? Plenty of places. He'd found half a dozen smoking in the boiler room one day, and the school itself was virtually empty. Quite a few of them just sloped off home though, and some didn't turn up at all. Anyway, like the headmaster, he wasn't really involved on Tuesday afternoons. It wasn't a bad idea, though, to get away from school occasionally—have a free afternoon. The headmaster had tried to do it for all the staff. Put all their free periods together and let them have a morning or an afternoon off. Trouble was that it meant a hell of a lot of work for the chap who did the timetabling. Him!

As he talked on Morse wondered whether he still felt bitter towards Phillipson; whether he would be all that eager to throw out a life-line to the drowning helmsman. He casually mentioned that he knew of Baines's ill luck in being pipped for the job; and bought more beer. Yes (Baines admitted), he'd been a bit unlucky perhaps, and more than once. He thought he could have run a school as well as most, and Morse felt he was probably right. Greedy and selfish (like most men), but shrewdly competent. Above all, thought Morse, he would have enjoyed power. And now that there no longer seemed much chance of power, perhaps a certain element of dark satisfaction in observing the inadequacies of others and quietly gloating over their misfortunes. There wasn't a word for it in English. The Germans called it *Schadenfreude*. Would Baines get the job if Phillipson left or if for some reason he *had* to leave? Morse thought he would be sure to. But how far would he go in actively promoting such a situation? Perhaps though, as usual, Morse was attributing too much cynical self-seeking to his fellow men, and he brought his attention back to the fairly ordinary man who sat opposite him, talking openly and amusingly about life in a comprehensive school.

"Did you ever teach Valerie yourself?" asked Morse.

Baines chuckled. "In the first form—just for a year. She didn't know a trapezium from a trampoline."

Morse grinned, too. "Did you like her?"

It was a sobering question, and the shrewdness gleamed again in Baines's eyes.

"She was all right." But it was an oddly unsatisfactory answer and Baines sensed it. He went on glibly about her academic prowess, or lack of it, and veered off into an anecdote about the time he'd found forty-two different spellings of "isosceles" in a first-year examination.

"Do you know Mrs. Taylor?"

"Oh, yes." He stood up and suggested there was just time for another pint. Morse knew that the momentum had been broken, quite deliberately, and he felt very tempted to refuse. But he didn't. Anyway, he was going to ask Baines a rather delicate favour.

Morse slept fitfully that night. Broken images littered his mind, like the broken glass strewn about the rubbish tip.

He tossed and turned; but the merry-go-round was out of control, and at 3:00 A.M. he got up to make himself a cup of tea. Back in bed, with the light left on, he tried to concentrate his closed, swift-darting eyes on to a point about three inches in front of his nose, and gradually the spinning mechanism began to slow down, slower and slower, and then it stopped. He dreamed of a beautiful girl slowly unbuttoning her low-cut blouse and swaying her hips sensuously above him as she slid down the zip at the side of her skirt. And then she put her long slim fingers up to her face and moved the mask aside, and he saw the face of Valerie Taylor.

Chapter Fourteen

> I am a man under authority.
> *St. Matthew*, ch. 8, v. 9

It wasn't too bad working with Morse. Odd sort of chap, sometimes, and should have got himself married long ago; everybody said that. But it wasn't too bad. He'd worked with him before, and enjoyed it most of the time. Sometimes he seemed a very ordinary sort of fellow. The real trouble was that he always had to find a complex solution to everything, and Lewis had enough experience of police work to know that most criminal activity owed its origins to simple, cheap and sordid motives, and that few of the criminals themselves had sufficiently intelligent or tortuous minds to devise the cunning stratagems that Morse was wont to attribute to them. In Morse's mind the simple facts of any case seemed somewhere along the line to get fitted out with hooks and eyes which rendered the possibility of infinite associations and combinations. What the great man couldn't do, for all his gifts, was put a couple of simple facts together and come up with something obvious. The letters from Valerie were a case in point. The first one, Peters had said, was pretty certainly written by Valerie herself. Why then not work on the assumption that it *was*, and go on from there? But no. Morse had to believe the letter was forged, just because it would fit better with some fantastical

117

notion that itself owed its abortive birth to some equally improbable hypothesis. And then there was the second letter. Morse hadn't said much about that; probably learned his lesson. But even if he had to accept that Valerie Taylor had written the letters, he would never be prepared to believe anything so simple as the fact that she'd got fed up with home and with school, and had just gone off, as hundreds of other girls did every year. Then why not Valerie? The truth was that Morse would find it all too easy; no fit challenge for that thoroughbred mind of his. Yes, that was it.

Lewis began to wish he could have a few days on his own in London; use his own initiative. He might find *something*. After all, Ainley probably had—well, according to Morse he had. But there again the chief was only guessing. There was no evidence for it. Wasn't it far more likely that Ainley hadn't found anything? If he was killed on the very day that he'd actually found some vital clue—after well over two years of finding nothing—it would be a huge coincidence. Too big. But no. Morse himself took such coincidences blithely in his stride.

He went to the canteen for a cup of tea and sat down by Constable Dickson.

"Solved the murder yet, sarge?"

"What murder?"

Dickson grinned. "Now don't tell me they've put old Morse on a missing persons case, 'cause I shan't believe you. Come on, sarge, spill the beans."

"No beans to spill," said Lewis.

"Come off it! I was on the Taylor business, too, you know. Searched everywhere we did—even dragged the reservoir."

"Well you didn't find the body. And if you don't have the body, Dickson boy, you don't have a murder, do you?"

"Ainley thought she was bumped off, though, didn't he?"

"Well, there's always the possibility, but ... Look here, Dickson." He swivelled round in his chair and faced the constable. "You kill somebody, right? And you've got a body on your hands, right? How do you get rid of it? Come on, tell me."

"Well, there's a hundred and one ways."

"Such as?"

"Well, for a start, there's the reservoir."

"But that was dragged, you say."

Dickson looked mildly contemptuous. "Yes, but I mean. A bloody great reservoir like that. You'd need a bit of luck, wouldn't you, sarge?"

"What else?"

"There was that furnace in the school boiler room. Christ, you wouldn't find much trace if they stuck you in there."

"The boiler room was kept locked."

"Come off it! S'posed to have been, you mean. Anyway, *somebody's* got keys."

"You're not much help, are you, Dickson?"

"Could have been buried easy enough, couldn't she? It's what usually happens to dead bodies, eh, sarge?" He was inordinately amused by his own joke, and Lewis left him alone in his glory.

He returned to the office and sat down opposite the empty chair. Whatever he thought about Morse it wasn't much fun without him ...

He thought about Ainley. *He* hadn't known about the letters. If he had ... Lewis was puzzled. Why *hadn't*

Morse worried more about the letters? Surely the two of them should be in London, not sitting on their backsides here in Kidlington. Morse was always saying they were a team, the two of them. But they didn't function as a team at all. Sometimes he got a pat on the back, but mostly he just did what the chief told him to. Quite right and proper, too. But he would dearly love to try the London angle. He could always suggest it, of course. Why not? Why indeed not? And if he found Valerie and proved Morse wrong? Not that he wanted to prove him wrong really, but Morse was such an obstinate blighter. In Lewis's garden ambition was not a weed that sprouted freely.

He noted that Morse had obviously read the notes he had made, and felt mildly gratified. Morse must have come back to the office after seeing the Taylors; and Lewis wondered what wonderful edifice his superior officer had managed to erect on the basis of those two interviews.

The phone rang and he answered it. It was Peters.

"Tell Inspector Morse it's the same as before. Different pen, different paper, different envelope, different postmark. But the verdict's the same as before."

"Valerie Taylor wrote it, you mean?"

Peters paused. "I didn't say that, did I? I said the verdict's the same as before."

"Same odds as before, then?"

He paused. "The degree of probability is just about the same."

Lewis thanked him and decided to communicate the information immediately. Morse had told him that if anything important came up, a message would always get through to him. Surely this was important enough? And while he was on the phone he would mention that idea of his. Sometimes it was easier on the phone.

He learned that Morse was in the witness box, but that he should be finished soon. Morse would ring back, and did so an hour later.

"What do you want, Lewis? Have you found the corpse?"

"No, sir. But Peters rang."

"Did he now?" A note of sudden interest crept into Morse's voice. "And what did the old twerp have to say, this time?" Lewis told him and felt surprised at the mild reception given to this latest intelligence. "Thanks for letting me know. Look, Lewis, I've finished here now and I'm thinking of taking the afternoon off. I had a bloody awful night's sleep and I think I'll go to bed. Look after my effects, won't you?"

To Lewis, he seemed to have lost interest completely. He'd tried his best to make a murder out of it; and now he'd learned he'd failed, he'd decided to go to bed! It was as good a time as any to mention that other little thing.

"I was just wondering, sir. Don't you think it might be a good idea if I went up to London. You know—make a few enquiries, have a look round—"

Morse interrupted him angrily from the other end of the line. "What the hell are you talking about, man? If you're going to work with me on this case, for God's sake get one thing into that thick skull of yours, d'you hear? Valerie Taylor isn't living in London or anywhere else. You got that? She's dead." The line was dead, too.

Lewis walked out of the office and slammed the door behind him. Dickson was in the canteen; Dickson was always in the canteen.

"Solved the murder yet, sarge?"

"No I have not," snarled Lewis. "And nor has Inspector bloody Morse."

He sat alone in the farthest corner and stirred his coffee with controlled fury.

Chapter Fifteen

> 'Tis a strange thing, Sam, that among us people can't agree the whole week because they go different ways upon Sundays.
>
> GEORGE FARQUHAR

The brief Indian Summer, radiant and beneficent, was almost at an end. On Friday evening the forecast for the weekend was unsettled, changeable weather with the possibility of high winds and rain; and Saturday was already appreciably cooler, with dark clouds from the west looming over North Oxfordshire. Gloomily the late-night weatherman revealed to the nation a map of the British Isles almost obliterated by a series of close, concentric millibars with their epicentrum somewhere over Birmingham, and prophesied in minatory tones of weak fronts and associated depressions. Sunday broke gusty and raw, and although the threatened rain storm held its hand, there was, at 9:00 A.M., a curiously-deadened, almost dreamlike quality about the early morning streets, and the few people there were seemed to move as in a silent film.

From Carfax (at the centre of Oxford) Queen Street leads westwards, very soon changing its name to Park End Street; and off Park End Street on the left-hand side and just opposite the railway station, is Kempis Street, where stands a row of quietly-senescent terraced houses. At five minutes past nine the door of one of these houses is opened, and a man walks to the end of the street, opens the faded-green doors of his garage and backs out his car. It is a dull black car, irresponsive, even in high summer, to any glancing sunbeams, and the chrome on the front and rear bumpers is rusted to a dirty brown. It is time he bought a new car, and indeed he has more than enough money to do so. He drives to St. Giles and up the Woodstock Road. It would be slightly quicker and certainly more direct to head straight up the Banbury Road; but he wishes to avoid the Banbury Road. At the top of the Woodstock Road he turns right along the ring-road for some three or four hundred yards and turns left at the Banbury Road roundabout. Here he increases his speed to a modest 45 m.p.h. and passes out of Oxford and down the long, gentle hill that leads to Kidlington. Here (inconspicuously, he hopes) he leaves his car in a side street which is only a few minutes' walk from the Roger Bacon Comprehensive School. It is a strange decision. It is more than that; it is an incomprehensible decision. He walks fairly quickly, pulling his trilby hat further over his eyes and hunching deeper into his thick, dark overcoat. He walks up the slight incline, passing the prefabricated hut in which the Clerk of Works directs (and will direct) the perpetual and perennial alterations and extensions to the school, and as deviously as he can he penetrates the sprawling amalgam of outbuildings, permanent and temporary, wherein the pupils of secondary school age are initiated into the mysteries of the Sciences and the Humanities. Guardedly his eyes glance hither and thither, but there is no one to be seen. Thence over the black tarmac of the central play area and towards the two-storeyed, flatroofed central administrative block, newly-built in yellow brick. The main door is locked; but he has a key. He enters quietly and unlocks the door. Within, there is a deathly silence about the familiar surroundings; his footsteps echo on the parquet flooring, and the smell of the floor polish takes him back to times of long ago. Again he looks around him and quickly mounts the stairs. The door to the secretary's office is locked; but he has a key, and enters and locks the door behind him. He walks over to the headmaster's study. The door is locked; but he has a key, and enters and feels a sudden fear. But there is no reason for the fear. He walks over to a large filing cabinet. It is locked; but he has a key, and opens it and takes out a file marked "Staff Appointments." He flicks through the thick file and replaces it; tries another, and another. At last he finds it. It is a sheet of paper he has never seen before; but it contains no surprises, for he has known its contents all along. In the office outside he turns on the electric switch of the copying machine. It takes only thirty seconds to make two copies (although he has been asked for only one). Carefully he replaces the original document in the filing cabinet, relocks the study door, unlocks and relocks the outer door, and makes his way down the stairs. Stealthily he looks outside. It is five minutes to ten. There is no one in sight as he lets himself out, relocks the main door and leaves the school premises. He is lucky. No one has seen him and he retraces his steps. A man is standing on the pavement by the car, but moves on, guiltily tugging a small white dog along the pavement and momentarily deferring the imminent defecation.

This same Sunday morning Sheila Phillipson is picking up the windfalls under the apple trees. The grass needs cutting again, for in spite of the recent weeks of sunshine a few dark ridges of longish grass are sprouting in dark green patches; and with rain apparently imminent, she will mention it to Donald. Or will she? He has been touchy and withdrawn this last week—almost certainly because of that girl! It is unlike him, though. Hereto he has assumed the duties and responsibilities of the headship with a verve and a confidence that have slightly surprised her. No. It isn't like him to worry. There must be something more to it; something wrong somewhere.

She stands with the basket of apples on her arm and looks around: the tall fencing that keeps them so private, the bushes and shrubs and ground-cover that blend so wonderfully with their variegated greens. It is almost terrifyingly beautiful. And the more she treasures it all the more frightened she is that she may lose it all. How she wants to keep everything just as it is! And as she stands beneath the apple-heavy boughs her face grows hard and determined. She *will* keep it all—for Donald, for the children, for herself. She will let nothing and no one take it from her!

Donald comes out to join her and says (praise be!) that it's high time he cut the grass again, and greets the promise of apple pie for dinner with a playfully-loving kiss upon her cheek. Perhaps after all she is worrying herself over nothing.

At midday the beef and the pie are in the oven, and as she prepares the vegetables she watches him cutting the lawn. But the shaded patterns of the parallel swathes seem not so neat as usual—and suddenly she bangs her hands upon the window and shouts hysterically: "Donald! For God's—" So nearly, so very nearly has he chewed up the electric flex of the lead with the blades of the mower. She has read of a young boy doing just that only a week ago: instantly and tragically fatal.

* * *

The Senior Tutor's secretary has had to come into Lonsdale College this Sunday morning. In common with many she feels convinced there are far too many conferences, and wonders whether the Conference for the Reform of French Teaching in Secondary Schools will significantly affect the notorious inability of English children to learn the language of any other nation. So many conferences, especially before the start of the Michaelmas Term! She is efficient and has almost everything ready for the evening's business: lists of those attending, details of their schools, programmes for the following two days' activities, certifications of attendance and the menus for the evening's banquet. There remain only the name-tags, and using the red ribbon and the upper case she begins typing the name and provenance of each of the delegates. It is a fairly simple and quick operation. She then cuts up the names into neat rectangles and begins to fit them into the small celluloid holders; MR. J. ABBOTT, The Royal Grammar School, Chelmsford; MISS P. ACKROYD, High Wycombe Technical College; MR. D. ACUM, City of Caernarfon School . . . and so on, to the end of the list.

She is finished by midday and takes all her bits and pieces to the Conference Room, where at 6:30 P.M. she will sit behind the reception desk and greet the delegates as they arrive. To be truthful, she rather enjoys this sort of thing. Her hair will be most cunningly coiffured, and on her name-tag she has proudly printed "Lonsdale College" as her own academic provenance.

With the new stretch of the M40 blasted through the heart of the Chilterns, the journey to and from London is now quicker than ever; and Morse feels reasonably satisfied with his day's work when he arrives back in Oxford just after 4:00 P.M. Lewis was quite right: there were one or two things that could only be checked in London, and Morse thinks that he has dealt with them. On his return he calls in at Police H.Q. and finds an envelope, heavily-sealed with Sellotape, and boldly marked for the attention of Chief Inspector Morse. The pieces are beginning to fall into place. He dials Acum's home number and waits.

"Hello?" It is a woman's voice.

"Mrs. Acum?"

"Yes, speaking."

"Could I have a word with your husband, please?"

"I'm afraid he's not here."

"Will he be in later?"

"Well, no. He won't. He's away on a Teachers' Conference."

"Oh, I see. When are you expecting him back, Mrs. Acum?"

"He said he hoped to be back Tuesday evening—fairly late, though, I think."

"I see."

"Can I give him a message?"

"Er, no. Don't worry. It's not important. I'll try to ring him later in the week."

"You sure?"

"Yes, that'll be fine. Thanks very much, anyway. Sorry to trouble you."

"That's all right."

Morse sits back and considers. As he's just said, it isn't really important.

*   *   *

Baines is not a man of regular habits, nor indeed of settled tastes. Sometimes he drinks beer, and sometimes he drinks Guinness. Occasionally, when a heavy burden weighs upon his mind, he drinks whisky. Sometimes he drinks in the lounge, and sometimes he drinks in the public bar; sometimes in the Station Hotel, and sometimes in the Royal Oxford, for both are near. Sometimes he doesn't drink at all.

Tonight he orders a whisky and soda in the lounge bar of the Station Hotel. It is a place with a very special and a very important memory. The bar is fairly small, and he finds he can easily follow long stretches of others' conversations; but tonight he is deaf to the chatter around him. It has been a worrying sort of day—though not worrying exactly; more a nervy, fluttery sort of day. Clever man, Morse!

Several of the customers are waiting for the London train; smartly-dressed, apparently affluent. Later there will be a handful who have missed the train and who will book in for the night if there are vacancies; relaxed, worldly men with generous expense allowances and jaunty anecdotes. And just once in a while there is a man who deliberately misses his train, who rings his wife and tells his devious tale.

It had been a chance in a thousand, really—seeing Phillipson like that. Phillipson! One of the six on the short-list, a list that had included himself! A stroke of luck, too, that *she* had not seen him when, just after 8:30, they had entered arm-in-arm. And then they had actually appointed Phillipson! Well, well, well. And the little secret glittered and gleamed like a bright nugget of gold in a miser's hoard.

Phillipson, Baines, Acum; headmaster, second master,

ex–Modern Languages master of the Roger Bacon
School, and all thinking of Valerie Taylor as they lay
awake that Sunday night listening as the wind howled
and the rain beat down relentlessly. At last to each of
them came sleep; but sleep uneasy and disturbed.
Phillipson, Baines, Acum; and tomorrow night one of the
three will be sleeping a sleep that is long and undis-
turbed; for tomorrow night at this same time one of the
three will be dead.

Chapter Sixteen

> They wish to know the family secrets
> and to be feared accordingly.
>
> JUVENAL, *Satire III*, 113

Morse woke from a deep, untroubled sleep at 7:30 A.M. and switched on Radio Oxford: trees uprooted, basements flooded, outbuildings smashed to matchwood. But as he washed and shaved, he felt happier than he had done since taking over the case. He saw things more clearly now. There was a long way still to go but at least he had made the first big breakthrough. He would have to apologise to Lewis—that was only fit and proper; but Lewis would understand. He backed out the Lancia and got out to lock the garage doors. The rain had ceased at last and everywhere looked washed and clean. He breathed deeply—it was good to be alive.

He summoned Lewis to his office immediately, cleared his desk and cheated by having a quick preliminary look at 1 Across: *Code name for a walrus* (5). Ha! The clue was like a megaphone shouting the answer at him. It was going to be his day!

Lewis greeted his chief defensively; he had not seen him since the previous Thursday morning. Where Morse had been he didn't know, and what he'd been doing he didn't really care.

"Look," said Morse. "I'm sorry I blasted your head off

last week. I know you don't worry about things like that, but I do."

It was a new angle, anyway, thought Lewis.

"And I feel I ought to apologise. It's not like me, is it, to go off the deep end like that."

It was hardly a question and Lewis made no reply.

"We're a team, Lewis, you and me—you must never forget that . . ." He went on and on and Lewis felt better and better. "You see, Lewis, the long and the short of it is that you were right and I was wrong. I should have listened to you." Lewis felt like a candidate who learns that he has been awarded grade 1 although he was absent for the examination.

"Yes," continued Morse, "I've had the chance to stand back and see things a little more clearly, and I think we can now begin to see what really happened."

He was becoming rather pompous and self-satisfied, and Lewis tried to bring him down to earth. As far as he knew, Morse had been nowhere near the office since Thursday morning.

"There's that report from Peters on Valerie's second letter, sir. You remember, I rang you about it."

Morse brushed the interruption aside. "That's not important, Lewis. But I'm going to tell you something that *is* important." He leaned back in the black leather chair and commenced an analysis of the case, an analysis which at several points had Sergeant Lewis staring at him in wide-eyed amazement and despair.

"The one person who has worried me all along in this case has been Phillipson. Why? Because it's clear that the man is hiding something, and to keep things dark he's been forced to tell us lies."

"He didn't lie about Blackwells, sir."

"No. But I'm not worried so much about what happened on the day when Valerie disappeared. That's where we've been making our mistake. We should have been concentrating much more on what happened *before* she disappeared. We should have been looking into the past for some incident, some relationship, *something*, that gives a coherent pattern to all the rest. Because, make no mistake, there *is* something buried away back there in the past, and if we can find it everything will suddenly click into place. It's the key, Lewis—a key that slips easily into the lock and when it turns it's smooth and silky and—hey presto! So, let's forget for a while who saw Valerie last and what colour knickers she was wearing. Let's go back long before that. For if I'm right, if I'm right . . ."

"You think you've found the key?"

Morse grew rather more serious. "I think so, yes. I think that what we've got to reckon with in this case is *power*, the power that someone, by some means or other, can exercise over someone else."

"Blackmail, you mean, sir?"

Morse paused before answering. "It may have been; I'm not sure yet."

"You think someone's blackmailing Phillipson, is that it?"

"Let's not rush, Lewis. Just suppose for a minute. Suppose you yourself did something shady, and no one found out. No one, that is, except for one other person. Let's say you bribed a witness, or planted false evidence or something like that. All right? If you got found out, you'd be kicked out of the force on your ear, and find yourself in jug, as likely as not. Your career would be ruined, and your family, too. You'd give a lot to keep things dark, and just let's suppose that I was the one who knew all about this, eh?"

"You'd have me by the . . ." Lewis thought better of it.

"I would, indeed. But not only that. I could also do some shady things myself, couldn't I? And get you to cover up for me. It would be dangerous, but it might be necessary. I could get you to compound the original crime you'd committed, by committing another, but committing it for *me*, not for yourself. From then on we'd sink or swim together, I know that; but we'd be fools to split on each other, wouldn't we?"

Lewis nodded, he was getting a bit bored.

"Just think, Lewis, of the ordinary people we come across every day. They do the same sort of things we do and have the same sort of hopes and fears as everybody else. And they're not really villains at all, but some of them occasionally do things they'd be frightened to death anyone else finding out about."

"Pinching a bag of sugar from the supermarket—that sort of thing?" Morse laughed.

"Your mind, as always, Lewis, leaps immediately to the limits of human iniquity! In the seventh circle of Dante's Hell we shall doubtless find the traitors, the mass murderers, the infant torturers and the stealers of sugar from the supermarkets. But that's the sort of thing I mean, yes. Now just let that innocent mind of yours sink a little lower into the depths of human depravity, and tell me what you find."

"You mean having another woman, sir?"

"How delicately you put things! Having another woman, yes. Jumping between the sheets with a luscious wench and thinking of nothing but that great lump of gristle hanging between your legs. And the little woman at home cooking a meal for you and probably pressing your pants or something. You make it all sound like having another pint of beer, Lewis; but perhaps you're right. It's not all that important in the long run. A quick blow-through, a bit of remorse and anxiety for a few days and then it's all over. And you tell yourself you're a damned fool and you're not going to do it again. But what, Lewis, *what if someone finds out*?"

"Bit of hard luck." He said it in such a way that Morse looked at him curiously.

"Have *you* ever had another woman?"

Lewis smiled. An old memory stirred and swam to the surface of his mind like a bubble in still water. "I daren't tell you, sir. After all I wouldn't want you to kick me out of the force, would I?"

The phone rang and Morse answered it. "Good . . . Good . . . That's good . . . Excellent." Morse's half of the conversation seemed singularly unenlightening and Lewis asked him who it was. "I'll come to that in a minute, Lewis. Now, where were we? Oh yes. I suspect—and, if I may say so, you tend to confirm my suspicion—that adultery is more widespread than even the League of Light would have us believe. And a few unlucky ones still get caught with their pants down, and a hell of a lot of others get away with it."

"What are you getting at, sir?"

"Simply this." He took a deep breath and hoped it wouldn't sound too melodramatic. "I think that Phillipson had an affair with Valerie Taylor, that's all."

Lewis whistled softly and slowly took it in. "What makes you think that?"

"No one reason—just lots of little reasons. And above

all, the fact that it's the only thing that makes sense of the whole wretched business."

"I think you're wrong, sir. There's an old saying, isn't there—if you'll excuse the language—about not shitting on your own doorstep. Surely it would be far too risky? Her at the school and him headmaster? I don't believe it, sir. He's not such a fool as that, surely?"

"No, I don't think he is. But as I told you, I'm trying to look back further than that, to the time, let's say, before he became headmaster."

"But he didn't know her then. He lived in Surrey."

"Yes. But he came to Oxford at least once, didn't he?" said Morse slowly. "He came up here when he was interviewed for the job. And in that sense, to use your own picturesque terminology, he wouldn't exactly be shitting on his own doorstep, would he?"

"But you just can't say things like that, sir. You've got to have some *evidence*."

"Yes. We shall need some evidence, you're quite right. But just forgetting the evidence for a minute, what worries me is whether it's a *fact* or not; and I think that we've just got to assume that it *is* a fact. We *could* get the evidence—I'm sure of that. We could get it from Phillipson himself; and I think, Lewis, that there are one or two other persons who could tell us a good deal if they had a mind to."

"You mean, sir, that you've not really got any evidence yet?"

"Oh, I wouldn't say that. One or two pointers, aren't there?"

"Such as?"

"Well, first of all there's Phillipson himself. *You* know he's hiding something as well as I do." As was his wont,

Morse blustered boldly through the weakest points in his argument. "He doesn't talk about the girl in a natural way at all—not about the girl *herself*. It's almost as if he's frightened to remember her—as if he feels guilty about her in some way." Lewis seemed stolidly unimpressed, and Morse left it. "And then there's Maguire. By the way, I saw him again yesterday."

Lewis raised his eyebrows. "Did you? Where was that?"

"I, er, I thought I ought to follow your advice after all. You were quite right, you know, about the London end. One or two loose ends to tie up, weren't there?"

Lewis opened his mouth, but got no further.

"When I first saw him," continued Morse, "it was obvious that he was jealous—plain miserably jealous. I think Valerie must have dropped the odd hint; nothing too specific, perhaps. And I tackled Maguire about it again yesterday, and—well, I'm sure there was a bit of gossip, at least among some of the pupils."

Lewis continued to sit in glum silence.

"And then there was George Taylor. According to him it was just about that time—when Phillipson first came for the job, that is—that Valerie began staying out late. Again, I agree, nothing definite, but another suggestive indication, wouldn't you say?"

"To be truthful, sir, I wouldn't. I think you're making it all up as you're going along."

"All right. I'll not argue. Just have a look at this." He handed to Lewis the document that Baines had so carefully packaged for him. It was a photocopy of the expenses form that Phillipson had submitted to the Governors after the headship interviews. From the form it was immediately apparent that he had not reached home that evening; he had claimed for B and B at the Royal Oxford, and had arrived home at lunchtime on the following day.

"He probably missed his train," protested Lewis.

"Don't think so," said Morse. "I've checked. The last of the interviews was over by a quarter to six, and there was a good train for Phillipson to catch at 8:35. And even if he'd missed that, there was another at 9:45. But he wouldn't miss it, would he? Two and three-quarter hours to get from Kidlington to Oxford? Come off it!"

"He probably felt tired—you know how it is."

"Not too tired to cock his leg round Valerie Taylor."

"It's just not fair to say that, sir."

"Isn't it, now? Well let me tell you something else, Lewis. I went to the Royal Oxford yesterday and found the old register. Do you know something? *There is no entry for any Phillipson that night.*"

"All right. He just tried to claim a few extra quid for nothing. He caught the train after all."

"I bet he wouldn't like me to check up with his wife about that!" Morse was now regaining his momentum.

"You've not checked with her, then?"

"No. But I checked up on something else. I went round to the Station Hotel just opposite. Very interesting. They looked out their old register for me, and I'll give you one guess who the last entry on the list was."

"He probably just got the names of the hotels muddled. They're pretty near each other."

"Could be. But you see, Lewis, *there's no Phillipson there either.* Let me show you what there was, though."

He passed over a photocopied sheet of paper and Lewis read what Morse had found:

"Mr. E. Phillips, 41 Longmead Road, Farnborough."

He sat silently, and then looked again at the copy of the expenses form that Morse had given him earlier. It was certainly odd. Very, very odd.

"And," continued Morse, "I've checked on something else. There's no Mr. Phillips who lives in Longmead Road, Farnborough, for the very simple reason there *is* no Longmead Road in Farnborough."

Lewis considered the evidence. Initials? Move on one from D to E. Easy. Phillipson? Just leave off the last two letters. Could be. But something else was staring him in the face. The home address (as given on the expenses form) of Mr. D. Phillipson was 14 Longmead Road, Epsom. Transpose the 1 and the 4, and move on one from E to F: Epsom to Farnborough.

"I should think Peters ought to be able to give us a line on the handwriting, sir."

"We'll leave him out of it." It sounded final.

"It's a bit suspicious, all right," admitted Lewis. "But where does Valerie Taylor fit in? Why her?"

"It's got to be her," said Morse. "It all adds up, don't you see?"

"No."

"Well, let's just assume that what I suspect is the truth. Agreed? *Assume*, nothing more. Now, where are we? For some reason Phillipson meets Valerie, probably in Oxford, probably at the station Buffet. He chats her up and—Bob's your uncle. Off they go to the Station Hotel—a bit of a roll round the bed, and she goes off home with a few quid in her pocket. I don't think she'd stay all night; probably a couple of hours or so— no more. It wouldn't be easy for her to leave the hotel after midnight, would it? Not without causing a bit of comment."

"I still don't see why it should be Valerie, though. And even if you're right, sir, what's it all got to do with Valerie disappearing?"

Morse nodded. "Tell me, Lewis. If *anyone* got to know about this little bit of philandering, who do you think it would be?"

"Phillipson could have told his wife, I suppose. You know, he would have felt guilty about it—"

"Mm." It was Morse's turn to display a lack of enthusiasm and Lewis tried again.

"I suppose Valerie could have told someone?"

"Who?"

"Her mum?"

"She was a bit scared of her mum, wasn't she?"

"Her dad, then?"

"Could be."

"I suppose someone could have seen them," said Lewis slowly.

"I'm pretty sure someone did," said Morse.

"And you think you know who it was?"

Again Morse nodded. "So do you, I think."

Did he? In such situations Lewis had learned to play it cleverly. "You mean . . . ?" He tried to look as knowing as his utter lack of comprehension would permit, and mercifully Morse took up his cue.

"Yes. He's the only person connected with the case who lives anywhere near there. You don't make an excursion to the Station Hotel if you live in Kidlington, do you? Come to think of it, you don't make an excursion to the Station Hotel wherever you live. The beer there's bloody awful."

Lewis understood now, but wondered how on earth

they'd ever managed to get this far on such a flimsy series of hypotheses. "He found out, you think?"

"Saw 'em, most probably."

"You've not tackled him about it yet?"

"No. I want to get a few things straight first. But I shall be seeing him, have no fear."

"I still don't see why you think it was Valerie."

"Well, let's look at things from her point of view for a minute. She gets herself pregnant, right?"

"So you say, sir."

"And so does Maguire."

"We've got no real evidence."

"No, not yet, I agree. But we may well have some fairly soon—you'll see. For the minute let's just assume she's pregnant. I'm pretty sure that Phillipson himself wouldn't have been the proud daddy; in fact, I shouldn't think he ever dreamed of touching her again. But if she were in trouble, daren't tell her parents, say—who would she go to? As I see it, she may well have gone to someone who owed her a favour, someone who had some sort of moral duty to help her, someone in fact who daren't *not* help her. In short she'd probably go to Phillipson. And, as I see it, they cooked up something between 'em. The Taylors—they'd almost certainly have to be in on it—the Taylors, Phillipson and Valerie. I should think that Phillipson arranged a place for her to go to in London, paid the abortion clinic, and let the whole thing look like a runaway schoolgirl lark. The Taylors are saved any local scandal and disgrace, Phillipson has paid his pound of flesh and Valerie is let off lightly for her sins. Yes, I think that's roughly what might have happened; only roughly, mind you."

"But how did she disappear?"

"Again I'm guessing. But I suspect that when she left home after lunch she took a minimum of things with her—hence the bag or basket, whatever it was; it had to look, you see, as if she was going off to school in the normal way—the neighbours and so on might see her. As it happens, they didn't—but that was pure chance. I should think she went down the main road, probably nipped into the ladies' lavatory by the shops and changed her school uniform for something a bit trendier (don't forget the bag, Lewis!), and met Phillipson who was waiting for her in his car further down the road near the roundabout. They've probably got her case in the boot already. He drove her down to the station in Oxford, gave her full instructions, parked somewhere in town, bought a book at Blackwells and got home by three o'clock. Easy." He stopped and looked hopefully at Lewis. "Well, something like that. What do you think?"

"And I suppose she just gets rid of the baby like you say, finds she likes London, gets in with a swinging set and forgets all about mum and dad and everything at home."

"Something like that," said Morse, without conviction.

"They put the police to a dickens of a lot of trouble for nothing, then, didn't they?"

"Probably never thought we'd make so much fuss."

"They'd have a good idea."

Morse was looking increasingly uneasy. "As I told you, Lewis, it's only a rough outline. Just remember that if Valerie had wanted to, she could have ruined Phillipson's career in a flash. Just think of the headlines! It'd be dynamite! And think of Valerie, too. She certainly wouldn't want to be carting a kid around at her age. And her parents . . ."

"A lot of parents don't seem to mind too much these days, sir."

Morse was feeling cross and showed it. "Well *they* did! They minded enough to go through with the whole bloody business; still are going through with it . . ."

Somewhere along the line the euphoria had turned to a saddened exasperation. He knew far better than Lewis could have told him that he hadn't really thought things through.

"You know, Lewis, something must have turned sour somewhere, mustn't it? Perhaps something went wrong . . ." He suddenly brightened. "We shall have to find out, shan't we?"

"You think Valerie's still alive then, sir?"

Morse backed down with commendable grace. "I suppose so, yes. After all she wrote home, didn't she? Or so you tell me."

He had a cheek, this man Morse, and Lewis shook his head in dismay. Everything had pointed to a straightforward case of a girl running away from home. As everyone (including Morse) had said, it happens all the time. And what a dog's breakfast he'd made of it all!

But Lewis had to concede that there might be something worth salvaging from all that complicated nonsense. Valerie and Phillipson. *Could* be true, perhaps. But why did he have to invent all that fanciful stuff about changing in ladies' lavatories? Oh dear. But something else was worrying him.

"You said, sir, that you thought Baines might have found out about Phillipson and this girl—whoever she was."

"I think he did. In fact, I think Baines knows a hell of a lot more about the whole caboodle than anybody."

"More than you, sir?"

"God, yes. He's been watching and waiting has Baines; and I suspect he'd be very happy for the truth—or most of it—to come out. Phillipson would be a dead duck then, and they'd have to appoint a new headmaster, wouldn't they? And they've got Baines—a faithful servant who's been there all those years, runner-up at the last appointment . . . why, I shouldn't think the Governors would even advertise."

"They'd have to, sir. It's the law."

"Oh . . . Anyway, he'd get the job—sure as eggs are eggs. And he'd love it. The thought of all that power, Lewis—power over other people's lives. That's what Baines is hankering after."

"Don't you think," said Lewis gently, "that it would be a good idea to get things on to a bit of a firmer footing, sir? I mean, why not question Phillipson and Baines and the Taylors? You'd probably get the truth out of one of them."

"Perhaps." Morse stood up and flexed his arms. "But you're going to be pleased with me, Lewis. At the beginning of this case I promised myself I'd stick to *facts*, and so far I've not done very well. But you see a reformed character before you, my friend. First, I've arranged to see Phillipson and Baines—together, mind you!—tomorrow afternoon. Good touch, eh, Lewis? *Tuesday* afternoon. Should be good, I reckon. No holds barred! And then—that phone call you heard. Metropolitan Police, no less. They're going to help us if they can; and they think they can. If Valerie did go up to London for an abortion, she'd have to go to some sort of clinic, wouldn't she? And we know exactly *when* she went. She might have changed her name and address and God knows what. But those boys in London are pretty sharp. If she *did* go to a clinic—even a shady, back-street clinic—I reckon we've got her on toast. And if they don't trace anything—well we shall have to think again, I suppose. But if we do find out where she went—and I think we shall—well, we're there, aren't we? She had no money of her own, that's for sure, and somebody, *somebody*, Lewis, had to fork out pretty handsomely. And then? Then we take it from there." Morse sat down again. He was trying hard, but was convincing no one, not even himself.

"You're not really very interested in finding her at all, are you, sir?"

The sparkle had gone from Morse's eyes: Lewis was right, of course. "To tell you the truth, I shan't give two buggers if we never find her. Perhaps we've found her, anyway. She may have been the girl sharing Maguire's flat. I don't think so. But if she was—so what? She may have been one of those strippers we saw; you remember, the one with the mask and the bouncy tits. So what? You know, Lewis, this whole case is beginning to get one almighty bore, and if all we're going to do is stir up a load of trouble and get poor old Phillipson the sack—I'd rather pack it up."

"It's not like you to back out of anything, sir."

Morse stared morosely at the blotting paper. "It's just not my sort of case, Lewis. I know it's not a very nice thing to say, but I just get on better when we've got a body—a body that died from unnatural causes. That's all I ask. And we haven't got a body."

"We've got a living body," said Lewis quietly.

Morse nodded. "I suppose you're right." He walked

across the room and stood by the door, but Lewis remained seated at the desk. "What's the matter, Lewis?"

"I just can't help wondering where she is, sir. You know, at this very minute she must be somewhere, and if only we knew we could just go along there and find her. Funny, isn't it? But we can't find her, and I don't like giving up. I just wish we *could* find her, that's all."

Morse walked back into the room and sat down again. "Mm. I'd not thought of it quite like that before ... I've been so cock-sure she was dead that I haven't really thought of her as being alive. And you're right. She's some-where; at this very second she's sitting *somewhere.*" The grey eyes were beginning to glow once more and Lewis felt happier.

"Could be quite a challenge, couldn't it, sir?"

"Ye-es. Perhaps it's not such a bad job after all—chasing a young tart like Valerie Taylor."

"You think we should try, then?"

"I'm beginning to think we should, yes."

"Where do we start?"

"Where the hell do you think? She's almost certainly sitting somewhere in a luxury flat plucking her eyebrows."

"But where, sir?"

"Where? Where do you think? London, of course. What was that postmark? E.C.4 wasn't it? She's within a few miles' radius of E.C.4. Sure to be!"

"That wasn't the postmark on the second letter she wrote."

"Second letter? Oh yes. What was the postmark on that?"

Lewis frowned slightly. "W.1. Don't you remember?"

"W.1, eh? But I wouldn't worry your head about that second letter, Lewis."

"You wouldn't?"

"No, I wouldn't bother about it at all. You see, Lewis, I wrote that second letter myself."

Chapter Seventeen

And all the woe that moved him so
   That he gave that bitter cry,
And the wild regrets, and the bloody sweats,
   None knew so well as I:
For he who lives more lives than one
   More deaths than one must die.
   OSCAR WILDE, *The Ballad of Reading Gaol*

There were over one hundred and twenty of them, and it was too many. Why, if each of them were given leave to speak only for a minute, that would be two hours! But anyway, Acum didn't think he wanted to say anything. The great majority of the delegates were in their forties and fifties, senior men and women who, judging from their comments and their questions, sent forth an annual stream of gifted linguists to assume their natural Oxbridge birthrights.

He had felt tired after his five-and-a-half-hours' drive the previous day, and this morning's programme, conducted in a genteel atmosphere of rarefied intellectuality, had hardly succeeded in fostering any real *esprit de corps*. Speaking on "Set Texts in the Sixth Form" the Senior Tutor had given voice softly and seriously to the delicate rhythms of Racine, and Acum began to wonder if the premier universities were not growing further and further out of touch with his own particular brand of comprehensive school. His main problem in the sixth was to recruit a handful of pupils who had just about reached the minimum requirement of a grade C in O-level French, and who, in the wake of their qualified triumphs,

had promptly mislaid the substance of their erstwhile
knowledge during two long months of carefree summer
freedom. He wondered if other schools were different; if
he himself, in some way, were to blame.

Fortunately the post-lunch discussion on the merits of
the Nuffield French experiment was infinitely lighter and
brighter, and Acum felt slightly more at home with his
co-delegates. The Senior Tutor, the rhythms of Racine
still rippling along through his mind, testified evangeli-
cally to the paramount need for a formal, grammatical
discipline in the teaching of all languages, including
modern languages. And if Racine and Molière were not
worth reading, reading with accuracy, and reading without the remotest possibility of misunderstanding arising
from mistranslation—then we all might just as well
forget literature and life. It sounded magnificent. And
then that burly, cheerful fellow from Bradford had
brought the academic argument down to earth with a
magnificent thud: give him a lad or a lass with t'gump-
tion to order t'pound of carrots at t'French greengrocer's
shop, any dair! The conference exploded in glorious
uproar. Slyly, a dignified old greybeard suggested that no
Englishman, even one who had the good fortune to learn
his native tongue in Yorkshire, had ever been confronted
with an insuperable language-barrier in finding his way
to a pissoir in Paris.

It was all good stuff now. The conference should have
passed a vote of thanks to the burly Bradfordian and his
pound of carrots. Even Acum nearly said something; and
almost every other member of the silent majority nearly
said something, too. There were just far too many there.
Ridiculous, really. No one would notice if you were there
or not. He was going out tonight, anyway. No one was

going to miss him if he slipped away from the conference after Hall. He would be back long before the porters' lodge was shut at 11:00 P.M.

The school bell rang at 4:00 P.M., and the last lesson of the day was over. Streams of children emerged from classrooms and, like a nest of ants uncovered, bewilderingly crossed and recrossed to cloakrooms, to bicycle sheds, to societies, to games practices and to sundry other pursuits. More leisurely, the teachers threaded their way back through the milling throngs to the staff room; some to smoke, some to talk, some to mark. And very soon most of them, teachers and pupils alike, would be making their way home. Another day was done.

Baines returned from teaching a fourth-year mathematics set and dropped a pile of thirty exercise books on to his table. Twenty seconds each—no more; only ten minutes the lot. He might as well get them marked straightaway. Thank the Lord it wasn't like marking English or History, with all that reading to do. His practised eye had learned to pounce upon the pages in a flash. Yes, he would dash them off now.

"Mr. Phillipson would like a word with you," said Mrs. Webb.

"Oh. Now?"

"As soon as you came in, he said."

Baines knocked perfunctorily and entered the study.

"Have a seat a minute, Baines."

Warily the second master took a seat. There was a serious edge to Phillipson's voice—like a doctor's about to inform you that you've only a few months more to live.

"Inspector Morse will be in again tomorrow afternoon.

You know that, don't you?" Baines nodded. "He wants to talk to us both—together."

"He didn't mention that to me."

"Well, that's what he's going to do." Baines said nothing. "You know what this probably means, don't you?"

"He's a clever man."

"No doubt. But he won't be getting any further, will he?" The tone of Phillipson's voice was hard, almost the tone of a master to his pupil. "You realise what I'm saying, don't you, Baines? Keep your mouth shut!"

"Yes, you'd like me to do that, wouldn't you?"

"I'm warning you!" The latent hatred suddenly blazed in Phillipson's eyes. No pretence now; only an ugly, naked hatred between them.

Baines got up, savouring supremely the moment of his power. "Don't push me too far, Phillipson! And just remember who you're talking to."

"Get out!" hissed Phillipson. The blood was pounding in his ears, and although a non-smoker he longed to light a cigarette. He sat motionless at his desk for many minutes and wondered how much longer the nightmare could go on. What a relief it would be to end it all—one way or another . . .

Gradually he grew calmer, and his mind wandered back again. How long ago was it now? Over three and a half years! And still the memory of that night came back to haunt him like a ghost unexorcised. That night . . . He could picture it all so vividly still . . .

He felt quite pleased with himself. Difficult to tell for certain, of course; but yes, quite pleased with himself really. As accurately as it could his mind retraced the stages of the day's events: the questions of the interviewing committee—wise and foolish; and his own answers—carefully considered . . .

Chapter Eighteen

In philological works ... a dagger † signifies an obsolete
word. The ... sign, placed before a person's name, signifies
deceased.

Rules for Compositors and Readers, O.U.P.

This same Monday night or, to be accurate, Tuesday
morning, Morse was not in bed until 2:00 A.M., overtired
and underbeered. The euphoria of the earlier part of the
day had now completely passed, partly as a result of
Lewis's sceptical disparagement, but more significantly
because of his own inability ever to fool himself for very
long. He still believed that some of the pieces had clicked
into place, but knew that many didn't fit at all; and a few
didn't even look like pieces of the same jigsaw. He recol-
lected how in the army he had been given a test for
colour-blindness. A sheet of paper on which a chaotically
confused conglomeration of colour-blocks were printed
had been magically metamorphosed when looked at
through differently-coloured filter slides; a red filter, and
there appeared an elephant; a blue filter, and a lion leaped
out at the eyes; a green filter, and behold the donkey!
Donkey ... He'd been reading something about a
donkey only a few days ago. Where had he read it?
Morse was not a systematic reader; he was a dipper-in.
He looked at the small pile of books on his bedside table
underneath the alarm clock. *The Road to Xanadu, A
Selection of Kipling's Short Stories, The Life of Richard
Wagner* and *Selected Prose of A. E. Housman*. It was in

Housman, surely, that bit about the donkey who couldn't make up its asinine mind which bundle of hay to start on first. Hadn't the stupid animal finally died of starvation? He soon found the passage:

> *An editor of no judgment, perpetually confronted with a couple of MSS to choose from, cannot but feel in every fibre of his being that he is a donkey between two bundles of hay.*

Two MSS, and no judgment! That summed it up perfectly. One MS told him that Valerie Taylor was alive, and the other told him she was dead. And he still didn't know which MS a man of judgment should settle for. Oh Lord! Which of the wretched MSS had the correct reading? Had either?

He knew that at this rate he would never go to sleep, and he told himself to forget it all and think of something else. He picked up Kipling and began re-reading his favourite short story, *Love O' Women*. He firmly believed that Kipling knew more about women than Kinsey ever had, and he came back to a passage marked with vertical lines in the margin:

> *. . . as you say, sorr, he was a man with an educashin, an' he used ut for his schames; an' the same educashin an' talkin' an' all that made him able to do fwhat he had a mind to wid a woman, that same wud turn back again in the long-run an' tear him alive.*

Phew!

He thought back on what he'd learned about Valerie's sex-life. Nothing much, really. He thought of Maguire, and half-remembered something Maguire had said that didn't quite ring true. But he couldn't quite get hold of it and the memory slipped away again like a bar of soap in the bath.

Educashin. Most people were more interesting for a bit of education. More interesting to women ... some of these young girls must soon get tired of the drib-drab, wishy-washy drivel that sometimes passed for conversation. Some of them liked older men for just that reason; interesting men with some show of pretence for cultured pursuits, with a smattering of knowledge—with something more in mind than fiddling for their bra-straps after a couple of whiskies.

What *was* Valerie like? Had she gone for the older men? Phillipson? Baines? But surely not Baines. Some of her teachers, perhaps? Acum? He couldn't remember the other names. And then he suddenly caught the bar of soap. He'd asked Maguire how many times he'd been to bed with Valerie, and Maguire had said a dozen or so. And Morse had told him to come off it and tell him the truth, fully expecting a considerably increased count of casual copulations. But no. Maguire had come down, hadn't he? "Well, three or four," he'd said. Something like that. Probably hadn't slept with her at all? Morse sat up and considered. Why, oh why, hadn't he pressed this point with Maguire when he had seen him yesterday? Was she really pregnant after all? He had assumed so, and Maguire had seemingly confirmed his suspicions. But was she? It made sense if she was. But made sense of what? Of the preconceived pattern that Morse was building up, and into which, willy-nilly, the pieces were being forced into their places.

If only he knew what the problem *was*. Then he

wouldn't be quite so restless, even if it proved beyond his powers. Problem! He remembered his old Latin master. Hm! Whenever *he* was confronted with an insoluble difficulty—a crux in the text, an absurdly complex chunk of syntax—he would turn to his class with a serious mien: "Gentlemen, having looked this problem boldly in the face, we must now, I think, pass on." Morse smiled at the recollection . . . It was getting very late. A crux in the Oxford Classical Text, marked by daggers . . . the daggered text . . . He was falling asleep. Texts, manuscripts, and a donkey in the middle braying and bellyaching, not knowing which way to turn . . . like Morse, like himself . . . His head fell to the right and his ear strained no more for the incomprehensible nocturnal clues. He fell asleep, the light still burning and Kipling's stories still held loosely in his hand.

Earlier the same evening Baines had opened his front door to find an unexpected visitor.

"Well, well! This *is* a surprise. Come in, won't you? Shall I take your coat?"

"No. I'll keep it on."

"Well, at least you'll have a drop of something to cheer you up, eh? Can I offer you a glass of something? Nothing much in, though, I'm afraid."

"If you like."

His visitor following behind, Baines walked through to the small kitchen, opened the fridge and looked inside. "Beer? Lager?"

"Lager."

Baines squatted on his haunches and reached inside. His left hand lay on the top of the fridge, the fingernails slightly dirty; his right hand reached far in as he bent forward. There were two bald patches on the top of his head, with a greying tuft of hair between them, temporarily thwarting the impending merger. He wore no tie, and the collar of his light-blue shirt was grubbily lined. He would have changed it the next day.

Chapter Nineteen

> One morn I miss'd him on the custom'd hill.
> THOMAS GRAY, *Elegy Written in a Country Churchyard*

Full morning assembly at the Roger Bacon Comprehensive School began at 8:50. The staff stood at the back of the main hall, wearing (at least those authorised to do so) the insignia of their respective universities; it was something the head insisted on. Punctual to the second, and flanked at some short distance in the rear by the second master and the senior mistress, Phillipson, begowned and behooded, walked from the back of the hall, and the pupils rose to their feet as the procession made its way down the central gangway, climbed the short flight of steps at the side and mounted on to the stage itself. The routine seldom varied: a hymn sung, a prayer intoned, a passage read from Holy Writ—and paid for one more day were the proper respects to the Almighty. The last unsynchronised "Amen" marked the end of morning devotions, and gave the cue to the second master to recall the attention of the assembled host to more terrestrial things. Each morning he announced, in clear, unhurried tones, any changes in the day's procedure necessitated by staff absences, house activities, the times and places of society meetings and the results of the sports teams. And, always, reserved until the end, he read with doomsday gravity a list of names; the names of pupils who would report outside the staff room immediately after the assembly was finished: the recalcitrants, the anarchists, the obstructionists, the truants, the skivers and the defectors in general from the rules that governed the corporate life of the establishment.

As the procession walked up the central aisle on Tuesday morning, and as the school rose en bloc from their seats, several heads turned towards each other and many whispered voices asked where Baines could be; not even the oldest pupils could remember him being away for a single day before. The senior mistress looked lopsided and lost: it was like the dissolution of the Trinity. Phillipson himself read the notices, referring in no way to the absence of his adjutant. The girls' hockey team had achieved a rare and decisive victory, and the school greeted the news with unwonted enthusiasm. The chess club would meet in the physics lab and 4C (for unspecified criminality) would be staying in after school. The following pupils, etc., etc. Phillipson turned away from the rostrum and walked out through the wings. The school chattered noisily and prepared to go to their classrooms.

At lunchtime Phillipson spoke to his secretary.

"No word from Mr. Baines yet?"

"Nothing. Do you think we should give him a ring?"

Phillipson considered for a moment. "Perhaps we should. What do you think?"

"Not like him to be away, is it?"

"No, it isn't. Give him a ring now."

Mrs. Webb rang Baines's Oxford number and the distant burring seemed to echo in a vaulted, ominous silence.

"There's no answer," she said.

* * *

At 2:15 P.M. a middle-aged woman took from her handbag the key to Baines's house; she cleaned for him three afternoons a week. Oddly, the door was unlocked and she pushed it open and walked in. The curtains were still drawn and the electric light was still turned on in the living room, as well as in the kitchen, the door to which stood open wide. And even before she walked through to the kitchen she saw the slumped figure of Baines in front of the refrigerator, a long-handled household knife plunged deep into his back, the dried blood forming a horrid blotch upon the cotton shirt, like a deranged artist's study in claret and blue.

She screamed hysterically.

It was 4:30 P.M. before the fingerprint man and the photographer were finished, and before the hump-backed surgeon straightened his afflicted spine as far as nature would permit.

"Well?" asked Morse.

"Difficult to say. Anywhere from sixteen to twenty hours."

"Can't you pin it down any closer?"

"No."

Morse had been in the house just over an hour, for much of which time he had been sitting abstractedly in one of the armchairs in the living room, waiting for the others to leave. He doubted they could tell him much, anyway. No signs of forcible entry, nothing stolen (or not apparently so), no fingerprints, no blood-stained footprints. Just a dead man, and a deep pool of blood and a fridge with an open door.

A police car jerked to a halt outside and Lewis came in. "He wasn't at school this morning, sir."

"Hardly surprising," said Morse, without any conscious humour.

"Do we know when he was murdered?"

"Between eight o'clock and midnight, they say."

"Pretty vague, sir."

Morse nodded. "Pretty vague."

"Did you expect something like this to happen?"

Morse shook his head. "Never dreamed of it."

"Do you think it's all connected?"

"What do you think?"

"Somebody probably thought that Baines was going to tell us what he knew." Morse grunted non-committally. "Funny, isn't it, sir?" Lewis glanced at his watch. "He'd have told us by now, wouldn't he? And I've been thinking, sir." He looked earnestly at the inspector. "There weren't many who knew you were going to see Baines this afternoon, were there? Only Phillipson really."

"Each of them could have told somebody else."

"Yes, but—"

"Oh, it's a good point. I see what you're getting at. How did Phillipson take the news, by the way?"

"Seemed pretty shattered, sir."

"I wonder where he was between eight o'clock and midnight," mumbled Morse, half to himself, as he eased himself out of the armchair. "We'd better try to look like detectives, Lewis."

The ambulance men asked if they could have the body, and Morse walked with them into the kitchen. Baines had been eased gently on to his right side, and Morse bent down and eased the knife slowly from the second master's back. What an ugly business murder was. It was a wooden-handled carving knife, "Prestige, Made in England," some 35–36 centimetres long, the cutting blade honed along its entire edge to a razor-sharp ferocity. Globules of fresh pink blood oozed from the wicked-looking wound, and gradually seeped over the stiff clotted mess that once had been a blue shirt. They took Baines away in a white sheet.

"You know, Lewis, I think whoever killed him was bloody lucky. It's not too easy to stab a man in the back, you know. You've got to miss the spinal column and the ribs and the shoulder blades, and even then you've got to be lucky to kill someone straight off. Baines must have been leaning forward, slightly over to his right, and exposing about the one place that makes it comparatively easy. Just like going through a joint of beef."

Lewis loathed the sight of death, and he felt his stomach turning over. He walked to the sink for a glass of water. The cutlery and the crockery from Baines's last meal were washed up and neatly stacked on the draining board, the dish cloth squeezed out and draped over the bowl.

"Perhaps the post mortem'll tell us what time he had his supper," suggested Lewis hopefully.

Morse was unenthusiastic. He followed Lewis to the sink and looked around half-heartedly. He opened the drawer at the right of the sink unit. The usual collection: teaspoons, tablespoons, wooden spoons, a fish slice, two corkscrews, kitchen scissors, a potato peeler, various meat skewers, a steel—and a kitchen knife. Morse picked up the knife and looked at it carefully. The handle was bone, and the blade was worn away with constant sharpening into a narrowed strip. "He's had this a good while," said Morse. He ran his finger along the blade; it had almost the same cruel sharpness as the blade that had lodged its head in Baines's heart.

"How many carving knives do you keep at home, Lewis?"

"Just the one."

"You wouldn't think of buying another one?"

"No point, really, is there?"

"No," said Morse. He placed the murder weapon on the kitchen table and looked around. There seemed singularly little point in any inspection, however intelligently directed, of the tins of processed peas and preserved plums that lined the shelves of the narrow larder.

"Let's move next door, Lewis. You take the desk; I'll have a look at the books."

Most of the bookshelves were taken up with works on mathematics, and Morse looked with some interest at a comprehensive set of text books on the *School Mathematics Project*, lined up in correct order from Book 1 to Book 10, and beside them the corresponding Teachers' Guide for each volume. Morse delved diffidently into Book 1.

"Know anything about modern maths, Lewis?"

"Modern maths? Ha! I'm an acknowledged expert. I do all the kids' maths homework."

"Oh." Morse decided to puzzle his brain no more on how 23 in base 10 could be expressed in base 5, replaced the volume and inspected the rest of Baines's library. He'd been numerate all right. But literate? Doubtful. On the whole Morse felt slightly more sympathy with Maguire's uncompromising collection.

As he stood by the shelves the grim, brutal fact of

Baines's murder slowly sank into his mind. As yet it figured as an isolated issue; he'd had no chance of thinking of it in any other context. But he would be doing so soon, very soon. In fact some of the basic implications were already apparent. Or was he fooling himself again? No. It meant, for a start, that the donkey knew for certain which bundle of hay to go for, and that, at least, was one step forward. Baines must have known something. Correction. Baines must have known virtually everything. Was that the reason for his death, though? It seemed the likeliest explanation. But who had killed him? Who? From the look of things the murderer must have been known to Baines—known pretty well; must have walked into the kitchen and stood there as Baines reached inside the fridge for something. And the murderer had carried a knife—surely that was a reasonable inference? Had brought the knife into the house. But how the hell did anyone carry a knife as big as that around? Stuff it down your socks, perhaps? Unless . . .

From across the room a low-pitched whistle of staggering disbelief postponed any answers that might have been forthcoming to these and similar questions. Lewis's facial expression was one of thrilled excitement mingled with pained incredulity.

"You'd better come over here straightaway, sir."

Morse himself looked down into the bottom right-hand drawer of the desk; and he felt the hairs at the nape of his neck grow stiff. A book lay in the drawer, an exercise book; an exercise book from the Roger Bacon Comprehensive School; and on the front of the exercise book a name, a most familiar name, was inscribed in capital letters: VALERIE TAYLOR: APPLIED SCIENCE. The two men looked at each other and said nothing. Finally Morse picked up the book gently, placing the top of each index finger along the spine; and as he did so, two loose sheets of paper fell out and fluttered to the floor. Morse picked them up and placed them on the desk. The sheets contained drafts of a short letter; a letter which began Dear Mum and Dad and ended Love Valerie. Several individual words were crossed out and the identical words, but with minor alterations to the lettering, written above them; and between the drafts were whole lines of individual letters, practised and slowly perfected: w's, r's, and t's. It was Lewis who broke the long silence.

"Looks as if you're not the only forger in the case, sir." Morse made no reply. Somewhere at the back of his mind something clicked smoothly into place. So far in the case he had managed to catch a few of the half-whispers and from them half-divine the truth; but now it seemed the facts were shouting at him through a megaphone.

Baines, it was clear, had written the letter to Valerie's parents; and the evidence for Valerie being still alive was down to zero on the scale of probabilities. In one way Morse was glad; and in another he felt a deep and poignant sadness. For life was sweet, and we each of us had our own little hopes, and few of us exhibited overmuch anxiety to quit this vale of misery and tears. Valerie had a right to live. Like himself. Like Lewis. Like Baines, too, he supposed. But someone had decided that Baines had forfeited his right to live any longer and stuck a knife through him. And Morse stood silently at Baines's desk and knew that everyone expected him to discover who that someone was. And perhaps he would, too. At the rate he was going he would be able to know the truth before the day was out. Perhaps all he had to do was look through the rest of the drawers and find the whole solution neatly copied out and signed. But he hardly expected to find much else, and didn't. For the next hour he and Lewis carefully and patiently vetted the miscellaneous contents of each of the other drawers; but they found nothing more of any value or interest, except a recent photoprint of Phillipson's expenses form.

The phone stood on the top of the desk, a white phone, the same phone that had rung at lunchtime when Mrs. Webb had called a man who then lay cold and dead beside the opened fridge. And then, suddenly, Morse noticed it. It had been under his nose all the time but he had ignored it because it was an item so naturally expected: a plastic, cream-coloured rectangular telephone index-system, whereby one pressed the alphabetical letter and the index opened automatically at the appropriate place. Half expecting to find his own illustrious self recorded, Morse pressed the "m"; but there was nothing on the ruled card. Clearly none of Baines's more intimate acquaintances boasted a surname beginning with "m." So Morse pressed "n"; and again he found no entry. And "o"; and with the same result. Probably Baines had only recently acquired the index? It looked reasonably new and maybe he had not yet transcribed the numbers from an older list. But no such list had yet been found. Morse pressed "p," and a slight shiver ran along his spine as he saw the one entry: Phillipson, with the headmaster's Oxford telephone number neatly appended thereto. Morse continued systematically through the remainder of the alphabet. Under "r" was the number of the Oxford branch of the RAC, but nothing more. And under "s," the number of a Sun Insurance agent. And then "t"; and once again the slight,

involuntary shiver down the spine. Taylor. And somewhere at the back of Morse's mind something else
clicked smoothly into place. Under "u," "v"—nothing.
Then "w," Mr. Wright, with an Oxford number: builder
and decorator. On to "x," "y," "z"—nothing. "a." Morse
looked carefully at the card and frowned, and whistled
softly. Only one entry: Acum, the personal number (not
the school's) written neatly in the appropriate column . . .

In all, there were fourteen entries only, most of which
were as innocently explicable as the RAC and the interior
decorator. And only three of the fourteen names
appeared to have the slightest connection with the case:
Acum, Phillipson, Taylor. Funny (wasn't it?) how the
names seemed to crop up in trios. First, it had been
Acum, Baines and Phillipson, and now Baines had got
himself crossed off the list and another name had
appeared almost magically in his place: the name of
Taylor. Somewhere, yet again, in the farthest unchartered
corners of Morse's mind, a little piece clicked smoothly
into place.

Although the curtains had been drawn back as soon as
the police arrived, the electric lights were still switched
on, and Morse finally switched them off as he stood on
the threshold. It was 5:30 P.M.

"What's next?" asked Lewis.

Morse pondered a while. "Has the wife got the chips
on, Lewis?"

"I 'spect so, sir. But I'm getting rather fond of dried-up
chips."

Chapter Twenty

Alibi (L. alibi, elsewhere, orig. locative—alius, other); the plea in a criminal charge of having been elsewhere at the material time.

Oxford English Dictionary

"He's not going to like it much."

"Of course he's not going to like it much."

"It's almost as good as saying we suspect him."

"Well? We do, don't we?"

"Among others, you mean, sir?"

"Among others."

"It's a pity they can't be just a bit more definite about the time." Lewis sounded uneasy.

"Don't worry about that," said Morse. "Just get a complete schedule—from the time he left school to the time he went to bed."

"As I say, sir, he's not going to like it very much."

Morse got up and abruptly terminated the conversation. "Well, he'll have to bloody well lump it, won't he?"

It was just after 6:30 P.M. when Morse pushed his way through the glass doors, left police H.Q. behind him and made his way slowly and thoughtfully towards the housing estate. He wasn't looking forward to it, either. As Lewis had said, it was almost as good as saying you suspected them.

The Taylors' green Morris Oxford was parked along

the pavement, and it was the shirt-sleeved George himself who answered the door, hastily swallowing a mouthful of his evening meal.

"I'll call back," began Morse.

"No. No need, inspector. Nearly finished me supper. Come on in." George had been sitting by himself in the kitchen finishing off a plate of stew and potatoes. "Cup o' tea?"

Morse declined and sat opposite George at the rickety kitchen table.

"What can I do for you, Inspector Morse?" He filled an outsize cup with deep-brown tea and lit a Woodbine. Morse told him of Baines's murder. The news had broken just too late for the final edition of the *Oxford Mail*, a copy of which lay spread out on the table.

George's reaction was flat and unconcerned. He'd known Baines, of course—seen him at parents' evenings. But that was all. It seemed to Morse curious that George Taylor had so little to say or (apparently) to feel on learning of the death of a fellow human being he had known; yet neither was there hint of machination or of malice in his eyes, and Morse felt now, as on the previous occasion they had met, that he rather liked the man. But sooner or later he had to ask him, in the hallowed phrases, to account for all his movements on the previous evening. For the moment he stood on the brink and postponed the evil moment; and mercifully George himself did a good deal of the work for him.

"The missus knew him better'n me. I'll tell her when she gets in. Mondays and Tuesdays she's allus off at Bingo down in Oxford."

"Does she ever win?" The question seemed oddly irrelevant.

"Few quid now and then. In fact she won a bit last night, I reckon. But you know how it is—she spends about a quid a night anyway. Hooked on it, that's what she is."

"How does she go? On the bus?"

"Usually. Last night, though, I was playing for the darts team down at the Jericho Arms, so I took her down with me, and she called in at the pub after she was finished and then came home with me. It's on the bus, though, usually."

Morse took a deep breath and jumped in. "Look, Mr. Taylor, it's just a formality and I know you'll understand, but, er, I've got to ask you exactly where you were last night."

George seemed not in the least put out or perturbed. In fact—or was it a nothing, an imperceptibility, a fleeting flash of Morse's imagination?—there might have been the merest hint of relief in the friendly eyes.

Lewis was already waiting when Morse arrived back in his office at 7:30 P.M., and the two men exchanged notes. Neither of them, it appeared, had been in too much danger of flushing any desperado from his lair. The alibis were not perfect—far from it; but they were good enough. Phillipson (according to Phillipson) had arrived home from school about 5:15 P.M.; had eaten, and had left home, alone, at 6:35 P.M. to see the Playhouse production of *St. Joan*. He had left his car in the Gloucester Green car park, and reached the theatre at 6:50 P.M. The play had lasted from 7:15 to 10:30 P.M., and apart from walking to the bar for a Guinness in the first interval he had not left his seat until just after 10:30 when he collected his car and drove back home. He remembered seeing the BBC2 news bulletin at 11:00 P.M.

"How far's Gloucester Green from Baines's house?" asked Morse.

Lewis considered. "Two, three hundred yards."

Morse picked up the phone and rang the path lab. No. The hump-backed surgeon had not yet completed his scrutiny of various lengths of Baines's innards. No. He couldn't be more precise about the time of death. Eight to midnight. Well, if Morse were to twist his arm it might be 8:30 to 11:30—even 11:00, perhaps. Morse cradled the phone, stared up at the ceiling for a while, and then nodded slowly to himself.

"You know, Lewis, the trouble with alibis is not that some people have 'em and some people don't. The real trouble is that virtually no one's likely to have a really water-tight alibi. Unless you've been sitting all night hand-cuffed to a couple of high court judges, or something."

"You think Phillipson could have murdered Baines, then?"

"Of course he could."

Lewis put his notebook away. "How did you get on with the Taylors, sir?"

Morse recounted his own interview with George Taylor, and Lewis listened carefully.

"So *he* could have murdered Baines, too."

Morse shrugged non-committally. "How far's the Jericho Arms from Baines's place?"

"Quarter of a mile—no more."

"The suspects are beginning to queue up, aren't they, Lewis?"

"Is Mrs. Taylor a suspect?"

"Why not? As far as I can see, she'd have had no

trouble at all. Left Bingo at 9:00 P.M. and called in at the Jericho Arms at 9:30 P.M. or so. On the way she walks within a couple of hundred yards of Baines's place, eh? And where does it all leave us? If Baines was murdered at about 9:30 last night—what have we got? Three of 'em—all with their telephone numbers on Baines's little list."

"And there's Acum, too, sir. Don't forget him."

Morse looked at his watch. It was 8:00 P.M. "You know, Lewis, it would be a real turn up for the books if Acum was playing darts in the Jericho Arms last night, eh? Or sitting at a Bingo board in the Town Hall?"

"He'd have a job wouldn't he, sir? He's in Caernarfon."

"I'll tell you one thing for sure, Lewis. Wherever Acum was last night he wasn't in Caernarfon."

He picked up the phone and dialled a number. The call was answered almost immediately.

"Hello?" The line crackled fitfully, but Morse recognised the voice.

"Mrs. Acum?"

"Yes. Who is it?"

"Morse. Inspector Morse. You remember, I rang you up—"

"Yes, of course I remember."

"Is your husband in yet?"

"No. I think I mentioned it to you, didn't I, that he wouldn't be back until late tonight?"

"How late will he be?"

"Not too late, I hope."

"Before ten?"

"I hope so."

"Has he got far to travel?"

"Quite a long way, yes."

"Look, Mrs. Acum. Can you please tell me where your husband has been?"

"I told you. He's been on a Teachers' Conference. Sixth form French."

"Yes. But where exactly was that?"

"Where? I'm not quite sure where he was staying."

Morse was becoming impatient. "Mrs. Acum, you know what I mean. Where was the conference? In Birmingham?"

"Oh, I'm sorry. I see what you mean. It was in Oxford, actually."

Morse turned to Lewis and his eyebrows jumped an inch. "In Oxford, you say?"

"Yes. Lonsdale College."

"I see. Well, I'll ring up again—about ten. Will that be all right?"

"Is it urgent, inspector?"

"Well, let's say it's important, Mrs. Acum."

"All right, I'll tell him. And if he gets back before ten, I'll ask him to ring you."

Morse gave her his number, rang off, and whistled softly. "It gets curiouser and curiouser, does it not, Lewis? How far is Lonsdale College from Kempis Street?"

"Half a mile?"

"One more for the list, then. Though I suppose Acum's got just as good, or just as bad, an alibi as the rest of 'em."

"Haven't you forgotten one possible suspect, sir?"

"Have I?" Morse looked at his sergeant in some surprise.

"Mrs. Phillipson, sir. Two young children, soon in bed, soon asleep. Husband safely out of the way for three hours or so. She's got as good a motive as anybody, hasn't she?"

Morse nodded. "Perhaps she's got a better motive than most." He nodded again and looked sombrely at the carpet.

With a startling suddenness, a large spider darted across the floor with a brief, electric scurry—and, as suddenly, stopped—frozen into a static, frightening immobility. A fat-bodied, long-legged spider, the angular joints of the hairy limbs rising high above the dark squat body. Another scurry—and again the frozen immobility—more frightening in its stillness than in its motion. It reminded Morse of a game he used to play at children's parties called "statues"; the music suddenly stopped and—still! Freeze! Don't move a muscle! Like the spider. It was almost at the skirting board now, and Morse seemed mesmerised. He was terrified of spiders.

"Did you see that whopper in Baines's bath?" asked Lewis.

"Shut up, Lewis. And put your foot on that bloody thing, quick!"

"Mustn't do that, sir. He's got a wife and kids waiting for him somewhere." He bent down and slowly moved his hand towards the spider; and Morse shut his eyes.

Chapter Twenty-one

John and Mary are each given 20p. John gives 1p to Mary.
How much more does Mary have than John?
Problem set in the 11 + examination

The urge to gamble is so universal, so deeply embedded
in unregenerate human nature that from the earliest days
the philosophers and moralists have assumed it to be evil.
Cupiditas, the Romans called it—the longing for the
things of this world, the naked, shameless greed for gain.
It is the cause, perhaps, of all our troubles. Yet how easy
it remains to understand the burning envy, felt by those
possessing little, for those endowed with goods aplenty.
And gambling? Why, gambling offers to the poor the
shining chance of something got for nothing.

Crude analysis! For to some it is gambling itself, the
very process and the very practice of gambling that is
so immensely pleasurable. So pleasurable indeed that
gambling needs, for them, no spurious *raison d'être*
whatsoever, no necessary prospect of the jackpots and
the windfalls and the weekends in Bermuda; just the
heady, heavy opiate of the gambling game itself with
the promise of its thousand exhilarating griefs and dangerous joys. Win a million on the wicked spinning-wheel
tonight, and where are you tomorrow night but back
around the wicked spinning-wheel?

Every society has its games, and the games are just as
revealing of the society as are its customs—for in a sense

they are its customs: heads or tails, and *rouge ou noir*; and double or quits and clunk, clunk, clunk, in the payoff tray as the triple oranges align themselves along the fruit machine; and odds of 10 to 1 as the rank outsider gallops past the post at Kempton Park; *and then came the first, saying, Lord, thy pound hath gained ten pounds. And he said unto him, Well done, thou good servant: because thou hast been faithful in a very little, have thou authority over ten cities.* And once a week a hope, a light-year distant, of half a million pounds for half a penny stake, where happiness is a line of Xs and a kiss from a buxom beauty queen. For some are lucky at the gambling game. And some are not, and lose more than they can properly afford and try to recoup their losses and succeed only in losing the little that is left; and finally, alas, all hope abandoned, sit them down alone in darkened garages and by the gas rings in the kitchens, or simply slit their throats—and die. And some smoke fifty cigarettes a day, and some drink gin or whisky; and some walk in and out of betting shops, and the wealthier reach for the phone.

But what wife can endure a gambling husband, unless he be a steady winner? And what husband will ever believe his wife has turned compulsive gambler, unless she be a poorer liar than Mrs. Taylor is. And Mrs. Taylor dreams she dwells in Bingo halls.

It had started some years back in the church hall at Kidlington. A dozen of them, no more, seated in rickety chairs with a clickety subfusc vicar calling the numbers with a dignified Anglican clarity. And then she had graduated to the Ritz in Oxford, where the acolytes sit comfortably in the curving tiers of the cinema seats and listen to the harsh metallic tones relayed by microphones across the giant auditorium. There is no show here of human compassion, little even of human intercourse. Only "eyes down" in a mean-minded race to the first row, the first column, the first diagonal completed. Many of the players can cope with several cards simultaneously, a cold, pitiless purpose in their play, their mental antennae attuned only to the vagaries of the numerical combinations.

The game itself demands only an elementary level of numeracy, and not only does not require but cannot possibly tolerate the slightest degree of initiative or originality. Almost all the players almost win; the line is almost complete, and the card is almost full. Ye gods! Look down and smile once more! Come on, my little number, come! I'm *there*, if only, if only, if only . . . And there the women sit and hope and pray and bemoan the narrow miss and curse their desperate luck, and talk and think "if only" . . .

Tonight Mrs. Taylor caught the No. 2 bus outside the Ritz and reached Kidlington at 9:35 P.M.; she decided she would call in at the pub.

It was 9:35 P.M., too, when Acum rang, a little earlier than expected. He had been fortunate with the traffic (he said); on to the A5 at Towcester and a good clear run for a further five uncomplicated hours. He had left Oxford at 3:15, just before the conference had officially broken up. Jolly good conference, yes. The Monday night? Just a minute; let's think. In hall for dinner, and then there had been a fairly informal question-and-answer session afterwards. Very interesting. Bed about 10:30; a bit tired. No, as far as he remembered—no, he *did* remember; he hadn't gone out at all. Baines dead? What? Could Morse repeat that? Oh dear; very sorry to hear it. Yes, of course he'd known Baines—known him well. When did he die? Oh, Monday. Monday evening? Oh, yesterday evening, the one they'd just been speaking about. Oh, he saw now. Well, he'd told Morse what he could—sorry it was so little. Not been much help at all, had he?

Morse rang off. He decided that trying to interview by telephone was about as satisfactory as trying to sprint in diver's boots. There was no option; he would have to go up to Caernarfon himself, if ... if what? Was it really likely that Acum had anything to do with Baines's death? If he had, he'd picked a pretty strange way of drawing almost inevitable attention to himself. And yet ... And yet Acum's name had been floating unobtrusively along the mainstream of the case from the very beginning, and yesterday he had seen Acum's telephone number in the index file on Baines's desk. Mm. He would have to go and see him. He ought to have seen him before now; for whatever else he was or wasn't Acum had been a central figure during that school summer when she'd disappeared. But ... but you don't just come down to Oxford for a meeting and decide that while you're there you'll murder one of your ex-colleagues. Or do you? Who would suspect? After all, it was quite by accident that he himself had learned of Acum's visit to Oxford. Had Acum presumed ... ? Augrrh! It was suddenly cold in the office and Morse felt tired. Forget it! He looked at his watch. 10:00 P.M. Just time for a couple of pints if he hurried.

He walked over to the pub and pushed his way into the overcrowded public bar. The cigarette smoke hung in blue wreaths, head-high like undispersing morning mist, and the chatter along the bar and at the tables was raucous and interminable, the subtleties of conversational silence quite unknown. Cribbage, dominoes and darts and every available surface cluttered with glasses: glasses with handles and glasses without, glasses empty, glasses being emptied and glasses about to be emptied, and then refilled with the glorious, amber fluid. Morse found a momentary gap at the bar and pushed his way diffidently forward. As he waited his turn, he heard the fruit machine (to the right of the bar) clunking out an occasional desultory dividend, and he leaned across the bar to look more carefully. A woman was playing the machine, her back towards him. But he knew her well enough.

The landlord interrupted a new and improbable line of thought. "Yes, mate?"

Morse ordered a pint of best bitter, edged his way a little further along the bar, and found himself standing only a few feet behind the woman playing the machine. She pushed her glass over the bar.

"Stick another double in there, Bert."

She opened an inordinately large leather handbag and Morse saw the heavy roll of notes inside. Fifty pounds? More? Had she had a lucky night at Bingo?

She had not seen Morse—he was sure of that—and he observed her as closely as he could. She was drinking whisky and swopping mildly ribald comments with several of the pub's habitués. And then she laughed—a coarse, common cackle of a laugh, and curiously and quite unexpectedly Morse knew that he found her attractive, dammit! He looked at her again. Her figure was still good, and her clothes hung well upon her. Yes, all right, she was no longer a beauty, he knew that. He noticed the finger nails bitten down and broken; noticed the index finger of her right hand stained dark-brown with nicotine.

But what the hell did it matter! Morse drained his glass and bought another pint. The germ of the new idea that had taken root in his mind would never grow this night. He knew why, of course. It was simple. He needed a woman. But he had no woman and he moved to the back of the room and found a seat. He thought, as he often thought, of the attractiveness of women. There had been women, of course; too many women, perhaps. And one or two who still could haunt his dreams and call to him across the years of a time when the day was fair. But now the leaves were falling round him: mid-forties; unmarried; alone. And here he sat in a cheap public bar where life was beer and fags and crisps and nuts and fruit machines and . . . The ashtray on the table in front of him was revoltingly full of stubs and ash. He pushed it away from him, gulped down the last of his beer and walked out into the night.

He was sitting in the bar of the Randolph Hotel with an architect, an older man, who talked of space and light and beauty, who always wore a bowler hat, who studied Greek and Latin verses, and who slept beneath a railway viaduct. They talked together of life and living, and as they talked a girl walked by with a graceful, gliding movement, and ordered her drink at the bar. And the architect nudged his young companion and gently shook his head in wistful admiration.

"My boy, how lovely, is she not? Extraordinarily, quite extraordinarily lovely."

And Morse, too, had felt her beautiful and necessary, and yet had not a word to say.

Turning in profile as she left the bar the young girl flaunted the tantalising, tip-tilted outline of her breasts beneath her black sweater, and the faded architect, the lover of the classical poets, the sleeper beneath the viaduct, stood up and addressed her with grave politeness as she passed.

"My dear young lady. Please don't feel offended with me, or indeed with my dear, young friend here, but I wish you to know that we find you very beautiful."

For a moment a look of incredulous pleasure glazed the painted eyes; and then she laughed—a coarse and common cackle of a laugh.

"Gee, boys, you ought to see me when I'm washed!" And she placed her right hand on the shoulder of the architect, the nails pared down to the quick and the index finger stained dark-brown with nicotine. And Morse woke up with a start in the early light of a cold and friendless dawn, as if some ghostly hand had touched him in his sleep.

Chapter Twenty-two

Life can only be understood backwards,
but it must be lived forwards.

SOREN KIERKEGAARD

Morse was in his office by 7:30 A.M.

When he was a child, the zenith of terrestrial bliss had been a long, luxuriating lie in bed. But he was no longer a child, and the fitful bouts of sleep the night before had left him tired and edgy. His thoughts as he sat at his desk were becoming obsessive and his ability to concentrate had temporarily deserted him. The drive to the office had been mildly therapeutic, and at least he had *The Times* to read. The leaders of the superpowers had agreed to meet at Vladivostok, and the economy continued its downhill slide towards inevitable disaster. But Morse read neither article. He was becoming increasingly less well-informed about the state of the nation and the comings and goings of the mighty. It was a cowardly frame of mind, he knew that, but not entirely reprehensible. Certainly it wasn't very sensible to know too much about some things, and he seemed to be becoming peculiarly susceptible to auto-suggestion. Even a casual reminder that a nervous break-down was no rarity in our society was enough to convince him that he would likely as not be wheeled off into a psychiatric ward tomorrow; and the last time he had braced himself to read an article on the causes of coronary thrombosis he had discovered that he exhibited every one of the

182

major symptoms and had worked himself into a state of advanced panic. He could never understand why doctors could be anything but hyper-hypochondriacs, and supposed perhaps they were. He turned to the back-page of *The Times* and took out his pen. He hoped it would be a real stinker this morning. But it wasn't. Nine and a half minutes.

He took a pad of paper and began writing, and was still writing when the phone rang an hour later. It was Mrs. Lewis. Her husband was in bed with a soaring temperature. Flu, she thought. He'd been determined to go in to work, but her own wise counsels had prevailed and, much it appeared to her husband's displeasure, she had called the doctor. Morse, all sympathy, praised the good lady's course of action and warned her that the stubborn old so-and-so had better do as she told him. He would try to call round a bit later.

Morse smiled weakly to himself as he looked through the hurriedly written notes. It had all been for Lewis's benefit, and Lewis would have revelled in the routine. Phillipson: ticket office at the Playhouse, check row and number; occupants of seats on either side; check, trace, interview. The same with the Taylors and with Acum. The Ritz, the Jericho Arms and Lonsdale College. Ask people, talk to people, check and recheck, slowly and methodically probe and reconstruct. Yes, how Lewis would have enjoyed it. And, who knows? Something might have come of it. It would be irresponsible to neglect such obvious avenues of enquiry. Morse tore the sheets across the middle and consigned them to the waste-paper basket.

Perhaps he ought to concentrate his attention on the knife. Ah yes, the knife! But what the dickens was he supposed to do with the knife? If Sherlock were around he would doubtless deduce that the murderer was about five feet six inches tall, had tennis elbow and probably enjoyed roast beef every other Sunday. But what was *he* supposed to say about it? He walked to the cabinet and took it out; and summoning all his powers of logical analysis he stared at it with a concentrated intensity, and discovered that into his open and receptive mind came nothing whatsoever. He saw a knife—no more. A household knife; and somewhere in the country, most probably somewhere in the Oxford area, there was a kitchen drawer without its carving knife. That didn't move forward the case one millimetre, did it? And could anyone really be sure whether a knife had been sharpened by a left- or a right-handed carver? Was it worth trying to find out? How fatuous the whole thing was becoming. But *how* the knife had been carried—now that was a much more interesting problem. Yes. Morse put the knife away. He sat back in the black leather chair, and once again he pondered many things.

The phone rang again at half-past ten, and Morse started abruptly and guiltily in his chair, and looked at the time in disbelief.

It was Mrs. Lewis again. The doctor had called. Pharyngitis. At least three or four days in bed. But could Morse come round? The invalid was anxious to see him.

He certainly looked ill. The unshaven face was pale and the voice little more than a batrachian croak.

"I'm letting you down, chief."

"Nonsense. You get better that's all. And be a good boy and do as the quack tells you."

"Not much option with a missus like mine." He smiled

wanly, and supporting himself on one arm reached for his glass of weakly-pale orange juice. "But I'm glad you've come, sir. You see, last night I had this terrible headache, and my eyes went all funny—sort of wiggly lines all the time. I couldn't recognise things very well."

"You've got to expect summat to go wrong with you if you're ill," said Morse.

"But I got to thinking about things. You remember the old boy on the Belisha crossing? Well, I didn't mention it at the time but it came back to me last night."

"Go on," said Morse quietly.

"It's just that I don't think he could see very well, sir. I reckon that's why he got knocked over and I just wondered if . . ."

Lewis looked at the inspector and knew instinctively that he had been right to ask him to come. Morse was nodding slowly and staring abstractedly through the bedroom window and on to the neatly-kept strip of garden below, the beds trimmed and weeded, where a few late roses lingered languidly on.

Joe was still in the old people's home at Cowley, and lay in the same bed, half propped up on his pillows, his head lolling to the side, his thin mouth toothless and gaping. The sister who had accompanied Morse along the ward touched him gently.

"I've brought you a visitor."

Joe blinked himself slowly awake and stared vaguely at them with unseeing eyes.

"It's a policeman, Mr. Godberry. I think they must have caught up with you at last." The sister turned to Morse and smiled attractively.

Joe grinned and his mouth moved in a senile chuckle.

His hand groped feebly along the locker for his spectacle case, and finally he managed to hook an ancient pair of National Health spectacles behind his ears.

"Ah, I remember you, sergeant. Nice to see you again. What can I do fo' you this time?"

Morse stayed with him for fifteen minutes, and realised how very sad it was to grow so old.

"You've been very helpful, Joe, and I'm very grateful to you."

"Don't forget, sergeant, to put the clock back. It's this month, you know. There's lots o' people forgits to put the clocks back. Huh. I remember once . . ."

Morse heard him out and finally got away. At the end of the ward he spoke again briefly to the sister.

"He's losing his memory a bit."

"Most of them do, I'm afraid. Nice old boy, though. Did he tell you to put the clock back?"

Morse nodded. "Does he tell everybody?"

"A lot of them seem to get a fixation about some little thing like that. Mind you, he's right, isn't he?" She laughed sweetly and Morse noticed she wore no wedding ring. *I hope you won't be offended, sister, if I tell you that I find you very attractive.*

But the words wouldn't come, for he wasn't an architect who slept beneath the railway viaduct, and he could never say such things. Just as she couldn't. Morse wondered what she was thinking, and realised he would never know. He took out his wallet and gave her a pound note.

"Put it in the Christmas fund, sister."

Her eyes held his for a brief moment and he thought they were gentle and loving; and she thanked him nicely and walked briskly away. Fortunately The Cape of Good Hope was conveniently near.

* * *

Clocks! It reminded him. There was a good tale told in Oxford about the putting back of clocks. The church of St. Benedict had a clock which ran by electricity, and for many years the complexities of putting back this clock had exercised the wit and wisdom of clergy and laity alike. The clock adorned the north face of the tower and its large hands were manoeuvred round the square, blue-painted dial by means of an elaborate lever device, situated behind the clock-face and reached via a narrow spiral staircase leading to the tower roof. The problem had been this. No one manipulating the lever immediately behind the clock-face could observe the effects of his manipulations, and so thick were the walls of the church tower that not even with a megaphone could an accomplice, standing outside the church, communicate to the manipulator the aforementioned effects. Each year, therefore, one of the churchwardens had taken upon himself to mount the spiral staircase, to manipulate the lever in roughly the right direction, to descend the staircase, to walk out of the church, to look upwards at the clock, to ascend the staircase once more, to give the lever a few more turns before descending again and repeating the process, until at last the clock was cajoled into a reluctant synchronisation. Such a lengthy and physically-daunting procedure had been in operation for several years, until a mild-looking thurifer, rumoured to be one of the best incense-swingers in the business, had with becoming diffidence suggested to the minister that to remove the fuse from the fuse-box and to replace it after exactly sixty minutes might not only prove more accurate but also spare the rather elderly churchwarden the prospect of a coronary thrombosis. This idea, discussed at considerable length and finally accepted by the church committee, had proved wonderfully effective, and was now a firmly-established practice.

Someone had told Morse the story in a pub, and he recalled it now. It pleased him. Lewis, but for his illness, would even now be running up and down the spiral staircase looking at his alibis. But that was out—at least for several days. It was up to Morse himself now to take the fuse away and set the clock aright. But not just for an hour—for much, much longer than that. In fact for two years, three months and more, to the day when Valerie Taylor had disappeared.

Chapter Twenty-three

> For having considered God and himself
> he will consider his neighbour.
> CHRISTOPHER SMART, *My Cat Jeoffrey*

Detective Constable Dickson soon realised he was on to something and he felt as secretly excited as the poor woman was visibly nervous. It was the sixth house he had visited, a house on the opposite side of the street from Baines's and nearer the main road.

"You know, madam, that Mr. Baines across the way was murdered on Monday night?" Mrs. Thomas nodded quickly. "Er, did you know Mr. Baines?"

"Yes, I did. He's lived in the street nearly as long as I have."

"I'm, er . . . we're, er, obviously anxious to find any witness who might have seen someone going into Baines's house that night—or coming out, of course." Dickson left it at that and looked at her hopefully.

In her late sixties now, scraggy-necked and flat-chested, Mrs. Thomas was a widow who measured her own life's joy by the health and happiness of her white cat, which playfully and lovingly gyrated in undulating spirals around her lower leg as she stood on the threshold of her home. And as she stood there she was almost glad that this young police officer had called, for she *had* seen something; and several times the previous evening and again this Wednesday morning she had decided she

189

ought to report it to someone. It would have been so easy in the first exciting hours when policemen had been everywhere; later, too, when they had come and placed their no-parking signs, like witches' hats, around the front of the house. Yet it was all so hazy in her mind. More than once she wondered if she could have imagined it, and she would die of shame if she were to put the police to any trouble for no cause. It had always been like that for Mrs. Thomas; she had hidden herself unobtrusively away in the corners of life and seldom ventured forth.

But, yes; she had seen something.

Her life was fairly orderly, if nothing else, and each evening of the week, between 9:30 and 10:00 P.M., she put out the two milk bottles and the two Co-op tokens on the front doorstep before bolting the door securely, making herself a cup of cocoa, watching the News at Ten and going to bed. And on Monday evening she had seen something. If only at the time she had thought it might be important! Unusual, certainly, but only afterwards had she realised exactly how unusual it had been: for never had she seen a woman knocking at Baines's door before. Had the woman gone in? Mrs. Thomas didn't think so, but she vaguely remembered that the light was burning in Baines's front room behind the faded yellow curtains. The truth was that it had all become so very frightening to her. Had the woman she had seen been the one who . . . ? Had she actually seen the . . . murderer? The very thought of it caused her to shiver throughout her narrow frame. Oh God, please not! Such a thing should never be allowed to happen to her—to her of all people. And as the panic rose within her, she again began to wonder if she'd dreamed it after all.

The whole thing was too frightening, especially since there was one thing that she knew might be very important. Very important indeed. "You'd better come in, officer," she said.

In the early afternoon she felt far less at ease than she had done with the constable. The man sitting opposite her in the black leather chair was pleasant enough, charming even; but his eyes were keen and hard, and there was a restless energy about his questions.

"Can you describe her, Mrs. Thomas? Anything special about her—anything at all?"

"It was just the coat I noticed—nothing else. I told the constable . . ."

"Yes, I know you did; but tell me. Tell me, Mrs. Thomas."

"Well, that's all really—it was pink, just like I told the constable."

"You're quite sure about that?"

She swallowed hard. Once more she was assailed by doubts from every quarter. She thought she was sure, she *was* sure, really, but could she just conceivably be wrong?

"I'm—I'm fairly sure."

"What sort of pink?"

"Well, sort of . . ." The vision was fading rapidly now, had almost gone.

"Come on!" snapped Morse. "You know what I mean. Fuchsia? Cyclamen? Er, lilac?" He was running out of shades of pink and received no help from Mrs. Thomas. "Light pink? Dark pink?"

"It was a fairly bright sort of . . ."

"Yes?"

It was no good, though; and Morse changed his tack and changed it again and again. Hair, height, dress, shoes, handbag—on and on. He kept it up for more than twenty minutes. But try as she might Mrs. Thomas was now quite incapable of raising any mental image whatsoever of Baines's late-night caller. Suddenly she knew that she was going to burst into tears, and she wanted desperately to go home. And just as suddenly it all changed.

"Tell me about your cat, Mrs. Thomas."

How he knew she had a cat, she hadn't the faintest idea, but the tension drained away from her like the pus from an abscess lanced by the dentist. She told him happily about her blue-eyed cat.

"You know," said Morse, "one of the most significant physical facts about the cat is so obvious that we often tend to forget it. A cat's face is flat between the eyes and so the eyes can work together. Stereoscopic vision they call it. Now, this is very rare among animals. You just think. The majority of animals have . . ." He went on for several minutes and Mrs. Thomas was enthralled. But more than that; she was excited. It was all so clear again and she interrupted his discourse on the facial structure of the dog and told him all about it. Cerise pink coat—it might have been a herring-bone pattern, no hat, medium height, brownish hair. About ten minutes to ten. She was pretty certain about the time because . . .

She left soon afterwards, happy and relieved, and a nice policeman saw her safely back to her own cosy front-parlour, where the short-haired white cat lay indolently upon the sofa, momentarily opening the mysterious, stereoscopic eyes to greet his mistress's return.

* * *

Cerise. Morse got up and consulted the O.E.D. "A light, bright, clear red, like the colour of cherries." Yes, that was it. For the next five minutes he stared vacantly through the window in the pose of Aristotle's thinker; and at the end of that time he lifted his eyebrows slightly and nodded slowly to himself. It was time to get moving. He knew a coat like that, although he'd only seen it once—the colour of bright-pink cherries in the summer time.

Chapter Twenty-four

"Is there anybody there?" said the Traveller
Knocking on the moonlit door.
WALTER DE LA MARE, *The Listeners*

Within the Phillipson family the financial arrangements were a matter of clear demarcation. Mrs. Phillipson herself had a small private income accruing from interest received on her late mother's estate. This account she kept strictly separate from all other monies; and although her husband had known the value of the original capital inheritance, he had no more idea of his wife's annual income than she did of her husband's private means. For Phillipson himself also had a private account, in which he accumulated a not negligible annual sum from his examining duties with one of the national boards, from royalties on a moderately successful textbook, written five years previously, on Nineteenth Century Britain, and from various incidental perks associated with his headship. In addition to these incomes there was, of course, Phillipson's monthly salary as a headmaster, and this was administered in a joint account on which both drew cash and wrote cheques for the normal items of household expenditure. The system worked admirably, and since by any standards the family was well-to-do, financial bickering had never blighted the Phillipsons' marriage; in fact financial matters had never caused the slightest concern to either party. Or had not done so until recently.

194

Phillipson kept his cheque book, his bank statements and all his financial c   :pondence in the top drawer of the bureau in the lounge, and he kept it locked. And in normal circumstances Mrs. Phillipson would no more have dreamed of looking through this drawer than of opening the private and confidential letters which came through the letter-box week after week from the examination board. It was none of her business, and she was perfectly happy to keep it that way—in normal circumstances. But circumstances had been far from normal these last two weeks, and she had not lived with Donald for over twelve years without coming to know his moods and his anxieties. For she slept beside him every night and he was her husband, and she knew him. She knew with virtual certainty that whatever had lain so heavily upon his mind these last few days was neither the school, nor the inspector whose visit had been so strangely upsetting, nor even the ghost of Valerie Taylor that flitted perpetually across the twilit zone of his subconscious fears. It was a man. A man she had come to think of as wholly evil and wholly malignant. It was Baines.

No specific incident had led her to open her husband's drawer and to examine the papers within; it was more an aggregation of many minor incidents which had driven her lively imagination to the terminus—a terminus which the facts themselves may never have reached, but towards which (as she fearfully foresaw their implications) they seemed inevitably to be heading. Did he know that she had her own key to the drawer? Surely not. For otherwise, if there were something he was anxious to hide, he would have kept the guilty evidence at school and not at home. And she *had* looked—only last week, and many things were now so frighteningly clear.

Assuredly she had heard the warning voices, and yet had looked and now could guess the truth: her husband was being blackmailed. And strangely enough she found that she could face the truth: it mattered less to her than she had dared to hope. But one thing was utterly certain. Never would she tell a living soul—never, never, never! She was his wife and she loved him, and would go on loving him. And if possible she would protect him; to the last ounce of her energy, to the last drop of her blood. She might even be able to do something. Yes, she might even be able to *do* something . . .

She seemed neither surprised nor dismayed to see him, for she had learned a great deal about herself the past few days. Not only was it better to face up to life's problems than to run away from them or desperately to pretend they didn't exist; it seemed far easier, too.

"Can we talk?" asked Morse.

She took his coat and hung it on the hall-stand behind the front door, beside an expensive-looking winter coat, the colour of ripening cherries.

They sat in the lounge, and Morse again noticed the photograph above the heavy mahogany bureau.

"Well, inspector? How can I help you?"

"Don't you know?" replied Morse quietly.

"I'm afraid not." She gave a little laugh and the hint of a smile played at the corners of her mouth. She spoke carefully, almost like a self-conscious teacher of elocution, the "d" and the "t" articulated separately and distinctly.

"I think you do, Mrs. Phillipson, and it's going to be easier for both of us if you're honest with me from the start because believe me, my love, you're going to be honest with me before we've finished."

The niceties were gone already, the words direct **and** challenging, the easy familiarity almost frightening. As **if** she were looking in on herself from the outside, she wondered what her chances were against him. It depended, **of** course, on what he knew. But surely there was nothing **he** *could* know?

"What am I supposed to be honest about?"

"Can't we keep this between ourselves, Mrs. Phillipson? That's why I've called now, you see, while your husband's still at school."

He noted the first glint of anxiety in the light-brown eyes; but she remained silent, and he continued. "If you're in the clear, Mrs. Phillipson—" He had repeated her name with almost every question, and she felt uncomfortable. It was like the repeated blows of a battering ram against a beleaguered city.

"*In the clear?* What *are* you talking about?"

"I think you called at Mr. Baines's house on Monday night, Mrs. Phillipson." The tone of his voice was ominously calm, but she only shook her head in semi-humorous disbelief.

"You can't really be serious, can you, inspector?"

"I'm always serious when I'm investigating murder."

"You don't think—you can't think that I had anything to do with *that*? On Monday night? Why, I hardly knew the man."

"I'm not interested in how well you knew him." It seemed an odd remark and her eyebrows contracted to a frown.

"What *are* you interested in?"

"I've told you, Mrs. Phillipson."

"Look, inspector. I think it's about time you told me

exactly why you're here. If you've got something you want to say to me, please say it. If you haven't . . ."

Morse, in a muted way, admired her spirited performance. But he had just reminded Mrs. Phillipson, and now he reminded himself: he was investigating murder.

When he spoke again his words were casual, intimate almost. "Did you like Mr. Baines?"

Her mouth opened as if to speak and, as suddenly, closed again; and whatever doubts had begun to creep into Morse's mind were now completely removed.

"I didn't know him very well. I just told you that." It was the best answer she could find, and it wasn't very good.

"Where were you on Monday evening, Mrs. Phillipson?"

"I was here of course. I'm almost always here."

"What time did you go out?"

"Inspector! I just told—"

"Did you leave the children on their own?"

"Of course I didn't—I meant I wouldn't. I could never—"

"What time did you get back?"

"Back? Back from where?"

"Before your husband?"

"My husband was out—that's what I'm telling you. He went to the theatre, The Playhouse—"

"He sat in row M, seat 14."

"If you say so, all right. But he wasn't home until about eleven."

"Ten to, according to him."

"All right, ten to eleven. What does—"

"You haven't answered my question, Mrs. Phillipson."

"What question?"

"I asked you what time *you* got home, not your husband." His questions were flung at her now with breakneck rapidity.

"You don't think I would go out and leave—"

"Go out? Where to, Mrs. Phillipson? Did you go on the bus?"

"I didn't go anywhere. Can't you understand that? How could I possibly go out and leave—"

Morse interrupted her again. She was beginning to crack, he knew that; her voice was high-pitched now amidst the elocutionary wreckage.

"All right—you didn't leave your children alone—I believe you—you love your children—of course you do—it would be illegal to leave them on their own—how old are they?"

Again she opened her mouth to speak, but he pushed relentlessly, remorselessly on.

"Have you heard of a baby-sitter, Mrs. Phillipson?— somebody who comes in and looks after your children while you go out—do you hear me?—while you go out—do you want me to find out who it was?—or do you want to tell me?—I could soon find out, of course— friends, neighbours—do you want me to find out, Mrs. Phillipson?—do you want me to go and knock next door?—and the door next to that?—of course, you don't, do you? You know, you're not being very sensible about this, are you, Mrs. Phillipson?" (He was speaking more slowly and calmly now.) "You see, I *know* what happened on Monday night. Someone saw you, Mrs. Phillipson; someone saw you in Kempis Street. And if you'd like to tell me why you were there and what you did, it would save a lot of time and trouble. But if you won't tell me, then I shall have to—"

Of a sudden she almost shrieked as the incessant flow of words began to overwhelm her. "I told you! I don't know what you're talking about! You don't seem to understand that, do you? *I just don't know what you're talking about!*"

Morse sat back in the armchair, relaxed and unconcerned. He looked about him, and once more fastened his gaze on the photograph of the headmaster and his wife above the large bureau. And then he looked at his wristwatch.

"What time do the children get home?" His tone was suddenly friendly and quiet, and Mrs. Phillipson felt the panic welling up within her. She looked at her own wristwatch and her voice was shaking as she answered him.

"They'll be home at four o'clock."

"That gives us an hour, doesn't it, Mrs. Phillipson. I think that's long enough—my car's outside. You'd better put your coat on—the pink one, if you will."

He rose from the armchair, and fastened the front buttons of his jacket. "I'll see that your husband knows if . . ." He took a few steps towards the door, but she laid her hand upon him as he moved past her.

"Sit down, please, inspector," she said quietly.

She had gone (she said). That was all, really. It was like suddenly deciding to write a letter or to ring the dentist or to buy some restorer for the paint brushes encrusted stiff with last year's gloss. She asked Mrs. Cooper next door to baby-sit, said she'd be no longer than an hour at the very latest, and caught the 9:20 P.M. bus from the stop immediately outside the house. She got off at Cornmarket, walked quickly through Gloucester Green and reached Kempis Street by about a quarter to ten. The light was shining in Baines's front window—

she had never been there before—and she summoned up all her courage and knocked on the front door. There was no reply. Again she knocked—and again there was no reply. She then walked along to the lighted window and tapped upon it hesitantly and quietly with the back of her hand; but she could hear no sound and could make out no movement behind the cheap yellow curtains. She hurried back to the front door, feeling as guilty as a young schoolgirl caught out of her place in the classroom by the headmistress. But still nothing happened. She had so nearly called the whole thing off there and then; but her resolution had been wrought-up to such a pitch that she made one last move. She tried the door—and found it unlocked. She opened it slightly, no more than a foot or so, and called his name.

"Mr. Baines?" And then slightly louder, *"Mr. Baines?"* But she received no reply. The house seemed strangely still and the sound of her own voice echoed eerily in the high entrance hall. A cold shiver of fear ran down her spine, and for a few seconds she felt sure that he was there, very near to her, watching and waiting . . . And suddenly a panic-stricken terror had seized her and she had rushed back to the lighted, friendly road, crossed over by the railway station and, with her heart pounding in her ribs, tried to get a grip on herself. In St. Giles she caught a taxi and arrived home just after ten.

That was her story, anyway. She told it in a flat, dejected voice, and she told it well and clearly. To Morse it sounded in no way like the tangled, mazy machinations of a murderer. Indeed a good deal of it he could check fairly easily: the baby-sitter, the bus conductor, the taxi-driver. And Morse felt sure that all would verify the outline of her story, and confirm the approximate times she'd given. But there was no chance of checking those fateful moments when she stood outside the door of Baines's house ... Had she gone in? And if she had, what terrible things had then occurred? The pros and cons were counter-poised in Morse's mind, with the balance tilting slightly in Mrs. Phillipson's favour.

"Why did you want to see him?"

"I wanted to talk to him, that's all."

"Yes. Go on."

"It's difficult to explain. I don't think I knew myself what I was going to say. He was—oh, I don't know—he was everything that's *bad* in life. He was mean, he was vindictive, he was—sort of calculating. He just delighted in seeing other people squirm. I'm not thinking of anything in particular, and I don't really know all that much about him. But since Donald has been headmaster he's—how shall I put it?—he's waited, hoping for things to go wrong. He was a cruel man, inspector."

"You hated him?"

She nodded hopelessly. "Yes, I suppose I did."

"It's as good a motive as any," said Morse sombrely.

"It might seem so, yes." But she sounded unperturbed.

"Did your husband hate Baines, too?" He watched her carefully and saw the light flash dangerously in her eyes.

"Don't be silly, inspector. You can't possibly think that Donald had anything to do with all this. I know I've been a fool, but you can't ... It's impossible. He was at the theatre all night. You know that."

"Your husband would have thought it was impossible for *you* to be knocking at Baines's door that night, wouldn't he? You were here, at home, with the children, surely?" He leaned forward and spoke more curtly again now. "Make no mistake, Mrs. Phillipson, it would have been a hell of a sight easier for him to leave the theatre than it was for you to leave here. And don't try to tell me otherwise!"

He sat back impassively in the chair. He sensed an evasion somewhere in her story, a half-truth, a curtain not yet fully drawn back; and at the same time he knew that he was almost there, and all he had to do was sit and wait. And so he sat and waited; and the world of the woman seated opposite him was slowly beginning to fall apart, and suddenly, dramatically, she buried her head in her hands and wept uncontrollably.

Morse fished around in his pockets and finally found a crumpled apology for a paper handkerchief, and pushed it gently into her right hand.

"Don't cry," he said softly. "It won't do either of us any good."

After a few minutes the tears dried up, and soon the sniveling subsided. "What *can* do us any good, inspector?"

"It's very easy, really," said Morse in a brisk tone. "You tell me the truth, Mrs. Phillipson. You'll find I probably know it anyway."

But Morse was wrong—he was terribly wrong. Mrs. Phillipson could do little more than reiterate her strange little story. This time, however, with a startling addition—an addition which caught Morse, as he sat there nodding sceptically, like an uppercut to the jaw. She hadn't wanted to mention it because . . . because, well, it seemed so much like trying to get herself out of a mess by pushing someone else into it. But she could only tell the truth, and if that's what Morse was after she thought she'd better tell it. As she had said, she ran along to the main street after leaving Baines's house and crossed over towards the Royal Oxford Hotel; and just before she reached the hotel she saw someone she knew—knew very well—come out of the lounge door and walk across the road to Kempis Street. She hesitated and her tearful eyes looked pleadingly and pathetically at Morse.

"Do you know who it was, inspector? It was David Acum."

Chapter Twenty-five

For oily or spotty skin, first cleanse face and throat, then pat with a hot towel. Smooth on an even layer of luxurious "Ladypak," avoiding the area immediately around the eyes.
Directions for applying a beauty mask

At 6:20 A.M. the following morning Morse was on the road: it would take about five hours. He would have enjoyed the drive more with someone to talk to, especially Lewis, and he switched on the Lancia's radio for the 7:00 A.M. news. The world seemed strangely blighted: abroad there were rumours of war and famine, and at home more bankruptcies and unemployment—and a missing lord who had been dredged up from a lake in east Essex. But the morning was fresh and bright, the sky serene and cloudless, and Morse drove fast. He had left Evesham behind him and was well on the way to Kidderminster before he met any appreciable volume of traffic. The 8:00 A.M. news came and went, with no perceptible amelioration of the cosmic plight, and Morse switched over to Radio Three and listened lovingly to the Brandenburg Concerto no. 5 in D. The journey was going well, and he was through Bridgnorth and driving rather too quickly round the Shrewsbury ring road by 9:00 A.M. when he decided that a Schönberg string quartet might be a little above his head, and switched off. He found himself vaguely pondering the lake in east Essex, and remembering the reservoir behind the Taylors' home, before switching that off, too, and concentrating with

appropriate care and attention upon the perils of the busy
A5. At Nesscliffe, some twelve miles north of Shrewsbury, he turned off left along the B4396 towards Bala.
Wales now, and the pale-green hills rose ever more
steeply. He was making excellent time and he praised the
gods that his journey was not being made on a dry Welsh
Sunday. He was feeling thirsty already. But he was
through Bala and swinging in the long left-handed loop
around Llyn Tegid (reservoir again!) long before the
pubs were open; and through the crowded streets of Port-
madog, festooned still with the multi-colored bunting of
high summer, and past the Lloyd George Museum in
Llanystumdwy, and still the hands on the fascia clock
were some few minutes short of eleven. He might just as
well drive on. At Four Crosses he turned right on to the
Pwllheli-Caernarfon road, and drove on into the Lleyn
Peninsula, past the triple peaks of the Rivals and on to
the coastal road, with the waters of Caernarfon Bay
laughing and glittering in the sunshine to his left. He
would stop at the next likely-looking hostelry. He had
passed one in the last village, but the present tract of road
afforded little for the thirsty traveller; and he was only
two or three miles south of Caernarfon itself when he
spotted the sign: BONTNEWYDD. Surely the village where
the Acums lived? He pulled in to the side of the road, and
consulted the file in his brief-case. Yes, it was. No. 16 St.
Beuno's Road. He enquired of an ageing passer-by and
learned that he was only a few 'undred yaards from St.
Beuno's Road, and that The Prince of Wales was just
around the corner. It was five minutes past eleven.

   As he sampled the local brew, he debated whether he
should call at the Acums' home. Did the modern languages master come home for lunch? Morse's original

plan had been to go direct to the City of Caernarfon School, preferably about lunchtime. But perhaps it would do no harm to have a little chat with Mrs. Acum first? Temporarily he shelved the decision, bought another pint, and considered the forthcoming interview. Acum had lied, of course, about not leaving the conference; for Mrs. Phillipson could not have had the faintest notion that Acum would be in Oxford on that Monday night. How could she? Unless ... but he dropped the fanciful line of thought. The beer was good, and at noon he was happily discussing with his host the sorry Sunday situation in the thirsty counties and the defacement of the Welsh road signs by the Nationalists. And ten minutes later, legs astraddle, he stood and contemplated the defacement of the landlord's lavatory walls by a person or persons unknown. Several of the graffiti were unintelligible to the non-Welsh-speaker; but one that was scrawled in his native tongue caught Morse's eye, and he smiled in approbation as his bladder achingly emptied itself:

"The penis mightier than the sword."

It was now 12:15 P.M., and if Acum were coming home to lunch, there was an obvious danger of his passing Morse in the opposite direction. Well, there was one pretty certain way of finding out. He left the Lancia at The Prince of Wales and walked.

St. Beuno's Road led off right from the main road. The houses were small here, built of square, grey, granite blocks, and tiled with the purplish-blue Ffestiniog slate. The grass in the tiny front gardens was of a green two or three shades paler than the English variety, and the soil looked tired and undernourished. The front door was painted a Cambridge blue, with the black number 16 dextrously worked in the florid style of a Victorian theatre-bill. Morse knocked firmly, and after a brief interval the door opened; but opened only slightly, and then to reveal a strangely incongruous sight. A woman stood before him, her face little more than a white mask, with slits left open for the eyes and mouth, a blood-red towel swathed around the top of her head where (as, alas, with most of the blondes) the tell-tale roots of the hair betrayed its darker origins. It was curious to witness the lengths to which the ladies were prepared to go in order to improve upon the natural gifts their maker had endowed them with; and in the depths of Morse's mind there stirred the dim remembrance of the fair-haired woman with the spotty face in the staff photograph of the Roger Bacon Comprehensive School. He knew that this must be Mrs. Acum. Yet it was not the beauty pack, smeared though it doubtless was with a practised skill, that chiefly held the inspector's wrapt attention. She was holding a meagre white towel to the top of her shoulders, and as she stood half hidden by the door, it was immediately apparent that behind the towel the woman was completely naked. Morse felt as lecherous as a billy-goat. A Welsh billy-goat, perhaps. It must have been the beer.

"I've called to see your husband. Er, it is Mrs. Acum, isn't it?"

The head nodded, and a hair-line fracture of the carefully assembled mask appeared at the corners of the white mouth. Was she laughing at him?

"Will he be back home for lunch?"

The head shook, and the top of the towel drooped

tantalisingly to reveal the beautifully-moulded outline of her breasts.

"He's at school, I suppose?"

The head nodded, and the eyes stared blandly through the slits.

"Well, I'm sorry to have bothered you, Mrs. Acum, especially at, er, such, er . . . We've spoken to each other before, you know—over the phone, if you remember. I'm Morse. Chief Inspector Morse from Oxford."

The red towel bobbed on her head, the mask almost breaking through into a smile. They shook hands through the door, and Morse was conscious of the heady perfume on her skin. He held her hand for longer than he need have done, and the white towel dropped from her right shoulder; and for a brief and beautiful moment he stared with shameless fascination at her nakedness. The nipple was fully erect and he felt an almost irresistible urge to hold it there and then between his fingers. Was she inviting him in? He looked again at the passive mask. The towel was now in place again, and she stood back a little from the door; it was fifty-fifty. But he had hesitated too long, and the chance, if chance it was, was gone already. He lacked, as always, the bogus courage of his own depravity, and he turned away from her and walked back slowly towards The Prince of Wales. At the end of the road he stopped, and looked back; but the light-blue door was closed upon him and he cursed the conscience that invariably thus doth make such spineless cowards of us all. It was perhaps something to do with status. People just didn't expect such base behaviour from a chief inspector, as if such eminent persons were somehow different from the common run of lewd humanity. How wrong they were! How wrong! Why, even the mighty had their little weaknesses. Good gracious, yes. Just think of old Lloyd George. The things they said about Lloyd George! And he was a prime minister . . .

He climbed into the Lancia. Oh God, such beautiful breasts! He sat motionless at the wheel for a short while, and then he smiled to himself. He reckoned that Constable Dickson could almost have hung his helmet there! It was an irreverent thought, but it made him feel a good deal better. He pulled carefully out of the car park and headed north on the final few miles of his journey.

Chapter Twenty-six

> Merely corroborative detail, to add artistic verisimilitude to an otherwise bald and unconvincing narrative.
>
> W. S. GILBERT, *The Mikado*

A small group of boys was kicking a football around at the side of a large block of classrooms which abutted on to the wide sports fields, where sets of rugby and hockey posts demarked the area of grass into neatly white-lined rectangles. The rest of the school was having lunch. The two men walked three times around the playing fields, hands in pockets, heads slightly forward, eyes downcast. They were about the same build, neither man above medium height; and to the football players they seemed unworthy of note, anonymous almost. Yet one of the two men pacing slowly over the grass was a chief inspector of police, and the other, one of their very own teachers, was a suspect in a murder case.

Morse questioned Acum about himself and his teaching career; about Valerie Taylor and Baines and Phillipson; about the conference in Oxford, times and places and people. And he learned nothing that seemed of particular interest or importance. The schoolmaster appeared pleasant enough—in a nondescript sort of way; he answered the inspector's questions with freedom and with what seemed a fair degree of guarded honesty. And so Morse told him, told him quietly yet quite categorically, that he was a liar, told him that he had indeed left

211

the conference that Monday evening, at about 9:30 P.M., told him that he had walked to Kempis Street to see his former colleague, Mr. Baines, and that he had been seen there; told him that, if he persisted in denying such a plain, incontrovertible statement of the truth, he, Morse, had little option but to take him back to Oxford where he would be held for questioning in connection with the murder of Mr. Reginald Baines. It was as simple as that! And, in fact, it proved a good deal simpler than even Morse had dared to hope; for Acum no longer denied the plain, incontrovertible statement of the truth which the inspector had presented to him. They were on their third and final circuit of the playing fields, far away from the main school buildings, by the side of some neglected allotments, where the ramshackle sheds rusted away sadly in despairing disrepair. Here Acum stopped and nodded slowly.

"Just tell me what you did, sir, that's all."

"I'd been sitting at the back of the hall—deliberately— and I left early. As you say, it was about half-past nine, or probably a bit earlier."

"You went to see Baines?" Acum nodded. "Why did you go to see him?"

"I don't know, really. I was getting a bit bored with the conference, and Baines lived fairly near. I thought I'd go and see if he was in and ask him out for a drink. It's always interesting to talk about old times, you know the sort of thing—what was going on at school, which members of the staff were still there, which ones had left, what they were doing. You know what I mean."

He spoke naturally and easily, and if he were a liar he seemed to Morse a fairly fluent one.

"Well," continued Acum, "I walked along there. I was

in a bit of a hurry because I knew the pubs would be closed by half-past ten and time was getting on. I had a drink on the way and it must have been getting on for ten by the time I got there. I'd been there before, and I thought he must be in because the light was on in the front room."

"Were the curtains drawn?" For the first time since they had been talking together, Morse's voice grew sharper.

Acum thought for a moment. "Yes, I'm almost certain they were."

"Go on."

"Well, I thought, as I say, that he must be in. So I knocked pretty loudly two or three times on the door. But he didn't answer, or at least he didn't seem to hear me. I thought he might be in the front room perhaps with the T.V. on, so I went to the window and knocked on it."

"Could you hear the T.V.? Or see it?"

Acum shook his head; and to Morse it was all beginning to sound like a record stuck in its groove. He knew for certain what was coming next.

"It's a funny thing, inspector, but I began to feel just a bit frightened—as if I were sort of trespassing and shouldn't really be there at all; as if he knew that I was there but didn't want to see me . . . Anyway, I went back to the door and knocked again, and then I put my head round the door and shouted his name."

Mores stood quite still, and considered his next question with care. If he was to get his piece of information, he wanted it to come from Acum himself without too much prompting.

"You put your head round the door, you say?"

"Yes. I just felt sure he was there."

"Why did you feel that?"

"Well, there was the light in the front room and . . ." He hesitated for a moment, and seemed to be fumbling around in his mind for some fleeting, half-forgotten impression that had given him this feeling.

"Think back carefully, sir," said Morse. "Just picture yourself there again, standing at the door. Take your time. Just put yourself back there. You're standing there in Kempis Street. Last Monday night . . ."

Acum shook his head slowly and frowned. He said nothing for a minute or two.

"You see, inspector, I just had this idea that he was somewhere about. I almost *knew* he was. I thought he might just have slipped out somewhere for a few seconds because . . ." It came back to him then, and he went on quickly. "Yes, that's it. I remember now. I remember why I thought he must be there. It wasn't just the light in the front window. There was a light on in the hall, too. And when I first knocked I could see the light in the hall because the front door was open. Not wide open, but standing ajar as if he'd just slipped out and would be back again any second."

"And then?"

"I left. He wasn't there. I just left, that's all."

"Why didn't you tell me all this when I rang you, sir?"

"I was frightened, inspector. I'd been there, hadn't I? And he was probably lying there all the time—murdered. I was frightened, I really was. Wouldn't you have been?"

Morse drove into the centre of Caernarfon, and parked his car alongside the jetty under the great walls of the first Edward's finest castle. He found a Chinese restaurant nearby, and greedily gulped down the oriental fare that was set before him. It was his first meal for twenty-four hours, and he temporarily dismissed all else from his mind. Only over his coffee did he allow his restless brain to come to grips with the case once more; and by the time he had finished his second cup of coffee he had reached the firm conclusion that, whatever improbabilities remained to be explained away, especially the reasons given for calling on Baines, both Mrs. Phillipson and David Acum had told him the truth, or something approximating to the truth, at least as far as their evidence concerned itself with the visits made to the house in Kempis Street. Their accounts of what had taken place there were so clear, so mutually complementary, that he felt he should and would believe them. That bit about the door being slightly open, for example—exactly as Mrs. Phillipson had left it before panicking and racing down to the lighted street. No. Acum could not have made that up. Surely not. Unless . . . It was the second time that he had qualified his conclusions with that sinister word "unless"; and it troubled him. Acum and Mrs. Phillipson. Was there any link at all between that improbable pair? If link there was, it had to have been forged at some point in the past, at some point more than two years ago, at the Roger Bacon Comprehensive School. Could there have been something? It was an idea, anyway. Yet as he drove out of the castle car park, he decided on balance that it was a lousy idea. In front of the castle he passed the statue to commemorate the honourable member for Caernarfon (Lloyd George, no less) and as he drove out along the road to Capel Curig, his brain was as jumbled and cluttered as a magpie's nest.

He stopped briefly in the pass of Llanberis, and watched the tiny figures of the climbers, conspicuous only by their bright orange anoraks, perched at dizzying heights on the sheer mountain faces that towered massively above the road on either side. He felt profoundly thankful that whatever the difficulties of his own job he was spared the risk, at every second, and every precarious hand- and foot-hold, of a vertical plunge to a certain death upon the rocks far, far below. Yet, in his own way, Morse knew that he too was scaling a peak and knew full well the blithe exhilaration of reaching to the summit. So often there was only one way forward, only one. And when one route seemed utterly impossible, one had to look for the nearly impossible alternative, to edge along the face of the cliff, to avoid the impasse, and to lever oneself painstakingly up to the next ledge, and look up again and follow the only route. On the death of Baines, Morse had considered only a small group of likely suspects. The murderer could, of course, have been someone completely unconnected with the Valerie Taylor affair; but he doubted it. There had been five of them, and he now felt that the odds against Mrs. Phillipson and David Acum had lengthened considerably. That left the Taylors, the pair of them, and Phillipson himself. It was time he tried to put together the facts, many of them very odd facts, that he had gleaned about these three. It must be one of them surely; for he felt convinced now that Baines had been murdered before the visits of Mrs. Phillipson and David Acum. Yes, that was the only way it could have been. He grasped the firm fact with both hands and swung himself on to a higher ledge, and discovered that from this vantage point the view seemed altogether different.

He drove to Capel Curig and there turned right on to the A5 towards Llangollen. And even as he drove he began to see the pattern. He ought to have seen it before; but with the testimony of Mrs. Phillipson and Acum behind him, it became almost childishly easy now to fit the pieces into quite a different pattern. One by one they clicked into place with a simple inevitability, as on and on he drove at high speed, passing Shrewsbury and, keeping to the A5, rattling along the old Watling Street and almost missing the turning off for Daventry and Banbury. It was now nearly 8:00 P.M. and Morse was feeling the effects of his long day. He found his mind wandering off to that news item he had heard about the unfortunate lord in the Essex reservoir; and as he was leaving the outskirts of Banbury an oncoming car flashed its lights at him. He realised that he had been drifting dangerously over the centre of the road, and jerked himself into a startled wakefulness. He resolved not to allow his concentration to waver one centimetre, opened the side window and breathing deeply upon the cool night air, sang in a mournful baritone, over and over again, the first and only verse he could remember of "Lead, Kindly Light."

He drove straight home and locked up the garage. It had been a long day, and he hoped he would sleep well.

Chapter Twenty-seven

> All happy families are alike, but each unhappy family is unhappy in its own way.
>
> LEO TOLSTOY

Lewis was getting better. He got up for a couple of hours just after Morse had arrived back in Oxford, with the aid of the banister made his careful way downstairs and joined his surprised wife on the sofa in front of the television set. His temperature was normal now, and though he felt weak on his legs and sapped of his usual energy, he knew he would soon be back in harness. Many of the hours in bed he had spent in thinking, thinking about the Taylor case; and that morning he had been suddenly struck by an idea so novel and so exciting that he had persuaded his wife to ring the station immediately. But Morse was out: off to Wales, they said. It puzzled Lewis: the Principality in no way figured in his own new-minted version of events, and he guessed that Morse had followed one of his wayward fancies about Acum, wasted a good many gallons of police petrol, and advanced the investigation not one whit. But that wasn't quite fair. In the hands of the chief inspector things seldom stood still; they might go sideways, or even backwards, and often (Lewis agreed) they went forwards. But they seldom stood still. Yes, Lewis had been deeply disappointed not to catch him. Everything—well, almost everything— fitted so perfectly. It had been that item on his bedside radio at eight o'clock that had started the chain reaction; that item about some big noise being washed up in a reservoir. He knew they had dredged the reservoir behind the Taylors' home; but you could never be sure in such a wide stretch of water as that; and anyway it didn't really matter much whether it was in the reservoir or somewhere else. That was just the starting point. And then there was that old boy at the Belisha crossing, and the basket, and—oh, lots of other things. How he wished he'd caught the chief at the station! The really surprising thing was that Morse hadn't thought of it himself. He usually thought of everything—and more! But later, as the day wore on, he began to think that Morse probably *had* thought of it. After all, it was Morse himself who had suggested, right out of the blue, that she was carrying a basket.

Laboriously, during the afternoon, Lewis wrote it all down, and when he had finished the initial thrill was already waning, and he was left only with the quiet certainty that it had indeed been, for him, a remarkable brainwave, and that there was a very strong possibility that he might be right. At 9:15 P.M., he rang the station himself, but Morse had still not shown up.

"Probably gone straight home—or to a pub," said the desk sergeant. Lewis left a message, and prayed that for the morrow the chief had planned no trip to the Western Isles.

Donald Phillipson and his wife sat silently watching the nine o'clock news on B.B.C. television. They had said little all evening, and now that the children were snugly tucked up in bed, the little had dried up to nothing. Once or twice each of them had almost asked a question of the other, and it would have been the same question: is there anything you want to tell me? Or words to that effect. But neither of them had braved it, and at a quarter-past ten Mrs. Phillipson brought in the coffee and announced that she was off to bed.

"You've had your fill tonight, haven't you?"

He mumbled something inaudible, and lumbered along unsteadily, trying with limited success to avoid bumping into her as they walked side by side along the narrow pavement. It was 10:45 P.M. and their home was only two short streets away from the pub.

"Have you ever tried to work out how much you spend a week on beer and fags?"

It hurt him, and it wasn't fair. Christ, it wasn't fair.

"If you want to talk about money, my gal, what about your Bingo. Every bloody night nearly."

"You just leave my Bingo out of it. It's about the one pleasure I've got in life, and don't you forget it. And some people *win* at Bingo; you know that, don't you? Don't tell me you're so ignorant you don't know that."

"Have you won recently?" His tone was softer and he hoped very much that she had.

"I've told you. You keep your nose out of it. I spend my own money, thank you, not yours; and if I win that's my business, isn't it?"

"You were lashing out a bit with your money tonight, weren't you? Bit free with your favours all round, if you ask me."

"What's that supposed to mean?" Her voice was very nasty.

"Well, you—"

"Look, if I want to treat some of my friends to a drink, that's my look out, isn't it? It's my money, too!"

"I only meant—"

They were at the front gate now and she turned on him, her eyes flashing. "And don't you ever dare to say anything again about my favours! Christ! You're a one to talk, aren't you—you—*bastard*!"

Their holiday together, the first for seven years, was due to begin at the week-end. The omens seemed hardly favourable.

It was half-past eleven when Morse finally laid his head upon the pillows. He shouldn't have had so much beer really, but he felt he'd deserved it. It would mean shuffling along for a pee or two before the night was out. But what the hell! He felt at peace with himself and with the world in general. Beer was probably the cheapest drug on the market, and he only wished that his G.P. would prescribe it for him on the National Health. Ah, this was good! He turned into the pillows. Old Lewis would be in bed, too. He would see Lewis first thing in the morning; and he was quite sure that however groggy his faithful sergeant was feeling he would sit up in his sick bed and blink with a pained, incredulous surprise. For tomorrow morning he would be able to reveal the identity of the murderer of Valerie Taylor and that of the murderer of Reginald Baines, to boot. Or, to be slightly more accurate, just the one identity; for it had been the same hand which had murdered them both, and Morse now knew whose hand it was.

Chapter Twenty-eight

An ill-favoured thing, sir, but mine own.
SHAKESPEARE, *As You Like It*

"How're you doing then, my old friend?"

"Much better, thanks. Should be fit again any day now."

"Now you're not to rush things, remember that. There's nothing spoiling."

"Isn't there, sir?" The tone of the voice caught the inspector slightly unawares, and he looked at Lewis curiously.

"What's on your mind?"

"I tried to get hold of you yesterday, sir." He sat up in bed and reached to the bedside table. "I thought I had a bright idea. I may be wrong, but ... Well, here it is anyway, for what it's worth." He handed over several sheets of notepaper, and Morse shelved his own pronouncements and sat down beside the bed. His head ached and he stared reluctantly at his sergeant's carefully-written notes.

"You want me to read all this?"

"I just hope it's worth reading, that's all."

And Morse read; and as he read a wan smile crept across his mouth, and here and there he nodded with rigorous approbation, and Lewis sank back into his pillows with the air of a pupil whose essay is receiving the alpha accolade. When he had finished, Morse took out his pen.

"Don't mind if I make one or two slight alterations, do you?" For the next ten minutes he went methodically through the draft, correcting the more heinous spelling errors, inserting an assortment of full-stops and commas, and shuffling several of the sentences into a more comprehensible sequence. "That's better," said Morse finally, handing back to a rueful-looking Lewis his amended masterpiece. It was an improvement, though. Anyone could see that.

To begin with, the evidence seemed to point to the fact that Valerie Taylor was alive. After all, her parents received a letter from her. But we then discovered that the letter was almost certainly not written by Valerie at all. So. Instead of assuming that she's alive, we must face the probability that she's dead, and we must ask ourselves the old question: who was the last person to see her alive? The answer is Joe Godberry, a short-sighted old fellow who ought never to have been in charge of a Belisha crossing in the first place. Could he have been wrong? He could, and in my view he was wrong; that is, he didn't see Valerie Taylor at all on the afternoon she disappeared. He says quite firmly that he did see her, but might he not have been mistaken? Might he just have seen someone who *looked* like Valerie? Well? Who looked like Valerie? Chief Inspector Morse himself thought that a photograph of Mrs. Taylor was one of her daughter Valerie, and this raises an interesting possibility. Could the person seen by Godberry have been *not Valerie but Valerie's mother*? (Lewis had underlined the words thickly, and it was at this point on his first reading that Morse had nodded his approval.) If it was Valerie's mother there are two important implications. First, that the last person to see Valerie alive was none other than her own mother, at lunchtime that same day. Second, that this person—Valerie's mother—had gone to a great deal of trouble to establish the fact that her daughter had left the house and returned to afternoon school. On this second point we know that mother and daughter were very similar in build and figure generally, and Mrs. Taylor is still fairly slim and attractive. (It was at this point that Morse nodded again.) What was the best way of convincing anyone who might notice, the neighbours, say, or the Belisha man or the shop assistants, that Valerie had left home after lunch that day? The answer is fairly obvious. The uniform of the school which Valerie attended was quite distinctive, especially the red socks and the white blouse. Mrs. Taylor could dress up in the uniform herself, run quickly down the road, keep on the far side of the crossing, and with a bit of luck there would be no trouble in persuading anyone, even the police, that her daughter had left home. We learned that on the particular Tuesday afternoon in question, Valerie would be most unlikely to be missed anyway. Games afternoon— and a real shambles. So. Let us assume that Mrs. Taylor dresses up as her daughter and makes her way towards school. Chief Inspector Morse suggested early on that the person seen by Godberry was perhaps carrying a basket or some such receptacle. (Lewis had made a sorry mess of the spelling.) Now, if she had been carrying *clothes* (heavily scored by Lewis) the situation is becoming very interesting. Once Mrs. Taylor has created the impression that Valerie has left for school, it is equally important that she should not create the further impression that

Valerie has returned home some five or ten minutes later. Because if someone sees Valerie, or someone who looks like Valerie, returning to the Taylors' house, the careful plan is ruined. When Valerie is reported missing, the enquiries will naturally centre on the house, not on the area around the school. But she can deal with this without too much trouble. In the basket *Mrs. Taylor has put her own clothes*. She goes into the ladies', just past the shopping area, and changes back into them, and then walks back, as unobtrusively as she can, probably by a roundabout route, to her own house. The real question now is this. Why all this palaver? Why should Mrs. Taylor have to go to all this trouble and risk? There can only be one answer. To create the firm impression that Valerie is alive *when in fact she is dead*. If Valerie had arrived home for lunch, and if Valerie did not leave the house again, we must assume that she was killed at some time during the lunch hour in her own home. And there was, it seems, only one other person in the Taylor household during that time: Valerie's own mother. It is difficult to believe, but the facts seem to point to the appalling probability that *Valerie was murdered by her own mother*. Why? We can only guess. There is some evidence that Valerie was pregnant. Perhaps her mother flew at her in a wild rage and struck her much harder than she intended to. We may learn the truth from Mrs. Taylor herself. The next thing is—what to do? And here we have the recorded evidence of the police files. The fact is that the police were not called in until the next morning. Why so much delay? Again an answer readily presents itself. (Morse had admired his sergeant's style at this point, and the nod had signified a recognition of a literary nicety rather than any necessary concurrence with the argument.) Mrs. Taylor had to get rid of the body. She waited, I think, obviously in great distress, until her husband arrived home about six; and then she told him what had happened. He has little option. He can't leave his poor wife to face the consequences of the terrible mess she's got herself into, and the two of them plan what to do. Somehow they get rid of the body, and I suspect the reservoir behind the house is the first place that occurs to them. I know that this was dragged at the time, but it's terribly easy to miss anything in so large a stretch of water. I can only suggest that it is thoroughly dragged again.

Lewis put the document back on the bedside table and Morse tapped him in congratulatory fashion upon the shoulder.

"I think it's time they made you up to inspector, my old friend."

"You think I may be right then, sir?"

"Yes," said Morse slowly, "I do."

Chapter Twenty-nine

Incest is only relatively boring.
Inscription on the lavatory wall of an Oxford pub

Lewis leaned back into his pillows, and felt content. He would never make an inspector, he knew that; didn't even want to try. But to beat old Morse at his own game—my goodness, that was something!

"Got a drop of booze in the house?" asked Morse.

Ten minutes later he was sipping a liberal helping of whisky as Lewis dunked a chunk of bread into his Bovril.

"There are one or two things you could add to your admirable statement, you know, Lewis." A slightly pained expression appeared on Lewis's face, but Morse quickly reassured him. "Oh, that's pretty certainly how it happened, I'm sure of that. But there are just one or two points where we can be even more specific, I think, and one or two where we shall need a clearer picture not so much of what happened as of why it happened. Let's just go over a few of the things you say. Mrs. Taylor dresses up as Valerie. I agree. You mention the school uniform and you rightly stress how distinctive this uniform is. But there's surely another small point. Mrs. Taylor would not only wish in a positive way to be mistaken for her daughter, but in a negative sort of way not to be recognised facially as who she was—Valerie's mother. After all it's the face that most of us look at—not the clothes.

And here I think her hair would be all-important. Their hair was the same colour, and Mrs. Taylor is still too young to have more than a few odd streaks of grey. When we saw her she wore her hair on the top of her head, but I'd like to bet that when she lets it down it gives her much the same sort of look that Valerie had; and with long shoulder-length hair, doubtless brushed forward over her face, I think the disguise would be more than adequate."

Lewis nodded; but as the inspector said, it was only a small point.

"Now," continued Morse, "we surely come to the central point, and one that you gloss over rather too lightly, if I may say so." Lewis looked stolidly at the counterpane, but made no interruption. "It's this. What could possibly have been the motive that led Mrs. Taylor to murder Valerie? Valerie! Her only daughter! You say that Valerie was pregnant, and although it isn't firmly established, I think the overwhelming probability is that she *was* pregnant; perhaps she had told her mother about it. But there's another possibility, and one that makes the whole situation far more sinister and disturbing. It isn't easy, I should imagine, for a daughter to hide a pregnancy from her mother for too long, and I think on balance it may well have been Mrs. Taylor who accused Valerie of being pregnant—rather than Valerie who told her mother. But whichever way round it was, it surely can't add up to a sufficient motive for murdering the girl. It would be bad enough, I agree. The neighbours would gossip and everyone at school would have to know, and then there'd be the uncles and aunts and all the rest of 'em. But it's hardly a rare thing these days to have an unmarried mother in the family, is it? It could have happened as you say it did, but I get the feeling that Valerie's pregnancy had been known to Mrs. Taylor for several weeks before the day she was murdered. And I think that on that Tuesday lunchtime Mrs. Taylor tackled her daughter—she may have tackled her several times before—on a question which was infinitely more important to her than whether her daughter was pregnant or not. A question which was beginning to send her out of her mind; for she had her own dark and terrifying suspicions which would give her no rest, which poisoned her mind day and night, and which she had to settle one way or the other. And that question was this: *who was the father of Valerie's baby?* To begin with I automatically assumed that Valerie was a girl of pretty loose morals who would jump into bed at the slightest provocation with some of her randy boyfriends. But I think I was wrong. I ought to have seen through Maguire's sexual boastings straightaway. He may have put his dirty fingers up her skirt once or twice, but I doubt that he or any of the other boys did much more. No. I should think that Valerie got an itch in her knickers as often—more often perhaps—than most young girls. But the indications all along the line were that her own particular weakness was *for older men.* Men about your age, Lewis."

"And yours," said Lewis. But the mood in the quiet bedroom was sombre, and neither man seemed much amused. Morse drained his whisky and smacked his lips.

"Well, Lewis? What do you think?"

"You mean Phillipson, I suppose, sir?"

"Could have been, but I doubt it. I think he'd learned his lesson."

Lewis thought for a moment and frowned deeply. Was it possible? Would it tie in with the other business?

"Surely you don't mean Baines, do you, sir? She must have been willing to go to bed with anyone if she let Baines . . ." He broke off. How sickening it all was!

Morse brooded awhile, and stared through the bedroom window. "I thought of it, of course. But I think you're right. At least I don't think she would have gone to bed *willingly* with Baines. And yet, you know, Lewis, it would explain a great many things if it *was* Baines."

"I thought you had the idea that he was seeing Mrs. Taylor—not Valerie."

"I think he was," said Morse. "But, as I say, I don't think it was Baines." He was speaking more slowly now, almost as if he were working through some new equation which had suddenly flashed across his mind; some new problem that challenged to some extent the validity of the case he was presenting. But reluctantly he put it aside, and resumed the main thread of his argument. "Try again, Lewis."

It was like backing horses. Lewis had backed the favourite, Phillipson, and lost; he'd then chosen an outsider, an outsider at least with a bit of form behind him, and lost again. There weren't many other horses in the race. "You've got the advantage over me, sir. You went to see Acum yesterday. Don't you think you ought to tell me about it?"

"Leave Acum out of it for the minute," said Morse flatly.

So Lewis reviewed the field again. There was only one other possibility, and he was surely a non-starter. Surely. Morse couldn't seriously . . . "You don't mean . . . you can't mean you think it was . . . George Taylor?"

"I'm afraid I do, Lewis, and we'd both better get used to the grisly idea as quickly as we can. It's not pleasant,

know; but it's not so bad as it might be. After all, he's not
her natural father, as far as we know, and so we're not
fishing around in the murky waters of genuine incest or
anything like that. Valerie would have known perfectly
well that George wasn't her real father. They all lived
together, and became as intimate as any other family. But
intimate with one vital difference. Valerie grew into a
young girl, and her looks and her figure developed, and
she was not his daughter. I don't know what happened.
What I do know is that we can begin to see one overwhelming motive for Mrs. Taylor murdering her own
daughter: the suspicion, gradually edging into a terrible
certainty, that her only daughter was expecting a baby
and that the father of that baby was her own husband. I
think that on that Tuesday Mrs. Taylor accused her
daughter of precisely that."

"It's a terrible thing," said Lewis slowly, "but perhaps
we shouldn't be too hard on her."

"I don't feel hard on anybody," rejoined Morse. "In
fact, I feel some sympathy for the wretched woman. Who
wouldn't? But if all this is true, you can see what the
likely train of events is. When George Taylor arrives
home he's caught up in it all. Like a fly in a spider's web.
His wife *knows*. It's no good him trying to wash his
hands of the whole affair: he's the *cause* of it all. So, he
goes along with her. What else can he do? What's more,
he's in a position, the remarkably fortunate position, of
being able to dispose, without suspicion and without too
much trouble, of virtually anything, including a body.
And I don't mean in the reservoir. George works at a
place where vast volumes of rubbish and waste are piled
high every day, and the same day buried without trace
below the ground. And don't forget that Taylor was a

man who worked on road construction—*driving a bulldozer*. If he arrives at work half an hour early, what's to
stop him using the bulldozer that's standing all ready,
with the keys invitingly hung up for him on a nail in the
shack? Nothing. Who would know? Who would care?
No, Lewis. I don't think they put her into the reservoir. I
think she lies buried out there on the rubbish dump."
Morse stopped for a second or two, and visualised the
course of events anew.

"I think that Valerie must have been put into a sack or
some sort of rubbish bag, and consigned for the long
night to the boot of Taylor's old Morris. And in the
morning he drove off early, and dumped her there, amid
all the other mouldering rubbish; and he started up the
bulldozer and buried her under the mounds of soil that
stood ready at the sides of the tip. That's about it, Lewis.
I'm very much afraid that's just about what happened. I
should have been suspicious before, especially about the
police not being called in until the next morning."

"Do you think they'll find her body after all this time?"

"I should think so. It'll be a horribly messy business—
but I should think so. The surveyor's department will
know roughly which parts of the tip were levelled when
and where, and I think we shall find her. Poor kid!"

"They put the police to a hell of a lot of trouble, didn't
they?"

Morse nodded. "It must have taken some guts to carry
it through the way they did, I agree. But when you've
committed a murder and got rid of the body, it might not
have been so difficult as you think."

A stray thought had been worrying Lewis as Morse
had expounded his views of the way things must have
happened.

"Do you think Ainley was getting near the truth?"

"I don't know," said Morse. "He might have had all sorts of strange ideas before he'd finished. But whether he got a scent of the truth or not doesn't really matter. What matters is that other people thought he was getting near the truth."

"Where do you think the letter fits in, sir?"

Morse looked away. "Yes, the letter. Remember the letter was probably posted before whoever sent it knew that Ainley was dead. I thought at the time that the whole point of it was to concentrate police attention away from the scene of the crime and on to London; and it seemed a possibility that the Taylors had cooked it up themselves because they thought Ainley was coming a bit too close for comfort."

"But you don't think so now?"

"No. Like you, I think we've got to accept the evidence that it was almost certainly written by Baines."

"Any idea why he wrote it?"

"I think I have, although—"

The front door bell rang in mid-sentence, and almost immediately Mrs. Lewis appeared with the doctor. Morse shook hands with him and got up to go.

"There's no need for you to go. Shan't be with him long."

"No, I'll be off," said Morse. "I'll call back this afternoon, Lewis."

He let himself out and drove back to the police H.Q. at Kidlington. He sat in his black leather chair and looked mournfully at his in-tray. He would have to catch up with his correspondence very soon. But not today. Perhaps he had been glad of the interruption in Lewis's bedroom, for there were several small points in his reconstruction of the case which needed further cerebration. The truth was that Morse felt a little worried.

Chapter Thirty

> Money often costs too much.
> RALPH WALDO EMERSON

For the next hour he sat, without interruption, without a single telephone call, and thought it all through, beginning with the question that Lewis had put to him: why had Baines written the letter to the Taylors? At twelve noon, he rose from his chair, walked along the corridor and knocked at the office of Superintendent Strange.

Half an hour later, the door reopened and the two men exchanged a few final words.

"You'll have to produce one," said Strange. "There's no two ways about it, Morse. You can hold them for questioning, if you like, but sooner or later we want a body. In fact, we've got to have a body."

"I suppose you're right, sir," said Morse. "It's a bit fanciful without a body, as you say."

"It's a bit fanciful *with* a body," said Strange.

Morse walked to the canteen, where the inevitable Dickson was ordering a vast plate of meat and vegetables.

"How's Sergeant Lewis, sir? Have you heard?"

"Much better. I saw him this morning. He'll be back any day."

He thought of Lewis as he ordered his own lunch, and knew that he had not finally resolved the question that his sergeant had put to him. Why had Baines written that letter? He had thought of all the possible reasons that anyone ever had for writing a letter, but was still not convinced that he had a satisfactory answer. It would come, though. There was still a good deal about Baines he didn't know, but he had set enquiries in progress several days ago, and even bank managers and income-tax inspectors didn't take all that long, surely.

He ought to have had a closer look through his in-tray; and he would. For the moment, however, he thought that a breath of fresh air would do him good, and he walked out into the main road, turned right and found himself walking towards the pub. He didn't wish to see Mrs. Taylor, and he was relieved to find that she wasn't there. He ordered a pint, left immediately he had finished it and walked down towards the main road. Two shops he had never paid any attention to before lay off a narrow service road at the top of Hatfield Way, one a general provisions store, the other a fresh fruiterer, and Morse bought a small bunch of black grapes for the invalid. It seemed a kind thought. As he walked out, he noticed a small derelict area between the side of the provisions store and the next row of council houses. It was no more than ten square yards in extent, with two or three bicycle racks, the bric à brac of builders' carts from years ago—half bricks, a flattened heap of sand; and strewing the area the inevitable empty cigarette cartons and crisps packets. Two cars stood in the small area, unobtrusive and unmolested. Morse stopped and took his bearings and realised that he was only some forty or fifty yards from the Taylors' house, a little further down towards the main road on the left. He stood quite still and gripped the bag of grapes more firmly. Mrs. Taylor was in the front garden

He could see her quite clearly, her hair piled rather untidily on top of her head, her back towards him, her slim legs more those of a schoolgirl than a mother. In her right hand she held a pair of secateurs, and she was bending over the rose trees and clipping off the faded blooms. He found himself wondering if he would have been able to recognise her if she suddenly rushed out of the gate in a bright school uniform with her hair flowing down to her shoulders; and it made him uneasy, for he felt that he *would* have been able to tell at once that she was a woman and not a girl. You couldn't really disguise some things, however hard you tried; and perhaps it was very fortunate for Mrs. Taylor that none of the neighbours *had* seen her that Tuesday lunchtime, and that old Joe Godberry's eyes had grown so tired and dim. And all of a sudden he saw it all plainly, and the blood tingled in his arms. He glanced around again at the small piece of waste land, shielded from the Taylors' home by the wall of the council house, looked again at the Taylors' front garden, where the wilted petals were now piled neatly at the edge of the narrow lawn, turned on his heel and walked back the long way round to police H.Q.

He had been right about his in-tray. There were detailed statements about Baines's financial position, and Morse raised his eyebrows in some surprise as he studied them, for Baines was better off than he had thought. Apart from insurance policies, Baines had over £5,000 in the Oxford Building Society, £6,000 tied up in a high-interest long-term loan with Manchester Corporation, £4,500 in his deposit account with Lloyds, as well as £150 in his current account with the same bank. It all added up to a tidy sum, and schoolmasters, even experienced second masters, weren't all that highly recompensed. The pay

cheques for the previous year had all been paid directly
into the deposit account, and Morse noticed with some
surprise that the withdrawals on the current account had
seldom amounted to more than thirty pounds per month
over that period. It seemed clear from the previous year's
tax returns that Baines had no supplementary monies
accruing to him from examination fees or private tuition,
and although he may have risked not declaring any such
further income, Morse thought that on the whole it was
unlikely. The house, too, belonged to Baines: the final
payment had been made some six years previously. Of
course, he may well have been left a good deal of money
by his parents and other relatives; but the fact remained
that Baines somehow had managed to live on about seven
or eight pounds a week for the last twelve months. Either
he was a miser or, what seemed more likely, he was
receiving a supply of ready cash fairly regularly from
some quarter or quarters. And it hardly needed a mind as
imaginative as Morse's to make one or two intelligent
deductions on that score. There must have been several
people who had shed no tears when Baines had died;
indeed there had been one person who had been unable to
stand it any longer and who had stuck him through with a
carving knife.

Chapter Thirty-one

> To you, Lord Governor,
> Remains the censure of this hellish villain—
> The time, the place, the torture. O enforce it!
> SHAKESPEARE, *Othello*, Act V

Lewis was sitting up in his dressing-gown in the front room when Morse returned at a quarter to three.

"Start next Monday, sir—Sunday if you want me—and I can't tell you how glad I am."

"It'll all be over then with a bit of luck," said Morse. "Still we may have another homicidal lunatic roaming the streets before then, eh?"

"You really think this is nearly finished, sir?"

"I saw Strange this morning. We're going ahead tomorrow. Bring in both the Taylors and then start digging up all the rubbish dump—if we have to; though I think George will cooperate, even if his wife doesn't."

"And you think it all links up with Baines's murder?"

Morse nodded. "You were asking this morning about Baines writing that letter, and the truth is I don't quite know yet. It could have been to put the police off the scent, or to put them on—take your pick. But I feel fairly sure that one way or another it would keep his little pot boiling."

"I don't quite follow you, sir."

Morse told him of Baines's financial position, and Lewis whistled softly. "He really was a blackmailer, then?"

"He was certainly getting money from somewhere, probably from more than one source."

"Phillipson, for sure, I should think."

"Yes. I think Phillipson had to fork out a regular monthly payment; not all that much perhaps, certainly not a ruinous sum for a man in Phillipson's position. Let's say twenty, thirty pounds a month. I don't know. But I shall know soon. There can be little doubt that Baines saw him the night he was going back home after his interview; saw him with a bit of stuff—more than likely Valerie Taylor. He could have ruined Phillipson's position straightaway, of course, but that doesn't seem to have been the way that Baines's warped and devious mind would usually work. It gave him power to keep the intelligence to himself—to himself, that is, and to Phillipson."

"He had as good a reason as anybody for killing Baines, didn't he?"

"He had, indeed. But he didn't kill Baines."

"You sound pretty sure of yourself, sir."

"Yes I am sure," said Morse quietly. "Let's just go on a bit. I think there was another member of staff Baines had been blackmailing."

"You mean Acum?"

"Yes, Acum. It seemed odd to me from the start that he should leave a fairly promising situation in the modern languages department here at the Roger Bacon, and take up a very similar position in a very similar school right up in the wilds of North Wales—away from his friends and family and the agreeable life of a university town like Oxford. I think that there must have been a little flurry of a minor scandal earlier in the year that Acum left. I asked him about it when I saw him yesterday, but he wouldn't have any of it. It doesn't matter much, though, and Phillipson will have to come clean anyway."

"What do you think happened?"

"Oh, the usual thing. Somebody caught him with one of the girls with his trousers down."

Lewis leaned his head to one side and smiled rather wearily. "I suppose you think it may have been Valerie Taylor, sir?"

"Why not?" said Morse. "She seems to have made most of the men put their hands on their cocks at some time, doesn't she? I should think that Phillipson got to know and Baines, too—oh yes, I'm sure Baines got to know—and they got together and agreed to hush things up if Acum would agree to leave as soon as it was practicable to do so. And I shouldn't think that Acum had any option. He'd be asked to leave whatever happened, and his wife would probably find out and—well, it would have seemed like the end of the world to a young fellow like Acum."

"And you think Baines had the bite on Acum?"

"Pretty certain of it. I should think that Acum" (Morse chose his words carefully) "—judging from the little I've seen of his wife—would have been a bloody fool to have ruined his career just for the sake of a brief infatuation with one of his pupils. And he didn't. He played the game and cleared out."

"And paid up."

"Yes. He paid up, though I shouldn't think Baines was stupid enough to expect too much from a former colleague who was probably fairly hard up anyway. Just enough, though. Just enough for Baines to relish another little show of power over one of his fellow human beings."

"I suppose you're going to tell me next that Baines had the bite on the Taylors as well."

"No. Just the opposite, in fact. I reckon that Baines was paying money to Mrs. Taylor."

Lewis sat up. Had he heard aright? "You mean Mrs. Taylor was blackmailing *Baines*?"

"I didn't say that, did I? Let's go back at bit. We've agreed that Baines got to know about Phillipson's little peccadillo at the Station Hotel. Now I can't imagine that Baines would merely be content with the Phillipson angle. I think that he began to grub around on the Taylor side of the fence. Now, Lewis. What did he find? You remember that George Taylor was out of work at the time, and that far from being a potential source of blackmail the Taylors were in dire need of money themselves. And especially Mrs. Taylor. Baines had met them several times at parents' evenings, and I should guess that he arranged to see Mrs. Taylor privately, and that he pretty soon read the temperature of the water correctly."

"But Baines wasn't the type of man who went around doing favours."

"Oh no. The whole thing suited Baines splendidly."

"But he gave her money, you think?"

"Yes."

"But she wouldn't take his money just like that, would she? I mean . . . she wouldn't expect . . ."

"Wouldn't expect to get the money for nothing? Oh no. She had something to give him in return."

"What was that?"

"What the hell do you think it was? You weren't born yesterday, were you?"

Lewis felt abashed. "Oh, I see," he said quietly.

"Once a week in term time, if you want me to keep

guessing. Tuesdays, likely as not, when he had the afternoon off. *Tuesday afternoons*, Lewis. Do you see what that means?"

"You mean," stammered Lewis, "that Baines probably . . . probably . . ."

"Probably knew more about the fate of Valerie Taylor than we thought, yes. I should think that Baines would park somewhere near the Taylors' house—not too near—and wait until Valerie had gone off back to school. Then he'd go in, get his pound of flesh, pay his stamp duty—"

"Bit dangerous, wasn't it?"

"If you're a bachelor like Baines and you're dying to spill your oats—well . . . After all, no one would *know* what was going on. Lock the door and—"

Lewis interrupted him. "But if they'd arranged to meet the day that Valerie disappeared it would have been crazy for Mrs. Taylor to have murdered her daughter."

"It was crazy anyway. I don't think she would have worried too much if the police force was out the front and the fire brigade was out the back. Listen. What I think may have happened on that Tuesday is this. Baines parked pretty near the house, probably in a bit of waste land near the shops, just above the Taylors' place. He waited until afternoon school had started, and then he saw something very odd. He saw Valerie, or who he thought was Valerie, leave by the front door and run down the road. Then he went up to the house and knocked—we didn't find a key, did we?—and he got no answer. It's all a bit odd. Has his reluctant mistress—well, let's hope she was reluctant—has she slipped out for a minute? He can almost swear she hasn't, but he can't be absolutely sure. He walks back, frustrated and disappointed, and scratches his balls in the car; and something tells him to wait. And about ten minutes later he sees Mrs. Taylor walking—probably walking in a great hurry—out of one of the side streets and going into the house. Has she been out over the lunchtime? Unusual, to say the least. But there's something odder still—far odder. Something that makes him sit up with a vengeance. Valerie—he would remember now—had left with a basket; and here is Valerie's mother returning *with the very same basket*. Does he guess the truth? I don't know. Does he go to the house again and knock? Probably so. And I would guess she told him she couldn't possibly see him that afternoon. So Baines walks away, and drives home, and wonders . . . Wonders even harder the next day when he hears of Valerie's disappearance."

"He guessed what had happened, you think?"

"Pretty sure he did."

Lewis thought for a minute. "Perhaps Mrs. Taylor just couldn't face things any longer, sir, and told him that everything was finished; and he in turn might have threatened to go to the police."

"Could be, but I should be very surprised if Baines was killed to stop him spilling the beans—or even some of them. No, Lewis. I just think that he was killed because he was detested so viciously that killing him was an act of superb and joyous revenge."

"You think that Mrs. Taylor murdered him, then?"

Morse nodded. "You remember the first time we saw Mrs. Taylor in the pub? Remember that large American-style handbag she had? It was a bit of a puzzle at first to know how anyone could ever cart such a big knife around. But the obvious way to do it is precisely the way Mrs. Taylor chose. Stick it in a handbag. She got the

Kempis Street at about a quarter-past nine, I should think, knocked on the door, told a surprised Baines some cock-and-bull story, followed him into the kitchen, agreed to his offer of a glass of something, and as he bends down to get the beer out of the fridge, she takes her knife out and—well, we know the rest."

Lewis sat back and considered what Morse had said. It all hung loosely together, perhaps, but he was feeling hot and tired.

"Go and have a lie down," said Morse, as if reading his thoughts. "You've had about enough for one day."

"I think I will, sir. I shall be much better tomorrow."

"Don't worry about tomorrow. I shan't do anything until the afternoon."

"It's the inquest in the morning, though, isn't it?"

"Formality. Pure formality," said Morse. "I shan't say much. Just get him identified and tell the coroner we've got the bloodhounds out. 'Murder by person or persons unknown.' I don't know why we're wasting public money on having an inquest at all."

"It's the law, sir."

"Mm."

"And tomorrow afternoon, sir?"

"I'm bringing the Taylors in."

Lewis stood up. "I feel a bit sorry for him, sir."

"Don't you feel a bit sorry for *her*?" There was a sharp edge on Morse's voice; and after he had gone Lewis wondered why he'd suddenly turned so sour.

At four o'clock that same afternoon, as Morse and Lewis were talking together and trying to unravel the twisted skein of the Valerie Taylor case, a tall military-looking man was dictating a letter to one of the girls from the typing pool. He had some previous experience of the young lady in question, and decided it would be sensible to make the letter even briefer than he had intended; for although it would contain no earth-shattering news, he was anxious for it to go in the evening post. He had tried to phone earlier but had declined to leave a message when he learned that the only man who could have any possible interest in the matter was out—whereabouts temporarily unknown. At four-fifteen the letter was signed and in the evening postbag.

The bombshell burst on Morse's desk at 8:45 A.M. the following morning.

Chapter Thirty-two

> When you have eliminated the impossible, whatever remains, however improbable, must be the truth.
> A. CONAN DOYLE, *The Sign of the Four*

"It's a mistake, I tell you. It's some clown of a sergeant who's ballsed the whole thing up." His voice was strident, exasperated. He was prepared to forgive a certain degree of inadequacy, but never incompetence of this order. The voice at the other end of the line sounded firm and assured, like a kindly parent seeking to assuage a petulant child.

"There's no mistake, I'm afraid. I've checked it myself. And for heaven's sake calm down a bit, Morse, my old friend. You asked me to do something for you, and I've done it. If it comes as a bit of a shock—"

"*A bit of a shock!* Christ Almighty, it's not just a bit of a shock, believe me; it's sheer bloody lunacy!"

There was a short delay at the other end. "Look, old boy, I think you'd better come up and see for yourself, don't you? If you still think it's a mistake—well, that's up to you."

"Don't keep saying 'if' it's a mistake. It *is* a mistake— you can put your shirt and your underpants on that, believe me!" He calmed himself down as far as he could and resumed the conversation in a tone more befitting his station. "Trouble is I've got a damned inquest today."

"Shouldn't let that worry you. Anybody can do that for you. Unless you've arrested somebody, of course."

"No, no," muttered Morse, "nothing like that. It would have been adjourned anyway."

"You sound a bit fed up one way or another."

"I bloody *am* fed up," snapped Morse, "and who wouldn't be. I've got the case all ready for bed and you send me a scratty little note that's blown the top off the whole f——— thing! How would *you* feel?"

"You didn't expect us to find anything—is that it?"

"No," said Morse, "I didn't. Not a load of cock like that, anyway."

"Well, as I say, you'll be able to see for yourself. I suppose it could have been somebody else with the same name, but it's a whacking big coincidence if that's the case. Same name, same dates. No, I don't think so. You'd be pushing your luck, I reckon."

"And I'm going on pushing it," rejoined Morse, "pushing it like hell, have no fear. Coincidences do happen, don't they?" It sounded more like a plea to the gods than a statement of empirical truth.

"Perhaps they do, sometimes. It's my fault, though. I should have got hold of you yesterday. I did try a couple of times in the afternoon, but . . ."

"You weren't to know. As far as you were concerned it was just one more routine enquiry."

"And it wasn't?" said the voice softly.

"And it wasn't," echoed Morse. "Anyway, I'll get there as soon as I can."

"Good. I'll get the stuff ready for you."

Chief Inspector Rogers of New Scotland Yard put down the phone and wondered why the letter he had dictated and signed the previous afternoon had blown up with such obvious devastation in Morse's face. The carbon copy, he noticed, was still lying in his out-tray, and he picked it up and read it through again. It still seemed pretty harmless.

CONFIDENTIAL.

For the attention of Det. Chief Inspector Morse,
Thames Valley Police H.Q.,
Kidlington, Oxon.

Dear Morse,

You asked for a check on the abortion clinics for the missing person, Valerie Taylor. Sorry to have taken so long about it, but it proved difficult. The trouble is all these semi-registered places where abortions still get done unofficially—no doubt for a whacking private fee. Anyway, we've traced her. She was at the East Chelsea Nursing Home on the dates you gave us. Arrived 4:15 P.M. Tuesday, under her own name, and left some time Friday A.M. by taxi. About three months pregnant. No complications. Description fits all along the line, but we could check further. She had a room-mate who might not be too difficult to trace. We await your further instructions.

Yours sincerely,

P.S. Don't forget to call when you're this way again. The beer at the Westminster is drinkable—just!

Chief Inspector Rogers shrugged his shoulders and put the carbon back in the out-tray. Morse! He always had been a funny old bird.

* * *

Morse himself sat back in his black leather chair and felt like a man who had just been authoritatively informed that the moon really was made of green cheese after all. Scotland Yard! They must have buggered it all up—must have done! But whatever they'd done, it was little use pretending he could go ahead with his intended schedule. What was the good of bringing two people in for questioning about the murder of a young girl if on the very day she was supposed to be lying dead in the boot of a car she had walked as large as life into some shabby nursing home in East Chelsea—of all places? For a few seconds Morse almost considered the possibility of taking the new information seriously. But he couldn't quite manage it. It just *couldn't* be right, and there was a fairly easy way of proving that it wasn't right. Central London lay no more than sixty miles away.

He went in to see Strange, and the superintendent, reluctantly, agreed to stand in for him at the inquest.

He rang Lewis, and told him he had to go off to London—he mentioned nothing more—and learned that Lewis would be reporting for duty again the next morning. That is, if he was needed. And Morse said, in a rather weak voice, that he thought he probably would be.

Chapter Thirty-three

She'll be wearing silk pyjamas when she comes.
                                    Popular song

By any reckoning Yvonne Baker was a honey. She lived alone—or to be accurate she rented a single flat—in a high-rise tenement block in Bethune Road, Stoke Newington. She would have preferred a slightly more central spot and a slightly more luxurious apartment. But from Manor House tube station in Seven Sisters Road, just ten minutes' walk away, she could be in Central London in a further twenty minutes; and anyone looking around the tasteful and expensive décor of her flat would have guessed (correctly) that, whether from money honourably earned in the cosmetic department of an exclusive store in Oxford Street, or from other unspecified sources of income, Miss Baker was a young woman of not unsubstantial means.

At half-past six she lay languorously relaxed upon her costly counterpane, idly painting her long, beautifully-manicured nails with a particularly revolting shade of sickly-green varnish. She wore a peach-coloured satin dressing-gown, her legs, invitingly long and slender, drawn up to her waist, her thoughts centred on the evening ahead of her. The real trouble with pyjama parties was that some of the guests hadn't quite the courage to conform to the code, and wore enough under their nightshirts or

pyjamas to defeat the whole object of the simple exercise.
At least *she* would show them. Some of the girls would
wear a bra and panties, but she wasn't going to. Oh no!
She experienced a tingle of excitement at the thought
of dancing with the men, and of knowing only too clearly
the effect that she would have upon them. It was a gorgeous feeling anyway, wearing so little. So sensuous, so
abandoned!

She finished her left hand, held it up before her like a
policeman stopping the traffic and flexed her fingers. She
then poured some removing fluid on to a wad of cotton
wool and proceeded to rub off all the varnish. Her hands
looked better without any nail polish, she decided. She
stood up, unfastened and took off her dressing-gown, and
carefully lifted out of one of the wardrobe drawers a pair
of palish-green pyjamas. She had a beautiful body, and
like so many of her admirers she was inordinately conscious of it. She admired herself in the long wall-mirror,
fastened all but the top button of her pyjama top and
began to brush her long, luxuriant, honey-coloured hair.
She would be collected by car at half-past seven, and she
glanced again at the alarm clock on her bedside table.
Three-quarters of an hour. She walked into the living
room, put a record on the turntable, and lit a cigarette of
quite improbable length.

The door bell rang at ten minutes to seven, and her first
thought was that the alarm clock must be slow again.
Well, if it was, so much the better. She walked gaily to
the door and opened it with a beaming smile upon her
soft, full lips, a smile which slowly contracted and finally
faded away as she stared at a man she had never seen
before, who stood rather woodenly upon the threshold.
Middle-aged and rather sour.

"Hullo," she managed.

"Miss Baker?" Miss Baker nodded. "I'm Chief Inspector Morse. I'd like to come in and have a word with you, if I may."

"Of course." A slightly worried frown puckered the meticulously plucked eyebrows as he stood aside and closed the door behind him.

As he explained the reason for his visit, she felt that he was about the only man within living memory upon whom she appeared to have no visibly erotic effect. In her pyjamas, too! He was brisk and business-like. Two years the previous June she had shared, had she not, a room in the East Chelsea Nursing Home with a girl named Valerie Taylor? He wanted to know about this girl. Everything she could conceivably remember—every single little thing.

The door bell rang again at twenty-five past seven and Morse told her in an unexpectedly peremptory tone to get rid of him, whoever he was.

"I hope you realise I'm going out to a party tonight, inspector." She sounded vexed, but in reality was not so vexed as she appeared. In an odd sort of way he was beginning to interest her.

"So I see," said Morse, eyeing the pyjamas. "Just tell him you'll be another half hour with me—at least." She decided she liked his voice. "And tell him I'll take you myself if he can't wait." She decided she'd rather like that.

Morse had already learned enough; and he knew—had known earlier, really—that what Rogers had written was true. There was now no doubt whatsoever that Valerie Taylor had somehow found her way into a London abortion clinic on the very same day on which she had disappeared. The doctor who ran the nursing home had been pleasantly co-operative, but had categorically refused to break what he termed the code of professional confidentiality by revealing the identity of the person or persons who had negotiated Miss Taylor's visit. It had amazed Morse that the affluent abortionist should have heard of, let alone practised, any code of professional confidentiality; but short of a forcible entry into his filing cabinets, the ambivalent doctor made it abundantly clear that further information was not forthcoming.

After explaining the situation to her pyjama-bottomed beau Miss Baker retired briefly to the bedroom, examined herself once more in the mirror, and wrapped her dressing-gown—not too tightly—around her. She was beginning to feel chilly.

"There was no need to worry too much about me," said Morse. "I'm pretty harmless with women, they say." For the first time she smiled at him, fully and freely, and immediately Morse wished she hadn't.

"I'll take it off again if you'll turn the fire on, inspector." She purred the words at him, and the danger bells were ringing in his head.

"I shan't keep you much longer, Miss Baker."

"Most people call me Yvonne." She smiled again and lay back in the armchair. No one ever called Morse by his Christian name.

"I'll turn on the fire if you're not careful," he said. But he didn't.

"You tell me she said she was from Oxford—not from Kidlington?"

"From where?"

"Kidlington. It's just outside Oxford."

"Oh, is it? No. She said Oxford, I'm sure of that."

Perhaps she would anyway, thought Morse. It did sound a bit more imposing. He had nearly finished. "Just one last thing, and I want you to think very hard, Miss— er, Yvonne. Did Miss Taylor mention to you at any stage who the father was? Or who she thought the father was?"

She laughed openly. "You're so beautifully delicate, inspector. But as a matter of fact she did, yes. She was quite a lass really, you know."

"Who was it?"

"She said something about one of her teachers. I remember that because I was a bit surprised to learn she was still a schoolgirl. She looked much older than that. She seemed much more . . . much more *knowing* somehow. She was nobody's fool, I can tell you that."

"This teacher," said Morse. "Did she say anything else about him?"

"She didn't mention his name, I don't think. But she said he'd got a little beard and it tickled her every time he . . . every time . . . you know."

Morse took his eyes from her and stared sadly down at the thick-piled, dark-green carpet. It had been a crazy sort of day.

"She didn't say what he taught? What subject?"

She thought a moment. "Do you know, I . . . I rather think she did. I think she said he was a French teacher or something."

He drove her into the West End, tried to forget that she was off to an open-ended orgy dressed only in the pyjamas he had eyed so lovingly in her flat, and decided that life had passed him by.

He dropped her in Mayfair, where she thanked him, a

little sadly, and turned towards him and kissed him fully
on the lips with her soft, open mouth. And when she was
gone, he looked after her, the flaired pale-green bottoms
of her pyjamas showing below the sleek fur coat. There
had been many bad moments that day, but as he sat there
in the Lancia slowly wiping the gooey, deep-orange lip-
stick from his mouth, he decided that this was just about
the worst.

Morse drove back to Soho and parked his car on the
double yellow lines immediately in front of the Pent
house Club. It was 9:00 P.M. At a glance he could see that
the man seated at the receipt of custom was not Maguire
as he hoped it would be. But he was almost past caring as
he walked into the foyer.

" 'Fraid you can't leave your car there, mate."

"Perhaps you don't know who I am," said Morse, with
the arrogant authority of a Julius Caesar or an Alexander
walking among the troops.

"I don't care who you are, mate," said the young man
rising to his feet, "you just can't . . ."

"I'll tell you who I am, sonny. My name's Morse.
M-O-R-S-E. Got that? And if anyone comes along and
asks you whose car it is tell 'em it's mine. And if they
don't believe you, just refer 'em to me, sonny boy—
sharpish!" He walked past the desk and through the lat-
ticed doorway.

"But . . ." Morse heard no more. The Maltese dwarf sat
dutifully at his post, and in a perverse sort of way Morse
was glad to see him.

"You remember me?"

It was clear that the little man did. "No need for tickets

sir. You go in. Ticket on me." He smiled weakly, but Morse ignored the offer.

"I want to talk to you. My car's outside." There was no argument, and they sat side by side in the front.

"Where's Maguire?"

"He's gone. He just gone. I do' know where."

"When did he leave?"

"Two day, three day."

"Did he have a girlfriend here?"

"Lots of girls. Some of the girls here, some of the girls there. Who know?"

"There was a girl here recently—she wore a mask. I think her name was Valerie, perhaps."

The little man thought he saw the light and visibly relaxed. "Valerie? No. You mean Vera. Oh yeah. Boys oh boys!" He was beginning to feel more confident now and his dirty hands expressively traced the undulating contours of her beautiful body.

"Is she here tonight?"

"She gone, too."

"I might have known it," muttered Morse. "She's buggered off with Maguire, I suppose."

The little man smiled, revealed a mouthful of large, brilliantly white teeth and shrugged his oversized shoulders. Morse repressed his strong desire to smash his fist into the leering face, and asked one further question.

"Did *you* ever take her out, you filthy little bastard?"

"Sometimes. Who know." He shrugged his shoulders again and spread out his hands, palms uppermost, in a typically Mediterranean gesture.

"Get out."

"You want to come in, mister policeman? See pretty girls, no?"

"Get out," snarled Morse.

For a while Morse sat on silently in his car and pondered many things. Life was down to its dregs, and he had seldom felt so desolate and defeated. He recalled his first interview with Strange at the very beginning of the case, and the distaste he had felt then at the prospect of trying to find a young girl in the midst of this corrupt and corrupting city. And now, again, he had to presume that she was alive. For all his wayward unpredictability, there was at the centre of his being an inner furnace of passion for truth, for logical analysis; and inexorably now the facts, almost all the facts, were pointing to the same conclusion—that he had been wrong, wrong from the start.

A constable, young, tall, confident, tapped sharply on the car window. "Is this your car, sir?"

Morse wound the window down and wearily identified himself.

"Sorry, sir. I just thought . . ."

"Of course you did."

"Can I be of any assistance, sir?"

"Doubt it," replied Morse. "I'm looking for a young girl."

"She live round here, sir?"

"I don't know," said Morse. "I don't even know if she lives in London. Not much hope for me, is there?"

"But you mean she's been seen round here recently?"

"No," said Morse quietly. "She's not been seen anywhere for over two years."

"Oh, I see, sir," said the young man, seeing nothing. "Well, perhaps I can't help much, then. Good night, sir." He touched his helmet, and walked off, uncomprehending, past the gaudy strip clubs and the pornographic bookshops.

"No," said Morse to himself, "I don't think you can."

He started the engine and drove via Shepherd's Bush and the White City towards the M40. He was back in his office just before midnight.

It did not even occur to him to go straight home. He was fully aware, even if he could give no explanation for it, of the curious fact that his mind was never more resilient, never sharper, than when apparently it was beaten. On such occasions his brain would roam restlessly around his skull like a wild and vicious tiger immured within the confines of a narrow cage, ceaselessly circumambulating, snarling savagely—and lethal. During the whole of the drive back to Oxford he had been like a chess player, defeated only after a monumental struggle, who critically reviews and analyses the moves and the motives for the moves that have led to his defeat. And already a new and strange idea was spawning in the fertile depths of his mind, and he was impatient to get back.

At three minutes to midnight he was poring over the dossiers on the Taylor case with the frenetic concentration of a hastily-summoned understudy who had only a few minutes in which to memorise a lengthy speech.

At 2:30 A.M. the night sergeant, carrying a steaming cup of coffee on a tray, tapped lightly and opened the door. He saw Morse, his hands over his ears, his desk strewn with documents, and an expression of such profound intensity upon his face that he quickly and gently put down the tray, reclosed the door and walked quickly away.

He called again at 4:30 A.M. and carefully put down a second cup of coffee beside the first, which stood where he had left it, cold, ugly-brown, untouched. Morse was fast asleep now, his head leaning back against the top of the black leather chair, the neck of his white shirt unfastened, and an expression on his face as of a young child for whom the vivid terrors of the night were past . . .

It had been Lewis who had found her. She lay supine upon the bed, fully-clothed, her left arm placed across the body, the wrist slashed cruelly deep. The white coverlet was a pool of scarlet, and blood had dripped its way through the mattress. Clutched in her right hand was a knife, a wooden-handled carving knife, "Prestige, Made in England," some 35–36 centimetres long, the cutting blade honed along its entire edge to a razor-sharp ferocity.

Chapter Thirty-four

Things are not always what they seem;
the first appearance deceives many.

PHAEDRUS

Lewis reported back for duty at eight o'clock and found a freshly-shaven Morse seated at his desk. He could scarcely hide his disappointment as Morse began to recount the previous day's events, and found himself quite unable to account for the inspector's sprightly tone. His spirits picked up, however, when Morse mentioned the crucial evidence given by Miss Baker, and after hearing the whole story, he evinced little surprise at the string of instructions that Morse proceeded to give him. There were several phone calls to make and he thought he began to understand the general tenor of the inspector's purpose.

At 9:30 he had finished, and reported back to Morse.

"Feel up to the drive then?"

"I don't mind driving one way, sir, but—"

"Settled then. I'll drive there, you drive back. Agreed?"

"When were you thinking of going, sir?"

"Now," said Morse. "Give the missus a ring and tell her we should be back about, er . . ."

"Do you mind me mentioning something, sir?"

"What's worrying you?"

"If Valerie was in that nursing home—"

261

"She was," interrupted Morse.

"—well, someone had to take her and fetch her and pay for her and everything."

"The quack won't tell us. Not yet, anyway."

"Isn't it fairly easy to guess, though?"

"Is it?" said Morse, with apparent interest.

"It's only a guess, sir. But if they were all in it together—you know, to cover things up . . ."

"All?"

"Phillipson, the Taylors and Acum. When you come to think of it, it would kill a lot of birds with one stone, wouldn't it?"

"How do you mean?"

"Well, if you're right about Phillipson and Valerie, he'd have a bit of a guilt complex about her and feel morally bound to help out, wouldn't he? And then there's the Taylors. It would save them any scandal and stop Valerie mucking up her life completely. And then there's Acum. It would get him out of a dickens of a mess at the school and save his marriage into the bargain. They've all got a stake in it."

Morse nodded and Lewis felt encouraged to continue. "They could have cooked it all up between them: fixed up the clinic, arranged the transport, paid the bill and found a job for Valerie to go to afterwards. They probably hadn't the faintest idea that her going off like that would create such a fuss, and once they started on it, well, they just had to go through with it. So they all stuck together. And told the same story."

"You may well be right."

"If I am, sir, don't you think it would be a good idea to fetch Phillipson and the Taylors in? I mean, it would save us a lot of trouble."

"Save us going all the way to Caernarfon, you mean?"

"Yes. If they spill the beans, we can get Acum brought down here."

"What if they all stick to their story?"

"Then we'll have to go and get him."

"I'm afraid it's not quite so easy as that," said Morse.

"Why not?"

"I tried to get Phillipson first thing this morning. He went off to Brighton yesterday afternoon—to a Headmasters' Conference."

"Oh."

"And the Taylors left by car for Luton airport at 6:30 yesterday morning. They're spending a week on a package tour in the Channel Islands. So the neighbours say."

"Oh."

"And," continued Morse, "we're still trying to find out who killed Baines, remember?"

"That's why you've asked the Caernarfon police to pick him up?"

"Yep. And we'd better not keep him waiting too long. It's about four and a half hours—non-stop. So we'll allow five. We might want to give the car a little rest on the way."

Outside a pub, thought Lewis, as he pulled on his overcoat. But Lewis thought wrong.

The traffic this Sunday morning was light and the police car made its way quickly up through Brackley and thence to Towcester where it turned left on to the A5. Neither man seemed particularly anxious to sustain much conversation, and a tacit silence soon prevailed between them, as if they waited tensely for the final wicket to fall in a test match. The traffic decelerated to a paralytic crawl at road works in Wellington, and suddenly Morse switched on full headlights and the blue roof-flasher, and wailing like a dalek in distress the car swept past the stationary column of cars and soon was speeding merrily along once more out on the open road. Morse turned to Lewis and winked almost happily.

Along the Shrewsbury ring-road, Lewis ventured a conversational gambit. "Bit of luck about this Miss Baker, wasn't it?"

"Ye-es."

Lewis looked at the inspector curiously. "Nice bit of stuff, sir?"

"She's a prick-teaser."

"Oh."

They drove on through Betws-y-coed: Caernarfon 25 miles.

"The real trouble," said Morse suddenly, "was that I thought she was dead."

"And now you think she's still alive?"

"I very much hope so," said Morse, with unwonted earnestness in his voice. "I very much hope so."

At five minutes to three they came to the outskirts of Caernarfon, where ignoring the sign directing traffic to the city centre Morse turned left on to the main Pwllheli Road.

"You know your way around here then, sir?"

"Not too well. But we're going to pay a brief visit before we meet Acum." He drove south to the village of Bontnewydd, turned left off the main road and stopped outside a house with the front door painted Cambridge blue.

"Wait here a minute."

Lewis watched him as he walked up the narrow front

path and knocked on the door; and knocked again. Clearly there was no one at home. But then of course David Acum *wouldn't* be there; he was three miles away, detained for questioning on the instructions of the Thames Valley Police. Morse came back to the car and got in. His face seemed inexplicably grave.

"No one in, sir?"

Morse appeared not to hear. He kept looking around him, occasionally glancing up into the driving mirror. But the quiet street lay preternaturally still in the sunny autumn afternoon.

"Shan't we be a bit late for Acum, sir?"

"Acum?" The inspector suddenly woke from his waking dreams. "Don't worry about Acum. He'll be all right."

"How long do you plan to wait here?"

"How the hell do I know!" snapped Morse.

"Well, if we're going to wait, I think I'll just—" He opened the nearside door and began to unfasten his safety-belt.

"Stay where you are." There was a note of harsh authority in the voice, and Lewis shrugged his shoulders and closed the door again.

"If we're waiting for Mrs. Acum, don't you think she may have gone with him?"

Morse shook his head. "I don't think so."

The time ticked on inexorably, and it was Morse who finally broke the silence. "Go and knock again, Lewis."

But Lewis was no more successful than Morse had been; and he returned to the car and slammed the door with some impatience. It was already half-past three.

"We'll give her another quarter of an hour," said Morse.

"But why are we waiting for *her*, sir? What's she got to do with it all? We hardly know anything about her, do we?"

Morse turned his light-grey eyes upon his sergeant and spoke with an almost fierce simplicity. "That's where you're wrong, Lewis. We know more about her—far more about her—than about anyone else in the whole case. You see, the woman living here with David Acum is not his real wife at all—she's the person we've been looking for from the very beginning." He paused and let his words sink in. "Yes, Lewis. The woman who's been living here for the past two years as Acum's wife is not his wife at all—*she's Valerie Taylor*."

Chapter Thirty-five

> "Now listen, you young limb," whispered Sikes. "Go softly up the steps straight afore you, and along the little hall, to the street door: unfasten it, and let us in."
>
> CHARLES DICKENS, *Oliver Twist*

Lewis's mouth gaped in flabbergasted disbelief as this astonishing intelligence partially percolated through his consciousness. "You can't mean . . ."

"But I *do* mean. I mean exactly what I say. And that's why we're sitting here waiting, Lewis. We're waiting for Valerie Taylor to come home at last."

For the moment Lewis was quite incapable of any more intelligent comment than a half-formed whistle. "Phew!"

"Worth waiting another few minutes for, isn't she? After all this time?"

Gradually the implications of what the inspector had just told him began to register more significantly in Lewis's mind. It meant . . . it meant . . . But his mental processes seemed now to be anaesthetised, and he gave up the unequal struggle. "Don't you think you ought to put me in the picture, sir?"

"Where do you want me to start?" asked Morse, in a slightly brisker tone.

"Well, first of all you'd better tell me what's happened to the *real* Mrs. Acum."

"Listen, Lewis. In this case you've been right more often than I have. I've made some pretty stupid blunders—

as you know. But at last we're getting near the truth, I think. You ask me what's happened to the real Mrs. Acum. Well, I don't know for certain. But let me tell you what I think may have happened. I've hardly got a shred of evidence for it, but as I see things it must have happened something like this.

"What do we know about Mrs. Acum? A bit prim and proper, perhaps. She's got a slim, boyish-looking figure and long shoulder-length blonde hair. Not unattractive maybe, in an unusual sort of way, but no doubt very self-conscious about the blotch of ugly spots all over her face. Then think about Valerie. She's a real honey, by all accounts. A nubile young wench, with a sort of animal sexuality about her that proves fatally attractive to the opposite sex—the men and the boys alike. Now just put yourself in Acum's place. He finds Valerie in his French class, and he begins to fancy her. He thinks she may have a bit of ability, but neither the incentive nor the inclination to make anything of it. Well, from whatever motives, he talks to her privately and suggests some extra tuition. Now let's try to imagine what might have happened. Let's say Mrs. Acum has joined a Wednesday sewing-class at Headington Tech.—I know, Lewis, but don't interrupt: it doesn't matter about the details. Where was I? Yes. Acum's free then on Wednesday evenings, and we'll say that he invites Valerie round to his house. But one night in March the evening-class is cancelled—let's say the teacher's got flu—and Mrs. Acum arrives home unexpectedly early, about a quarter to eight, and she finds them both in bed together. It's a dreadful humiliation for her, and she decides that their marriage is finished. Not that she necessarily wants to ruin Acum's career. She may feel she's to blame in some way: perhaps she doesn't enjoy sex; perhaps she can't have any children—I don't know. Anyway, as I say, it's finished between them. They continue to live together, but they sleep in different rooms and hardly speak to each other. And however hard she tries, she just can't bring herself to forgive him. So they agree to separate when the summer term is over, and Acum knows it will be better for both of them if he gets a new post. Whether he told Phillipson the truth or not, doesn't really matter. Perhaps he didn't tell him anything when he first handed in his resignation; but he may well have had to say something when Valerie tells him that she's expecting a baby and that he's almost certainly the father. So, as you yourself said this morning, Lewis, they all decide to put their heads together. Valerie, Acum, Phillipson and Mrs. Taylor—I don't know about George. They arrange the clinic in London and fix up the house in North Wales here, where Valerie comes immediately after the abortion, and where Acum will join her just as soon as the school term ends. And Valerie arrives and acts the dutiful little wife, decorating the place and getting things straight and tidy; *and she's still here.* Where the real Mrs. Acum is, I don't know; but we should be able to find out easily enough. If you want me to make a guess, I'd say she's living with her mother, in a little village somewhere near Exeter."

For several minutes Lewis sat motionless within the quiet car, until aroused at length by the very silence he took a yellow duster from the glove compartment and wiped the steamy windows. Morse's imaginative reconstruction of events seemed curiously convincing, and several times during the course of it Lewis's head had nodded an almost involuntary agreement.

Morse himself suddenly looked once more at his wrist-watch. "Come on, Lewis," he said. "We've waited long enough."

The side gate was locked, and Lewis clambered awkwardly over. The small top window of the back kitchen was open slightly, and by climbing on to the rain-water tub he was able to get his arm through the narrow gap and open the latch of the main window. He eased himself through on to the draining board, jumped down inside and breathing heavily walked to the front door to let the inspector in. The house was eerily silent.

"No one here, sir. What do we do?"

"We'll have a quick look round," said Morse. "I'll stay down here. You try upstairs."

The steps on the narrow flight of stairs creaked loudly as Lewis mounted aloft, and Morse stood below and watched him, his heart pounding against his ribs.

There were only two bedrooms, each of them opening almost directly off the tiny landing: one to the right, the other immediately in front. First Lewis tried the one to his right, and peered round the door. The junk room obviously. A single bed, unmade, stood against the far wall; and the bed itself and the rest of the limited space available were strewn with the necessary and the unnecessary oddments that had yet to find for themselves a permanent place in the disposition of the Acum household: several bell-jars of home-made wine, bubbling intermittently; a vacuum cleaner, with its box of varied fitments; dusty lampshades; old curtain rails; the mounted head of an old, moth-eaten deer; and a large assortment of other semi-treasured bric à brac that cluttered up the little room. But nothing else. Nothing.

Lewis left the room and tried the other door. It would

be the bedroom, he knew that. Tentatively he pushed open the door slightly further and became aware of something scarlet lying there upon the bed, bright scarlet—the colour of new-spilt blood. He opened the door fully now and went inside. And there, draped across the pure white coverlet, the arms neatly folded across the bodice, the waist tight-belted and slim, lay a long, red-velvet evening dress.

Chapter Thirty-six

> No one does anything from a single motive.
> S. T. COLERIDGE, *Biographia Literaria*

They sat downstairs in the small kitchen.

"It looks as if our little bird has flown."

"Mm." Morse leaned his head upon his left elbow and stared blankly through the window.

"When did you first suspect all this, sir?"

"Sometime last night, it must have been. About half past three, I should think."

"This morning, then."

Morse seemed mildly surprised. It seemed a long, long time ago.

"What put you on to it, though?"

Morse sat up and leaned his back against the rickety kitchen chair. "Once we learned that Valerie was probably still alive, it altered everything, didn't it? You see, from the start I'd assumed she was dead."

"You must have had *some* reason."

"I suppose it was the photograph more than anything," replied Morse. "The one of the genuine Mrs. Acum that Mrs. Phillipson showed me. It was a clear-cut, glossy photograph—not like the indistinct and out-of-date one we've got of Valerie. Come to think of it, I doubt if either of us will recognise Valerie when we *do* see her. Anyway, I met who I *thought* was Mrs. Acum when I first

272

came up here to Caernarfon, and although she had a towel round her head I couldn't help noticing that she wasn't a natural blonde at all. The roots of her hair were dark, and for some reason" (he left it at that) "the detail, well, just stuck with me. She'd dyed her hair, anyone could see that."

"But we don't know that the real Mrs. Acum is a natural blonde."

"No, that's true," admitted Morse.

"Not much to go on then, is it?"

"There was something else, Lewis."

"What was that?"

Morse paused before replying. "In the photograph I saw of Mrs. Acum, she had a sort of, er, sort of a boyish figure, if you know what I mean."

"Bit flat-chested you mean, sir?"

"Yes."

"So?"

"The woman I saw here—well, she wasn't flat-chested, that's all."

"She could have been wearing a padded bra. You just can't tell for certain, can you?"

"Can't you?" A gentle, wistful smile played momentarily about the inspector's mouth, and he enlightened the innocent Lewis no further. "I ought to have guessed much earlier. Of course I should. They just don't have anything in common at all: Mrs. Acum—and Valerie Taylor. Huh! I don't think you'd ever find anyone less like a blue-stocking than Valerie. And I've spoken to her *twice* over the phone, Lewis! More than that, I've actually *seen* her!" He shook his head in self-reproach. "Yes. I really should have guessed the truth a long, long time ago."

"From what you said, though, sir, you didn't see much of her, did you? You said she had this beauty-pack—"

"No, not much of her, Lewis. Not much..." His thoughts were very far away.

"What's all this got to do with the car-hire firms you're trying to check?" asked Lewis suddenly.

"Well, I've got to try to get *some* hard evidence against her, haven't I? I thought, funnily enough, of letting her give me the evidence herself, but . . ."

Lewis was completely lost. "I don't quite follow you."

"Well, I thought of ringing her up this morning first thing and tricking her into giving herself away. It would have been very easy, really."

"It would?"

"Yes. All I had to do was to speak to her in French. You see, the real Mrs. Acum is a graduate from Exeter, remember? But from what we know about poor Valerie's French, I doubt she can get very much further than *bonjour*."

"But *you* can't speak French either can you, sir?"

"I have many hidden talents of which as yet you are quite unaware," said Morse a trifle pompously.

"Oh." But Lewis had a strong suspicion that Morse knew about as much (or as little) French as he did. And what's more, he'd had no answer to his question. "Aren't you going to tell me why you'll be checking on the car hire firms?"

"You've had enough shocks for one day."

"I don't think one more'll make much difference," replied Lewis.

"All right, I'll tell you. You see, we've not only found Valerie; *we've also found the murderer of Baines.*

Lewis opened and closed his mouth like a stranded goldfish, but no identifiable vocable emerged.

"You'll understand soon enough," continued Morse. "It's fairly obvious if you think about it. She has to get from Caernarfon to Oxford, right? Her husband's got the car. So, what does she do? Train? Bus? There aren't any services. And anyway, she's got to get there quickly, and there's only one thing she can do and that's to hire a car."

"But we don't know yet that she *did* hire a car," protested Lewis. "We don't even know she can drive."

"We shall know soon enough."

The "ifs" were forgotten now, and Morse spoke like a minor prophet enunciating necessary truths. And with gradually diminishing reluctance, Lewis was beginning to sense the inevitability of the course of events that Morse was sketching out for him, and the inexorable logic working through the enquiry they'd begun together. A young schoolgirl missing, and more than two years later a middle-aged schoolmaster murdered; and no satisfactory solution to either mystery. Just two insoluble problems. And suddenly, in the twinkling of an eye, there were no longer two problems—no longer even one problem; for somehow each had magically solved the other.

"You think she drove from here that day?"

"And back," said Morse.

"And it was Valerie who . . . who killed Baines?"

"Yes. She must have got there about nine o'clock, as near as dammit."

Lewis's mind ranged back to the night when Baines was murdered. "So she could have been in Baines's house when Mrs. Phillipson and Acum called," he said slowly.

Morse nodded. "Could have been, yes."

He stood up and walked along the narrow hallway. From the window in the front room he could see two small boys, standing at a respectful distance from the police car and trying with cautious curiosity to peer inside. But for the rest, nothing. No one left and no one came along the quiet street.

"Are you worried, sir?" asked Lewis quietly, when Morse sat down again.

"We'll give her a few more minutes," replied Morse, looking at his watch for the twentieth time.

"I've been thinking, sir. She must be a brave girl."

"Mm."

"And he was a nasty piece of work, wasn't he?"

"He was a shithouse," said Morse with savage conviction. "But I don't think that Valerie would ever have killed Baines just for her own sake."

"What *was* her motive then?"

It was a simple question and it deserved a simple answer, but Morse began with the guarded evasiveness of a senior partner in the Circumlocution Office.

"I'm a bit sceptical about the word 'motive,' you know, Lewis. It makes it sound as if there's just got to be one—one big, beautiful motive. But sometimes it doesn't work like that. You get a mother slapping her child across its face because it won't stop crying. Why does she do it? You can say she just wants to stop the kid from bawling its head off, but it's not really true, is it? The motive lies much deeper than that. It's all bound up with lots of other things: she's tired, she's got a headache, she's fed up, she's just plain disillusioned with the duties of motherhood. Anything you like. When once you ask yourself what lies in the murky depths below what Aristotle called the immediate cause . . . You know anything about Aristotle, Lewis?"

"I've heard of him, sir. But you still haven't answered my question."

"Ah, no. Well, let's just consider for a minute the position that Valerie found herself in that day. For the first time for over two years, I should think, she finds herself completely on her own. Since Acum came to join her, he's no doubt been pretty protective towards her, and for the first part of their time together here he's probably been anxious for Valerie not to be caught up in too much of a social whirl. She stays in. *And she'd bleached her hair*—probably right at the beginning. Surprising, isn't it, Lewis, how so many of us go to the trouble of making a gesture—however weak and meaningless? A sop to Cerberus, no doubt. As you know, Acum's real wife had long, blonde hair—that's the first thing anyone would notice about her; it's the first thing I noticed about her when I saw her photograph. Perhaps Acum asked her to do it; it may have helped his conscience. Anyway, he must have been glad she *did* dye her hair. You remember the photograph of Valerie in the Colour Supplement? If he saw it, he must have been a very worried man. It wasn't a particularly clear photograph, I know. It had been taken over three years previously, and a young girl changes a good deal—especially between leaving school and becoming to all intents and purposes a married woman. But it still remained a photograph of Valerie and, as I say, I should think Acum was jolly glad about her hair. As far as we know, no one *did* spot the likeness."

"Perhaps they don't read the *Sunday Times* in Caernarfon."

For all his anti-Welsh prejudices, Morse let it go. "She's on her own at last, then. She can do what she likes. She probably feels a wonderful sense of freedom, freedom to do something for herself—something that now, for the first time, *can* in fact be done."

"I can see all that, sir. But *why*? That's what I want to know."

"Lewis! Put yourself in the position Valerie and her mother and Acum and Phillipson and God knows who else must have found themselves. They've all got their individual and their collective secrets—big and little—and somebody else knows all about them. Baines knows. Somehow—well, we've got a jolly good idea how—he got to know things. Sitting all those years in that little office of his, with the telephone there and all the correspondence, he's been at the nerve-centre of a small community—the Roger Bacon School. He's second master there, and it's perfectly proper that he *should* know what's going on. All the time his ears are tuned in to the slightest rumours and suspicions. He's like a bug in the Watergate Hotel: he picks it all up and he puts it all together. And it gives to his sinister cast of character just the nourishment it craves for—the power over other people's lives. Think of Phillipson for a minute. Baines can put him out of a job any day he chooses—but he doesn't. You see, I don't think he gloried so much in the actual exercise of his power as—"

"He did actually blackmail Phillipson, though, didn't he?"

"I think so, yes. But even blackmail wouldn't be as sweet for a louse like Baines as the thought that he *could* blackmail—whenever he wanted to."

"I see," said the blind man.

"And Mrs. Taylor. Think what he knows about her: about the arrangements for her daughter's abortion, about her elaborate lies to the police, about her heavy drinking, about her money troubles, about her anxiety that George Taylor—the only man who's ever treated her with any decency—should be kept in the dark about some of her wilder excesses."

"But surely everybody must have known she went to Bingo most nights and had a drop of drink now and then?"

"Do you know how much she spent on Bingo and fruit machines? Even according to George it was a pound a night, and she's hardly likely to tell him the truth, is she? And she drinks like a fish—you know she does. Lunchtimes as well."

"So do you, sir."

"Yes, but . . . well, I only drink in moderation, you know that. Anyway, that's only the half of it. You've seen the way she dresses. Expensive clothes, shoes, accessories—the lot. And jewellery. You noticed the diamonds on her fingers? God knows what they're worth. And do you know what her husband is? He's a dustman! No, Lewis. She's been living way, way beyond her means—you must have realised that."

"All right, sir. Perhaps that's a good enough motive for Mrs. Taylor, but—"

"I know. Where does Valerie fit in? Well, I should think Mrs. Taylor probably kept in touch with her daughter by phone—letters would be far too dangerous—and Valerie must have had a pretty good idea of what was going on: that her mother was getting hopelessly mixed up with Baines—that she was getting like a

drug-addict, loathing the whole thing in her sane
moments but just not being able to do without it. Valerie
must have realised that one way or another her mother's
life was becoming one long misery, and she probably
guessed how it was all likely to end. Perhaps her mother
had hinted that she was coming to the end of her tether
and couldn't face up to things much longer. I don't know.

"And then just think of Valerie herself. Baines knows
all about her, too: her promiscuous background, her night
with Phillipson, her affair with Acum—and all its consequences. He knows the lot. And at any time he can ruin
everything. Above all he can ruin David Acum, because
once it gets widely known that he's likely to start fiddling
around with some of the girls he's supposed to be
teaching, he'll have one hell of a job getting a post in *any*
school, even in these permissive days. And I suspect,
Lewis, that in a strange sort of way Valerie has gradually
grown to love Acum more than anyone or anything she's
ever wanted. I think they're happy together—or as happy
as anyone could hope to be under the circumstances. Do
you see what I mean, then? Not only was her mother's
happiness threatened at every turn by that bastard Baines,
but equally the happiness of David Acum. And one day
she suddenly found herself with the opportunity of doing
something about it all: at one swift, uncomplicated
swoop to solve *all* the problems, and she could do that by
getting rid of Baines."

Lewis pondered awhile. "Didn't she ever think that
Acum might be suspected, though? He was in Oxford
too—she knew that."

"No, I don't suppose she gave it a thought. I mean, the
chance that Acum himself would go along to Baines'

place at the very same time as she did—well, it's a thousand to one against, isn't it?"

"Odd coincidence, though."

"It's an odd coincidence, Lewis, that the forty-sixth word from the beginning and the forty-sixth word from the end of the Forty-sixth Psalm in the Authorised Version should spell 'Shakespear.' "

Aristotle, Shakespeare and the Book of Psalms. It was all a bit too much for Lewis, and he sat in silence deciding that he'd missed out somewhere along the educational line. He'd asked his questions and he'd got his answers. They hadn't been the best answers in the world, perhaps, but they just about added up. It was, one could say, satisfactory.

Morse stood up and went over to the kitchen window. The view was magnificent, and for some time he stared across at the massive peaks of the Snowdon range. "We can't stay here for ever, I suppose," he said at last. His hands were on the edge of the sink, and almost involuntarily he pulled open the right-hand drawer. Inside he saw a wooden-handled carving knife, new, "Prestige, Made in England," and he was on the point of picking it up when he heard the rattle of a Yale key in the front-door lock. Swiftly he held up a finger to his mouth and drew Lewis back with him against the wall behind the kitchen door. He could see her quite clearly now, the long, blonde hair tumbling over her shoulders, as she fiddled momentarily with the inner catch, withdrew the key and closed the door behind her.

Thinly-veiled anger yet little more than mild surprise showed on her face as Morse stepped into the hallway. "That's your car outside, I suppose." She said it in a

bleak almost contemptuous voice. "I'd just like to know
what right you think you've got to burst into my house
like this!"

"You've every right to feel angry," said Morse
defencelessly, lifting up his left hand in a feeble gesture
of pacification. "I'll explain everything in a minute, I
promise I will. But can I just ask you one question first?
That's all I ask. Just one question. It's very important."

She looked at him curiously, as if he were slightly mad.

"You speak French, don't you?"

"Yes." Frowning, she put down her shopping basket
by the door, and stood there quite still, maintaining the
distance between them. "Yes, I do speak French. What's
that—?"

Morse took the desperate plunge. "*Avez-vous appri
français à l'école?*"

For a brief moment only she stared at him with blank
uncomprehending eyes, before the devastating reply slid
smoothly and idiomatically from her tutored lips. "*Oui
Je l'ai étudié d'abord à l'école et après pendant trois an
à l'Université. Alors je devrais parler la langue asse
bien, n'est-ce pas?*"

"*Et avez-vous rencontré votre mari à Exeter?*"

"*Oui. Nous étions étudiants là-bas tous les deux
Naturellement, il parle français mieux que moi. Mais i
est assez évident que vous parlez français comme u
Anglais typique, et votre accent est abominable.*"

Morse walked back into the kitchen with the air of an
educationally subnormal zombie, sat down at the table
and held his head between his hands. Why had he both
ered anyway? He had known already. He had known a
soon as she had closed the front door and turned her fac
towards him—a face still blotched with ugly spots.

"Would you both like a cup of tea?" asked Mrs. Acum, as the embarrassed Lewis stepped forward sheepishly from behind the kitchen door.

Chapter Thirty-seven

The gaudy, blabbing and remorseful day
Is crept into the bosom of the sea.

Henry IV, PART II

As he slumped back in the passenger seat, Morse pre
sented a picture of stupefied perplexity. They had le
Caernarfon just after 9:00 P.M., and it would be well int
the early hours before they arrived in Oxford. Each le
the other to his private thoughts, thoughts that criss
crossed ceaselessly the no-man's-land of failure an
futility.

The interview with Acum had been a very strang
affair. Morse seemed entirely to have lost the thread c
the enquiry, and his early questions had been almos
embarrassingly apologetic. It had been left to Lewis t
press home some of the points that Morse had earlie
made, and after an initial evasiveness Acum had seeme
almost glad to get it all off his chest at last. And as he di
so, Lewis was left wondering where the inspector's trai
of thought had jumped the rails and landed in such a hea
of crumpled wreckage by the track; for many of Morse'
assumptions had been correct, it seemed. Almost uncar
nily correct.

Acum (on his own admission now) had indeed bee
attracted to Valerie Taylor and several times had inte
course with her; including a night in early April (n
March) when his wife had returned home early o

Tuesday (not Wednesday) evening from night school in Oxpens (not Headington) where she was attending art (not sewing) classes. Her teacher was down with shingles (not with flu), and the class was cancelled. It was just after eight o'clock (not a quarter to) when Mrs. Acum had returned and found them lying together across the settee (not in bed), and the upshot had been veritably volcanic, with Valerie, it seemed, by far the least confounded of that troubled trio. There followed, for Acum and his wife, a succession of bleak and barren days. It was all over between them—she insisted firmly upon that; but she agreed to stay with him until their separation could be effected with a minimum of social scandal. He himself decided he must move in any case, and applied for a job in Caernarfon; and although he had been questioned by Phillipson at some length about his motives for a seemingly meaningless move to a not particularly promising post, he had told him nothing of the truth. Literally nothing. He could only pray that Valerie would keep her mouth shut, too.

Not until about three weeks before her disappearance had he spoken personally to Valerie again, when she told him that she was expecting a baby, a baby that was probably his. She appeared (or so it seemed to Acum) completely confident and unconcerned and told him everything would be all right. She begged of him one thing only: that if she were to run away he would say nothing and know nothing—that was all; and although he had pressed her about her intentions, she would only repeat that she would be all right. Did she need any money? She told him she would let him know, but, smiling slyly as she told him, she said that she was going to be all right. Everything was "all right." Everything was always "all right" with Valerie. (It was at this point in Lewis's interrogation, and only at this point, that Morse had suddenly pricked up his ears and asked a few inconsequential questions.) It appeared, however, that the money side of things was not completely "all right," for only a week or so before the day she disappeared Valerie had approached Acum and told him she would be very grateful for some money if he could manage it. She hadn't pressed her claim on him in any way, but he had been only too glad to help; and from the little enough they had managed to save—and with his wife's full knowledge—he had raised one hundred pounds. And then she had gone; and like everyone else he hadn't the faintest idea where she had gone to, and he had kept his silence ever since, as Valerie had asked him to.

Meanwhile in the Acum household the weeping wounds were at last beginning to heal; and with Valerie gone they had tried, for the first time since that dreadful night, to discuss their sorry situation with some degree of rationality and mutual understanding. He told her that he loved her, that he realised now how very much she meant to him, and how desperately he hoped that they would stay together. She had wept then, and said she knew how disappointed he must be that she could have no children of her own . . . And as the summer term drew towards its close they had decided—almost happily decided—that they would stay together, and try to patch their marriage up. In any case there had never been the slightest question of divorce: for his wife was a Roman Catholic.

So, continued Acum, they had moved together to North Wales, and life was happy enough now—or had been so until the whole thing had once more exploded in their faces with the murder of Reggie Baines, of which (he swore on his solemn honour) he was himself completely innocent. Blackmail? The whole idea was laughable. The only person who had any hold on him was Valerie Taylor, and of Valerie Taylor he had seen or heard nothing whatsoever since the day of her disappearance. Whether she were alive or whether she were dead, he had no idea—no idea at all.

There the interview had finished. Or almost finished. For it was Morse himself who had administered the *coup de grâce* which finally put his tortured and tortuous theory out of all its pain.

"Does your wife drive a car?"

Acum looked at him with mild surprise. "No. She's never driven a yard in her life. Why?"

Lewis relived the interview as he drove on steadily through the night. And as he recalled the facts that Acum had recounted, he felt a deepening sympathy with the sour, dejected, silent figure slumped beside him, smoking (unusually) cigarette after cigarette, and feeling (if the truth be told) unconscionably angry with himself . . .

Why had he gone wrong? *Where* had he gone wrong? The questions re-echoed in Morse's mind as if repeated by some interminable interlocutor installed inside his brain. He thought back to his first analysis of the case—the one in which he had cast Mrs. Taylor as the murderer not only of Reginald Baines but also of her daughter Valerie. How easy now to see why *that* was wrong! His reasoning had run aground upon the Rock Improbable and the Rock Impossible: the glaring improbability that Mrs. Taylor had murdered her only daughter (mothers just didn't do that sort of thing very often, did they?); and the plain impossibility that *anyone* had murdered Valerie on the day she disappeared, since three days later, alive and well, she had climbed into the back of a taxi outside a London abortion clinic. Yes, the first analysis had been brutally smashed to pieces by the facts, and now lay sunk without a trace beneath the sea. It was as simple as that.

And what of the second analysis? *That* had seemed on the face of it to answer all the facts, or nearly all of them. What had gone wrong with that? Again his logic had foundered upon the Reef of Unreason: the glaring improbability that Valerie Taylor had either sufficient motive or adequate opportunity to murder a man who seemed to pose little more than a peripheral threat to her future happiness; and the plain impossibility that the woman living with David Acum was Valerie Taylor. She wasn't. She was Mrs. Acum. And Analysis One lay side by side with Analysis Two—irrecoverable wrecks upon the ocean floor.

Almost frenetically Morse tried to wrench his thoughts away from it all. He tried to conjure up a dream of fair women; and, failing this he essayed to project upon his mind a raw, uncensored film of rank eroticism; he tried so very hard . . . But still the wretched earth-bound realities of the Taylor case crowded his brain, forbade those flights of half-forbidden fancies, and jolted him back to his inescapable mood of gloom-ridden despondency. Facts, facts, facts! Facts that one by one he once again reviewed as they marched and counter-marched across his mind. If only he'd stuck to the facts! Ainley was dead—that was a fact. Somebody had written a letter the very day after he died—that was a fact. Valerie had been alive on the days immediately following her disappearance—that was a fact. Baines was dead—that was a fact.

Mrs. Acum was Mrs. Acum—that was a fact. But where did he go from there? He began to realise how few the facts had been; how very, very few. A lot of possible facts; a fair helping of probable facts; but few that ranked as positive facts. And once again the facts remarshalled themselves and marched across the parade ground . . . He shook his head sharply and felt he must be going mad.

Lewis, he could see, was concentrating hard upon the road. Lewis! Huh! It had been Lewis who had asked him the one question, the only question, that had completely floored him: *Why had Baines written the letter?* Why? He had never grappled satisfactorily with that question, and now it worried away at his brain again. Why? Why? Why?

It was as they swept along the old Watling Street, past Wellington, that Morse in a flash conceived a possible answer to this importunate question; an answer of astonishing and devastating simplicity. And he nursed his new little discovery like a frightened mother sheltering her only child amid the ruin of an earthquake-stricken city . . . The merry-go-round was slowing now . . . the pubs were long shut and the chips were long cold . . . his mind was getting back to normal now . . . This was better! Methodically he began to undress Miss Yvonne Baker.

Lewis had the road virtually to himself now. It was past 1:00 A.M. and the two men had not exchanged a single word. Strangely, the silence had seemed progressively to reinforce itself, and conversation now would seem as sacrilegious as a breaking of the silence before the cenotaph.

As he drove the last part of the journey his mind roved back beyond the oddly-unreal events of the last few hours, and dwelt again on the early days of the Valerie Taylor case. She'd just hopped it, of course—he'd said so right at the beginning: fed up with home and school she'd yearned for the brighter lights, the excitement and the glamour of the big city. Got shot of the unwanted baby, and finished up in a groovy, swinging set. Contented enough; even happy, perhaps. The last thing she wanted was to go back home to her moody mother and her stolid step-father. We all felt like that occasionally. We'd all like a fresh start in a new life. Like being born again ... He'd felt like running away from home when he was her age ... Concentrate, Lewis! Oxford 30 miles. He glanced at the inspector and smiled quietly to himself. The old boy was fast asleep.

They were within ten miles of Oxford when Lewis became vaguely conscious of Morse's mumbled words, muddled and indistinct; just words—words without coherent meaning. Yet gradually the words assumed a patterned sequence that Lewis almost understood. "Bloody photographs—wouldn't recognise her—huh!—bloody things—huh!"

"We're here, sir." It was the first time he had spoken for more than five hours, and his voice sounded unnaturally loud.

Morse shrugged himself awake and blinked around him. "I must have dozed off, Lewis. Not like me, is it?"

"Would you like to drop in at my place for a cup of coffee and a bite to eat?"

"No. But thanks all the same." He eased himself out of the car like a chronic arthritic, yawned mightily and stretched his arms. "We'll take tomorrow off, Lewis. Agreed? We've just about deserved it, I reckon."

Lewis said he reckoned, too. He parked the police car, backed out his own and waved a weary farewell.

Morse entered Police H.Q. and made his way along the dimly-lit corridor to his office, where he opened his filing cabinet and riffled through the early documents in the Valerie Taylor case. He found it almost immediately, and as he looked down at the so familiar letter, once more his mind was sliding easily along the shining grooves. It must be. It must be!

He wondered if Lewis would ever forgive him.

Chapter Thirty-eight

And then there were two.

Ten Little Indians

"... *not generally appreciated. We all normally assum[e]*
that the sex instinct is so obviously overriding, so prim[i]-
tively predominant that it must ..." Morse, newly
woken and surprisingly refreshed, switched over t[o]
Radio Three; and thence to Radio Oxford. But none [of]
the channels seemed anxious to inform him of the time [of]
day, and he turned back to Radio Four. "... *and abov[e]*
all, of course, by Freud. Let us assume, for example, the[t]
we have been marooned on a desert island for three day[s]
without food, and ask ourselves which of the bodil[y]
instincts most craves its instant gratification." Wit[h]
sudden interest Morse turned up the volume: the voic[e]
was donnish, slightly effeminate. "*Let us imagine that [a]*
beautiful blonde appears with a plate of succulent stea[k]
and chips ..." Leaning over to turn the volume highe[r]
still, Morse inadvertently nudged the tuning knob, an[d]
by the time he had re-centred the station it was cle[ar]
that the beautiful blonde had lost on points. "... *as w[e]*
tuck into the steak and ..." Morse switched off. "She[l]-
erp, you poncy twit!" he said aloud, got out of be[d,]
pulled on his clothes, walked downstairs and dialled th[e]
speaking clock. "At the first stroke it will be eleven-
twenty-eight—and forty seconds." She sounded nice, a[nd]

292

Morse wondered if she were a blonde. It was over twenty-four hours since he had eaten, but for the moment steak and chips was registering a poor third on the instinct index.

Without bothering to shave he walked round to the Fletchers' Arms where he surveyed with suspicion a pile of "freshly-cut" ham sandwiches beneath their plastic cover and ordered a glass of bitter. By 12:45 P.M. he had consumed four pints, and felt a pleasing lassitude pervade his limbs. He walked slowly home and fell fully-clothed into his bed. This was the life.

He felt lousy when he woke again at 5:20 P.M., and wondered if he were in the old age of youth or the youth of old age.

By 6:00 P.M. he was seated in his office, clearing up the litter from his desk. There were several messages lying there, and one by one he relegated them to an in-tray which never had been clear and never would be clear. There was one further message, on the telephone pad: "Ring 01-787 24392." Morse flicked through the telephone book and found that 787 was the S.T.D. code for Stoke Newington. He rang the number.

"Hello?" The voice was heavy with sex.

"Ah. Morse here. I got your message. Er, can I help?"

"Oh, inspector," purred the voice. "It was yesterday I tried to get you, but never mind. I'm so glad you rang." The words were slow and evenly spaced. "I just wondered if you wanted to see me again—you know, to make a statement or something? I wondered if you'd be coming down again . . . perhaps?"

"That's very kind of you, Miss—er, Yvonne. But I think Chief Inspector Rogers will be along to see you.

We shall need a statement, though—you're quite right
about that."

"Is he as nice as you are, inspector?"

"Nowhere near," said Morse.

"All right, whatever you say. But it would be so nic
to see you again."

"It would, indeed," said Morse with some conviction
in his voice.

"Well, I'd better say goodbye then. You didn't min
me ringing, did you?"

"No, er, no, of course I didn't. It's lovely to hear you
voice again."

"Well, don't forget if you're ever this way you mus
call in to see me."

"Yes, I will," lied Morse.

"I really would love to see you again."

"Same here."

"You've got my address, haven't you?"

"Yes, I've got it."

"And you'll make a note of the phone number?"

"Er, yes. Yes, I'll do that."

"Goodbye, then, till we see each other again." Fro
the tone of her voice Morse guessed she must be lyin
there, her hands sensuously sliding along those beautif
limbs; and all he had to do was to say, yes, he'd be ther
London wasn't very far away, and the night was still s
young. He pictured her as she had been on the night th
he had met her, the top button of the pyjama jack
already undone; and in his mind's eye his fingers gent
unfastened the other buttons, one by one, and slow
drew the sides apart.

"Goodbye," he said sadly.

*　*　*

He walked to the canteen and ordered black coffee.

"I thought you were taking the day off," said a voice behind him.

"You must love this bloody place, Lewis!"

"I rang up. They said you were here."

"Couldn't you stick it at home?"

"No. The missus says I get under her feet."

They sat down together, and it was Lewis who put their thoughts into words. "Where do we go from here, sir?"

Morse shook his head dubiously. "I don't know."

"Will you tell me one thing?"

"If I can."

"Have you *any* idea at all about who killed Baines?"

Idly Morse stirred the strong black coffee. "Have you?"

"The real trouble is we seem to be eliminating all the suspects. Not many left, are there?"

"We're not beaten yet," said Morse with a sudden and unexpected lift of spirits. "We got a bit lost in the winding mazes, and we still can't see the end of the road, but . . ." He broke off and stared through the window. In a sudden gust of wind a shower of leaves rained down from the thinning trees.

"But what, sir?"

"Somebody once said that the end is the beginning, Lewis."

"Not a particularly helpful thing to say, was it?"

"Ah, but I think it was. You see, we know what the beginning was."

"Do we?"

"Oh yes. We know that Phillipson met Valerie Taylor one night, and we know that when he was appointed

headmaster he discovered that she was one of his own
pupils. That was where it all began, and that's where
we've got to look now. There's nowhere else to look."

"You mean . . . Phillipson?"

"Or Mrs. Phillipson."

"You don't think—"

"I don't think it matters much which of them you
go for. They had the same motive; they had the same
opportunity."

"How do we set about it?"

"How do *you* set about it, you mean. I'm leaving it to
you, Lewis."

"Oh."

"Want a bit of advice?" Morse smiled weakly. "Bit of
a cheek, isn't it, me giving you advice?"

"Of course I want your advice," said Lewis quietly.
"We both know that."

"All right. Here's a riddle for you. You look for a leaf
in the forest, and you look for a corpse on the battlefield.
Right? Where do you look for a knife?"

"An ironmonger's shop?"

"No, not a *new* knife. A knife that's been used—used
continuously; used so much that the blade is wearing
away."

"A butcher's shop?"

"Warmer. But we haven't got a butcher in the case,
have we?"

"A kitchen?"

"Ah! Which kitchen?"

"Phillipson's kitchen?"

"They'd only have one knife. It would be missed,
wouldn't it?"

"Perhaps it *was* missed."

"I don't think so, somehow, though you'll have to check. No, we need to find a place where knives are in daily use; a lot of knives; a place where no one would notice the loss of a single knife; a place at the very heart of the case. Come on, Lewis! Lots of people cutting up spuds and carrots and meat and everything . . ."

"The canteen at the Roger Bacon School," said Lewis slowly.

Morse nodded. "It's an idea, isn't it?"

"Ye-es." Lewis pondered for a while and nodded his agreement. "But you say you want *me* to look into all this? What about you?"

"I'm going to look into the only other angle we've got left."

"What's that?"

"I've told you. The secret of this case is locked away in the beginning: Phillipson and Valerie Taylor. You've got one half; I've got the other."

"You mean . . . ?" Lewis had no idea what he meant.

Morse stood up. "Yep. You have a go at the Phillipsons. I shall have to find Valerie." He looked down at Lewis and grinned disarmingly. "Where do you suggest I ought to start looking?"

Lewis stood up, too. "I've always thought she was in London, sir. You know that. I think she just . . ."

But Morse was no longer listening. He felt the icy fingers running along his spine, and there was a sudden wild elation in the pale grey eyes. "Why not, Lewis? Why not?"

He walked back to his office, and dialled the number immediately. After all, she *had* invited him, hadn't she?

Chapter Thirty-nine

> The only way of catching a train I ever discovered is to miss the one before.
>
> G. K. CHESTERTON

"Mummy?" Alison managed a very important frown upon her pretty little face as her mother tucked her early into bed at 8:00 P.M.

"Yes, darling?"

"Will the policemen be coming to see daddy again when he gets back?"

"I don't think so, darling. Don't start worrying your little head about that."

"He's not gone away to prison or anything like that has he?"

"Of course he hasn't, you silly little thing! He'll be back tonight, you know that, and I'll tell him to come in and give you a big kiss—I promise."

Alison was silent for a few moments. "Mummy, he's not done anything wrong, has he?"

"No, you silly little thing. Of course he hasn't."

Alison frowned again as she looked up into her mother's eyes. "Even if he *did* do something wrong, he'd still be my daddy, wouldn't he?"

"Yes. He'd still be your daddy, whatever happened."

"And we'd forgive him, wouldn't we?"

"Yes, my darling . . . And you'd forgive mummy, too

wouldn't you, if she did something wrong? Especially
f . . ."

"Don't worry, mummy. God forgives everybody,
doesn't he? And my teacher says that we must all try to
be like him."

Mrs. Phillipson walked slowly down the stairs, and her
eyes were glazed with tears.

Morse left the Lancia at home and walked down from
North Oxford to the railway station. It took him almost
an hour and he wasn't at all sure why he'd decided to do
t; but his head felt clear now and the unaccustomed exercise had done him good. At twenty-past eight he stood
outside the Station Buffet and looked around him. It was
dark, but just across the way the street lights shone on the
first few houses in Kempis Street. So close! He hadn't
quite realised just how close to the railway station it was.
A hundred yards? No more, certainly. Get off the train on
Platform Two, cross over by the subway, hand your
ticket in . . . For a second or two he stood stock still and
felt the old familiar thrill that coursed along his nerves.
He was catching the 8:35 train—the same train that
Phillipson could have caught that fateful night so long
ago . . . Paddington about 9:40. Taxi. Let's see . . . Yes,
with a bit of luck he'd be there about 10:15.

He bought a first-class ticket and walked past the bar-
rier on to Platform One, and almost immediately the
loudspeaker intoned from somewhere in the station roof
above: "The train now arriving at Platform One is for
Reading and Paddington only. Passengers for . . ." But
Morse wasn't listening.

He sat back comfortably and closed his eyes. Idiot!
diot! It was all so simple really. Lewis had found the

pile of books in the store-room and had sworn there'd
been no dust upon the top one; and all Morse had done
had been to shout his faithful sergeant's head off. Of
course there had been no dust on the top book! Someone
had taken a book from the top of the self-same pile—a
book that was doubtless thick with dust by then. Taken it
recently, too. So very recently in fact that the book at the
top of the remaining pile was virtually free from dust
when Lewis had picked it up. Someone. Yes, a someone
called Baines who had taken it home and studied it very
hard. *But not because he'd wished to forge a letter in
Valerie Taylor's hand.* That had been one of Morse's
biggest mistakes. There was, as he had guessed the night
before, a blindingly obvious answer to the question of
why Baines had written the letter to Valerie's parents.
The answer was that he hadn't. Mr. and Mrs. Taylor had
received the letter on the Wednesday morning and had
been of two minds about taking it to the police—George
Taylor himself had told Morse exactly that. Why? Obviously because they couldn't decide whether it had come
from Valerie or not: it might just have been a hoax. It
must surely have been Mrs. Taylor who had taken it to
Baines; and Baines had very sensibly taken an exercise
book from the store-room and written out his own parallel version of the brief message, copying as accurately
as he could the style and shape of Valerie's own lettering as he found it in the Applied Science book. And then
he'd compared the letter from Valerie with his own painstaking effort, and pronounced to Mrs. Taylor that at
least in his opinion the letter seemed completely genuine.
That was how things must have happened. And there was
something else, too. The logical corollary of all this was
that Mr. and Mrs. Taylor had no idea at all about where

Valerie was. For more than two years they had heard
nothing whatsoever from her. And if both of them were
genuinely puzzled about the letter, there seemed one further inescapable conclusion: *the Taylors were completely
in the clear.* Go on, Morse! Keep going! With a smooth
inevitability the pieces were falling into place. Keep
going!

Well, if this hypothesis were correct, the overwhelming probability was that Valerie was alive and that
she had written the letter herself. It was just as Peter said
it was; just as Lewis said it was; just as Morse himself
had said it *wasn't.* Moreover, as he had learned the previous evening, there was a very interesting and suggestive piece of corroborative evidence. Acum had given it
to him: Valerie was always using the expression "all
right," he'd said. And on his return Morse had checked
the letter once again:

> *Just to let you know I'm alright so don't worry. Sorry
> I've not written before but I'm alright.*

And Ainley (poor old Ainley!) had not only known that
she was still alive; he'd actually found her—Morse felt
sure of that now. Or, at the very least, he'd discovered
where she could be found. Stolid, painstaking old
Ainley! A bloody sight better than he himself would ever
be. (Hadn't Strange said the same thing—right at the
beginning?) Valerie could never have guessed the full
extent of the hullabaloo that her disappearance had
caused. After all, hundreds of young girls went missing
every year. Hundreds. But had she suddenly learned of it,
so long after the event? Had Ainley actually met her and
told her? It seemed entirely probable now, since the very

next day she had sat down and written to her parents for the very first time. That was all. Just a brief scratty little letter! And that prize clown Morse had been called in. Big stuff. Christ! What a mess, what a terribly unholy mess he'd made of everything!

They were well into the outskirts of London now, and Morse walked out to the corridor and lit a cigarette. Only one thing worried him now: the thought that had flashed across his mind as he stood outside the Station Buffet and looked across at Kempis Street. But he'd know soon enough now; so very soon he'd know it all.

Chapter Forty

> For she and I were long acquainted
> And I knew all her ways.
>
> A. E. HOUSMAN, *Last Poems*

t was just after ten-thirty when he paid and tipped the
axi-driver: it cost him more than the return first-class
are to London. At the bottom of the building he found,
as before, the lift for the even-numbered floors on his left
and that for the odd on his right. He remembered the
loor. Of course he did.

She was radiant. That was the best epithet for her,
although there were many others. She wore a thin black
weater in which her full and bra-less breasts bobbed
rresistibly; and a long black skirt, slit high along her leg
and leaving a sublime uncertainty of what she wore
below. Her mouth, just as he had seen it last, was stickily
eductive, the lips moist and slightly parted, the teeth so
gleaming white. O Lord, have mercy on our souls!

"What would you like to drink, inspector? Whisky?
Gin?"

"Whisky, please. Lovely."

She disappeared into the kitchen, and Morse moved
quickly over to a small shelf of books beside the deeply-
eathered divan. Rapidly he flicked open the front cover
f the books there, and as rapidly replaced them. Only
ne of them held his attention, and that only for a few

303

seconds, when the grey eyes momentarily flashed with a glint of satisfaction, if not surprise.

He was seated on the divan when she returned with a large whisky in a cut-glass tumbler and sat down beside him.

"Aren't *you* drinking?"

Her eyes met his and held them. "In a minute," she whispered, linking her arm through his, the tips of her fingers gently tracing slow designs along his wrist.

Softly he took her hand in his, and for a short sweet second the thrill was that of a sharp electric shock that shot along his veins, and a zig-zag current that sparked across his temples. He looked down at her delicately fingered left hand, and saw across the bottom of the index finger the faint white line of an old scar—like the scar that was mentioned in the medical report on Valerie Taylor, when she had cut herself with a carving knife— in Kidlington, when she was a pupil at the Roger Bacon School.

"What shall I call you?" she asked suddenly. "I can't go on calling you 'inspector' all night, can I?"

"It's a funny thing," said Morse. "But no one ever calls me by my Christian name."

Lightly she touched his cheek with her lips, and her hand moved slowly along his leg. "Never mind. If you don't like your name, you can always change it, you know. There's no law against that."

"No, there isn't. I could always change it if I wanted to, I suppose. Just like you changed yours."

Her body stiffened and she took her hand away. "And what on earth is *that* supposed to mean?"

"You told me your name was Yvonne the last time

saw you. But that isn't your real name, is it? Is it, Valerie?"

"*Valerie?* You can't possibly . . ." But she was unable to articulate her thoughts beyond that point, and a look of profound perplexity appeared to cross her beautiful face. She stood up. "Look, inspector, or whatever your name is, my name's Yvonne Baker—you'd better get that straight before we go any further. If you don't believe me you can ring the couple on the floor below. I was at school in Seven Sisters Road with Joyce—"

"Go ahead," said Morse blandly. "Ring up your old school pal if you want to. Why not tell her to come up to see us?"

A look of anger flashed across her face and momentarily made it less than beautiful. She hesitated; then walked over to the phone and dialled a number.

Morse leaned back and sipped his whisky contentedly. Even from across the room he could hear the muted, metallic purrs with perfect clarity; he found himself mentally counting them . . . Finally she put down the phone and came back to sit beside him once more. He reached to the book-shelf, abstracted a small hard-bound copy of *Jane Eyre* and opened the front cover. Inside was the label of the Roger Bacon Comprehensive School, on which Valerie's own name appeared, appended to those of her literary predecessors:

Angela Lowe	5C
Mary Ann Baldwin	5B
Valerie Taylor	5C

He passed it across to her. "Well?"
She shook her head in exasperation. "Well what?"

"Is it yours?"

"Of course it isn't mine. It's Valerie's—you can see
that. She gave it to me to read in the clinic. It was one of
her O-level set books, and she thought I'd enjoy reading
it. But I never got round to it and I . . . I just forgot to
give it her back, that's all."

"And that's your story?"

"It isn't a *story*. It's the *truth*. I don't know—"

"What went wrong at home, Valerie? Did you—"

"Oh *God*! What the hell are you on about? I'm not
Valerie. It's . . . I . . . I just don't know where to start.
Look, my parents live in Uxbridge—can you understand
that? I can ring them. *You* can ring them. I—"

"I know your parents, Valerie. You got so fed up with
them that you left them. Left them without a word of
explanation—at least until Ainley found you. And then at
long last you *did* write home—"

"What are you *talking* about? *Ainley*? Who's he?
I've . . . Oh, what's the good!" Her voice had grown
shrill and harsh, but suddenly she subsided almost helplessly against the back of the divan. "All right, inspector.
Have it your way. You tell *me* what happened."

"You wrote home then," continued Morse. "You
hadn't realised what a terrible fuss you'd caused until
Inspector Ainley saw you. But Ainley was killed. He was
killed in a road accident on his way back to Oxford on
the very same day he saw you."

"I'm sorry to interrupt, inspector. But I thought I was
Yvonne Baker. When did I suddenly change to Valerie
Taylor?" Her voice was quite calm now.

"You met Yvonne in the abortion clinic. You were fed
up with home, fed up with school; and Yvonne . . . well,
probably, she put the idea into your head. For argument's

sake, let's say she was a girl with lots of money, rich parents—probably going off to Switzerland or somewhere for a year's holiday after it was all over. Why not take her name? Start a new life? You've nothing to lose, have you? You'd decided not to go back home, whatever happened. You hardly saw your mother anyway, except at lunch times, and her only real interests in life were booze and Bingo—and men, of course. And then there's your step-father: not very bright, perhaps, but likeable enough, in an odd sort of way. That is until he started getting a bit too fond of his beautiful step-daughter. And your mother got to know about that, I think, and when you got yourself pregnant, she suspected a terrible thing. She suspected that he might well be the father, didn't she? And she flew into an almighty rage about it, and for you this was the last straw. You just had to go; and you *did* go. But fortunately you had someone to help you: your headmaster. There's no need to go into all that—but *you* know all about it as well as I do. You could count on him—always. He fixed up the clinic, and he gave you some money. You'd probably packed a case the night before and arranged to meet him somewhere to stow it away safely in the boot of his car. And then on the Tuesday he picked you up just after school had started for the afternoon and took you to the railway station. You only had a bag with you—no doubt with your clothes in it—and you changed on the train and arrived at the clinic. Shall I go on?"

"Yes please. It's quite fascinating!"

"You just interrupt me if I go wrong, that's all."

"But . . ." She gave it up and sat there silently shaking her head.

"I'm guessing now," continued Morse, "but I should

think Yvonne put you on to a job—let's say a job in
West End store. The school-leavers hadn't crowded th
market yet, and it was fairly easy for you. You'd need
testimonial or a reference, I realise that. But you ran
Phillipson and told him the position, and he took care c
that. It was your first job. No bother. No employmer
cards, or stamps or anything. So, that was that."

Morse turned and looked again at the chic, sophisti
cated creature beside him. They wouldn't recognise he
back in Kidlington now, would they? They'd remembe
only the young schoolgirl in her red socks and her whit
blouse. They would always attract the men, these two–
mother and daughter alike. Somehow they shared th
same intangible yet pervasive sensuality, and "the Lor
had fashioned them so very fair."

"Is that the finish?" she asked quietly.

Morse's reply was brusque. "No, it's not. Where wei
you last Monday night?"

"Last Monday night? What's that got to do with you?

"What train did you catch the night that Baines wa
killed?"

She looked at him in utter astonishment now. "Wh
train are you talking about? I haven't—"

"Didn't you go there that night?"

"Go *where*?"

"You know where. You probably caught the 8:15 fro
Paddington and arrived in Oxford at about 9:30."

"You must be *mad*! I was in Hammersmith last Monda
night."

"Were you?"

"Yes, I *was*. I always go to Hammersmith on Monda
nights."

"Go on."

"You really want to know?" Her eyes grew softer again, and she shook her head sadly. "If you must know there's a sort of . . . sort of party we have there every Monday."

"What time?"

"Starts about nine."

"And you were there last Monday?"

She nodded, almost fiercely.

"You go every Monday, you say?"

"Yes."

"Why aren't you there tonight?"

"I . . . well, I just thought . . . when you rang . . ." She looked at him with doleful eyes. "I didn't think it was going to be like this."

"What time do these parties finish?"

"They don't."

"You stay all night, you mean."

She nodded.

"Sex parties?"

"In a way."

"What the hell's that supposed to mean?"

"You know. The usual sort of thing: films to start with . . ."

"Blue films?"

Again she nodded.

"And then?"

"Oh God! Come off it. Are you trying to torture yourself, or something?"

She was far too near the truth, and Morse felt miserably embarrassed. He got to his feet and looked round recklessly for his coat. "You'll have to give me the address, you realise that."

"But I can't. I'd—"

"Don't worry," said Morse wearily. "I shan't pry any
more than I have to."

He looked once more around the expensive flat. She
must earn a lot of money, somehow; and he wondered
if it was all much compensation for the heartache and
the jealousy that she must know as well as he. Or perhaps
we weren't all the same. Perhaps it wasn't possible to
live as she had done and keep alive the finer, tenderer
compassions.

He looked across at her as she sat at a small bureau
writing something down: doubtless the address of the
bawdy house in Hammersmith. He had to have that,
whatever happened. But did it matter all that much? He
knew instinctively that she was there that night, among
the wealthy, lecherous old men who gloated over pornographic films, and pawed and fondled the figures of the
high-class prostitutes who sat upon their knees unfas-
tening their flies. So what? He was a lecherous old man
too, wasn't he? Very nearly, anyway. Just a sediment of
sensitivity still. Just a little. Just a little.

She came over to him, and for a moment she was very
beautiful again. "I've been very patient with you,
inspector, don't you think?"

"I suppose so, yes. Patient, if not particularly
co-operative."

"Can I ask *you* a question?"

"Of course."

"Do you want to sleep with me tonight?"

The back of Morse's throat felt suddenly very dry.
"No."

"You really mean that?"

"Yes."

"All right." Her voice was brisker now. "Let me

'co-operative' then, as you call it." She handed him a sheet of notepaper on which she had written two telephone numbers.

"The first one's my father's. You may have to drag him out of bed, but he's almost certainly home by now. The other one's the Wilsons, downstairs. As I told you, I was at school with Joyce. I'd like you to ring them both, please."

Morse took the paper and said nothing.

"Then there's this." She handed him a passport. "I know it's out of date, but I've only been abroad once. To Switzerland, three years ago last June."

With a puzzled frown Morse opened the passport and the unmistakable face of Miss Yvonne Baker smiled up at him in gentle mockery from a Woolworth polyfoto. Three years last June ... whilst Valerie Taylor was still at school in Kidlington. Well before she ... before ...

Morse took off his coat and sat down once again on the divan. "Will you ring your friends below, Yvonne? And if you're feeling very kind, can I please ask you to pour me another whisky? A stiff one."

At Paddington he was informed that the last train to Oxford had departed half an hour earlier. He walked into the cheerless waiting room, put his feet up on the bench and soon fell fast asleep.

At 3:30 A.M. a firm hand shook him by the shoulder, and he looked up into the face of a bearded constable.

"You can't sleep here, sir. I shall have to ask you to move on, I'm afraid."

"You surely don't begrudge a man a bit of kip, do you officer?"

"I'm afraid I shall have to ask you to move on, sir."

Morse almost told him who he was. But simulta
neously the other sleepers were being roused and he
wondered why he should be treated any differently from
his fellow men.

"All right, officer." Huh! "All right": that's what
Valerie would have said. But he put the thought aside and
walked wearily out of the station. Perhaps he'd have more
luck at Marylebone. He needed a bit of luck somewhere.

Chapter Forty-one

> Pilate saith unto him, What is truth?
> *St. John*, ch. 18

Donald Phillipson was a very worried man. The sergeant had been very proper, of course, and very polite: "routine enquiries," that was all. But the police were getting uncomfortably close. A knife that might be missing from the school canteen—that was perfectly understandable: but from his own kitchen! And it was no great surprise that he himself should be suspected of murder: but Sheila! He couldn't talk to Sheila, and he wouldn't let her talk to him: the subject of Valerie Taylor and, later, the murder of Baines lay between them like a no-man's-land, isolated and defined, upon which neither dared to venture. How much did Sheila know? Had she learned that Baines was blackmailing him? Had she learned or half-guessed the shameful reason? Baines himself may have hinted at the truth to her. Baines! God rot his soul! But whatever Sheila had done or intended to do on the night that Baines was killed was utterly unimportant, and he wished to know nothing of it. Whichever way you looked at it, it was he, Donald Phillipson, who was guilty of murdering Baines.

The walls of the small study seemed gradually to be closing in around him. The cumulative pressures of the past three years had now become too strong, and the

313

tangled web of falsehood and deceit had enmeshed his very soul. If he were to retain his sanity he had to do *something*; something to bring a period of peace to a conscience tortured to its breaking-point; something to atone for all the folly and the sin. Again he thought of Sheila and the children and he knew that he could hardly face them for much longer. And interminably his thoughts went dancing round and round his head and always settled to the same conclusion. Whichever way you looked at it, it was he and only he who was guilty of murdering Baines.

Morning school was almost over, and Mrs. Webb was tidying up her desk as he walked through.

"I shan't be in this afternoon, Mrs. Webb."

"No. I realise that, sir. You never are on Tuesdays."

"Er, no. Tuesday afternoon, of course. I'd, er . . . I'd forgotten for the minute."

It was like hearing the phone in a television play: he knew there was no need to answer it himself. He still felt wretchedly tired and he buried his head again in the pillows. Having found no more peace at Marylebone than at Paddington, he had finally arrived back in Oxford at 8:05 A.M., and had taken a taxi home. One way or another it had been an expensive débâcle.

An hour later the phone rang again. Shrill, peremptory now, registering at a higher level of his consciousness and shaking his head awake, he reached for the receiver on the bedside table. He yawned an almighty "Yeah?" into the mouthpiece and levered himself up to a semi-vertical position.

"Lewis? What the hell do you want?"

"I've been trying to get you since two o'clock, sir. t's—"

"What? What time is it now?"

"Nearly three o'clock, sir. I'm sorry to disturb you but 've got a bit of a surprise for you."

"Huh! I doubt it."

"I think you ought to come, though. We're at the station."

"Who do you mean by 'we'?"

"If I told you that, sir, it wouldn't be a surprise, would it?"

"Give me half an hour," said Morse.

He sat down at the table in Interview Room One. In front of him lay a document, neatly typed but as yet unsigned, and he picked it up and read it:

"I have come forward voluntarily to the police to make this statement, and I trust that to some extent this may weigh in my favour. I wish to plead guilty to the murder of Mr. Reginald Baines, late second master of the Roger Bacon Comprehensive School, Kidlington, Oxon. The reasons I had for killing him are not, in my view, strictly relevant to the criminal procedings that will be brought against me, and there are certain things which everyone should have the right to hold sacrosanct. About the details of the crime, too, I wish for the present to say nothing. I am aware that the question of deliberate malice and premeditation may be of great importance, and for this reason I wish to notify my lawyer and to take the benefit of his advice.

I hereby certify that this statement was made by me in the presence of Sergeant Lewis, C.I.D., Thames

Valley Police, on the day and at the time subscribed

Your obedient servant,"

Morse looked up from the sheet of typing and turned his light-grey eyes across the table.

"You can't spell 'proceedings,'" he said.

"Your typist, inspector. Not me." Morse reached for his cigarettes and offered them across. "No thank you, I don't smoke."

Without dropping his eyes, Morse lit a cigarette and drew upon it deeply. His expression was a mixture of vague distaste and tacit scepticism. He pointed to the statement. "You want this to go forward?"

"Yes."

"As you wish."

They sat silently, as if neither had anything further to say to the other. Morse looked across to the window, and outside on to the concrete yard. He'd made so many stupid blunders in the case; and no one was likely to thank him overmuch for making yet another. It was the only sensible solution, perhaps. Or *almost* the only sensible solution. Did it matter? Perhaps not. But still upon his face remained the look of dark displeasure.

"You don't like me much, do you, inspector?"

"I wouldn't say that," replied Morse defensively. "It's just . . . it's just that you've never got into the habit of telling me the truth, have you?"

"I've made up for it now, I hope."

"Have you?" Morse's eyes were hard and piercing, but to his question there was no reply.

"Shall I sign it now?"

Morse remained silent for a while. "You think it

better this way?" he asked very quietly. But again there was no reply, and Morse passed across the statement and stood up. "You've got a pen?"

Sheila Phillipson nodded, and opened her long, expensive leather hand-bag.

"Do you believe her, sir?"

"No," said Morse simply.

"What do we do, then?"

"Ah, let her cool her heels in a cell for a night. I dare say she's got a good idea what happened, but I just don't think she killed Baines, that's all."

"She's covering up for Phillipson, you think?"

"Could be. I don't know." Morse stood up. "And I'll tell you something else, Lewis: I don't bloody well care! I think whoever killed Baines deserves a life peerage—not a life sentence."

"But it's still our job to find out who did, sir."

"Not for much longer, it isn't. I've had a bellyful of this lot—and I've failed. I'm going to see Strange in the morning and ask him to take me off the case."

"He won't be very happy about that."

"He's never very happy about anything."

"It doesn't sound like you, though, sir."

Morse grinned almost boyishly. "I've disappointed you, haven't I, Lewis?"

"Well, yes, in a way—if you're going to pack it all in now."

"Well, I am."

"I see."

"Life's full of disappointments, Lewis. I should have thought you'd learned that by now."

* * *

Alone Morse walked back to his office. If the truth could be told he felt more than a little hurt by what Lewis had just said. Lewis was right, of course, and had spoken with such quiet integrity: *but it's still our job to find out who did it.* Yes, he knew that; but he'd tried and tried and *hadn't* found out who did it. Come to think of it, he hadn't even found out if Valerie Taylor were alive or dead . . . Just now he'd tried to believe Sheila Phillipson but the plain fact was that he couldn't. Anyway, if what she said were true, it was much better for someone else to finish off the formalities. Much better. And if she were just shielding her husband . . . He let it go. He had sent Lewis round to see Phillipson, but the headmaster was neither at home nor at school, and for the time being the neighbours were looking after the children.

Whatever happened, this Tuesday afternoon was now the end, and he thought back to that first Tuesday afternoon in Phillipson's study . . . What, if anything, had he missed in the case? What small, apparently insignificant detail that might have set him on the proper track? He sat for half an hour and thought and thought, and thought himself nowhere. It was no good: his mind was stale and the wells of imagination and inspiration were dry as the Sahara sands. Yes, he *would* see Strange in the morning and hand it all over. He could still make a decision when he wanted to, whatever Lewis might think.

He walked over to the filing-cabinet and for the last time took out the mass of documents on the case. They now filled two bulging box-files, and pulling back the spring clips Morse tipped the contents of each haphazardly on to his desk. At least he ought to put the stuff into some sort of order. It wouldn't take all that long, and his mind positively welcomed the prospect of an hour or two of fourth-grade clerical work. Neatly and methodically he began stapling odd notes and sheets to their respective documents, and ordering the documents themselves into a chronological sequence. He remembered the last time he had tipped the contents (not so bulky then) on to his desk, when Lewis had noticed that odd business about the lollipop-man. A red herring, that, as it turned out. Yet it *could* have been a vitally important point, and he himself had missed it. Had he missed anything else amidst this formidable bumf? Ah, forget it! It was too late now, and he continued with his task. Valerie's reports next. They'd better go into some sort of order, too, and he shuffled them into their sequence. Three reports a year: Autumn term; Spring term; Summer term. No reports at all for the first year in the school, but all the others were here—except one: the report for the Summer term of the fourth year. Why was that? He hadn't noticed that before . . . The brain was whirring into life once more—but no! Morse snapped off the current impatiently. It was nothing. The report was just lost; lots of things got lost. Nothing at all sinister about that . . . Yet in spite of himself he stopped what he was doing and sat back again in the black leather chair, his finger tips together on his lower lip, his eyes resting casually on the school reports that lay before him. He'd read them all before, of course, and knew their contents well. Valerie had been one of those many could-do-better-if-she-tried pupils. Like all of us . . . In fact, the staff at the Roger Bacon School could quite easily have dispensed with terminal reports in Valerie's case: they were all very much the same, and one would have done quite as well as another. Any one. The last one, for example—the report on her Spring term's progress (or rather lack of it) in the year in which

she'd disappeared. Idly Morse looked down at it again
Acum's signature was there beside the French: "Coul
do so well if only she tried. Her accent is surprisingl
good, but her vocabulary and grammar are still ver
weak." Same old comment. In fact there was only on
subject in which Valerie had apparently not hidden he
light beneath the bushel of her casual indifference; an
oddly enough that was Applied Science and Technology
Funny, really, girls tackling subjects like that. But th
curriculum had undergone mysterious developments sinc
his own school days. He picked up the earlier reports an
read some of the comments of the science staff: "Goo
with her hands"; "A good term's work"; "Has goo
mechanical sense." He got up from his chair and wer
over to the shelf where earlier he'd stacked Valerie's ol
exercise books. It was there: Applied Science and Tech
nology. Morse flicked through the pages. Yes, the wor
was good, he could see that—surprisingly good . . . *Hol
it a minute!* He looked through the book again, mor
carefully now, and read the headings of the syllabu
Work; Energy; Power; Velocity Ratio; Efficiency c
Machines; Simple Machines; Levers; Pulleys; Simpl
Power-transmission Systems; Car Engines; Clutches . .

He walked back to his desk slowly, like a man in
dreamlike daze, and read the last Spring-term report onc
more: French, and Applied Science and Technology . . .

Suddenly the hair on his flesh stood erect. He felt
curious constriction in his throat, and a long shiv
passed icily down his spine. He reached for the phor
and his hand shook as he dialled the number.

Chapter Forty-two

I came fairly to kill him honestly.
BEAUMONT and FLETCHER, *The Little French Lawyer*

Valerie Taylor unscrewed the latest tube of skin-lotion—her sixth prescription. The last time she'd been to the doctor he'd asked rather pointedly if she were worried about anything; and perhaps she was. But not to *that* extent. She'd never worried overmuch about anything, really: just wanted to live in the present and enjoy herself ... Carefully she smeared some of the white cream over the ugly spots. How she prayed they would go! Over a month now—and still they persisted, horribly. She'd tried almost everything, including those face-mask things: in fact she had been wearing one of them when Chief Inspector Morse had called. Mm. She thought of Morse. Bit old, perhaps, but then she'd always felt attracted to the older men. Not that David was old. Quite young, really, and he'd been awfully nice to her, but ...

Morse's face, when she'd answered him in French! She smiled at the recollection. Phew! What a bit of luck that had been! Just as well she'd been with David on those two trips to France with his sixth-formers, although she'd probably have been all right anyway. It had taken a fair bit of cajoling on David's part, but as it turned out she'd really enjoyed her two years in the French Conversation Class at Caernarfon Tech. At the very least it was a chance to get out once a week, and it got so boring being on her own in the house all day. Nothing to do, nothing much to do if she *did* get out more. Not that she blamed David, but . . .

Bloody spots! She wiped off the lotion and applied a new layer. It might be better to leave them alone—let the sun get at them. But the sky this Tuesday evening was a sullen grey, and the weather would soon be getting cold again; far colder than it would be in the south. Like last winter. Brrh! She didn't intend to face another winter like that . . . The washing-up was done and David sat downstairs in the living room marking exercise books. He was always marking exercise books. He would be awfully upset, of course, but . . .

She stepped over to the wardrobe and took out the long, red velvet dress she'd taken to the cleaners last week. Inclining her head slightly, she held it against her body and stood before the mirror. Dinner-dates, parties, dancing . . . It had been such a long time since she'd been out—been out *properly*, that is . . . The dark roots of her hair had now grown almost half an inch into the pseudo-blonde, and it all began to look so *obvious*. She would buy another bottle of "Poly-bleach" tomorrow. Or would she bother? After all, she'd got to Oxford and back pretty easily . . . Not that she would hire a car again. Couldn't afford it, for a start. Much easier to get a bus into Bangor and then hitch-hike down the A5. A lot of men still drove the roads and hoped that every mile they'd see a lone, attractive girl. Yes, that would be much easier, and the A5 went all the way to London . . .

It was a good job she'd mentioned the car to David. That really *had* worried her—whether they'd check upon the car-hire firms. She'd not told David the truth, of course; just said she'd gone to see her mother. Yes, she'd admitted how silly and dangerous it was, and had promised David never to think of doing it again. But it had been a very sensible precaution, that—warning him to tell them that she couldn't drive. If they ever asked, that was. And Morse had asked, it seemed. Clever man, Morse . . . She'd been a fraction naughty—hadn't she?— the first time he had called. Yes. And the second time— phew! That had perhaps been the very worst moment of all, when she'd opened the door and found him looking through her kitchen drawer. She'd bought a new one, naturally, but it had been *exactly* the same sort of knife, brand new . . . Funny, really; he hadn't even mentioned it . . .

Valerie looked at herself once more in the mirror. The spots looked better now, and she closed the bedroom door behind her . . . Morse! She smiled to herself as she walked down the creaking stairs. His face! *Oui. Je l'ai étudié d'abord à l'école et après . . .*

The phone rang in Caernarfon Police H.Q., and the switchboard put the call through to the duty inspector.

"All right. Put him on." He clamped his hand firmly over the mouthpiece and mumbled a few hurried words *sotto voce* to the sergeant sitting opposite. "It's Morse again."

"Morse, sir?"

"Yes, you remember. That fellow from Oxford who buggered us all about at the weekend. I wonder what . . . Hello. Can I help you?"

Epilogue

> There are tears of things and mortal matters
> touch the heart.
>
> VIRGIL, *Aeneid I*

It was not until Saturday morning that a somewhat disgruntled Lewis was at last summoned into Morse's office to hear something of the final developments.

The Caernarfon police had felt (with some justification, admitted Morse) that they had insufficient evidence on which to hold Valerie Taylor—even if they accepted Morse's vehement protestations that the woman living as Mrs. Acum *was* indeed Valerie Taylor. And when Morse himself had arrived on Wednesday morning, it had been too late: the driver of the 9:50 A.M. bus from Bontnewydd to Bangor had remembered her clearly; and a petrol-pump attendant had noticed her ("So would you have done, officer!") as she stood beside the forecourt waiting to thumb a lift down the A5.

Lewis had listened carefully, but one or two things still puzzled him. "So it must have been Baines who wrote the letter?"

"Oh yes. It couldn't have been Valerie."

"I wouldn't be *too* sure, sir. She's a pretty clever girl."

And I'm a clown, thought Morse. The car, the French, and the spots: a combination of circumstance and coincidence which had proved too much even for *him*

324

accept; a triple-oxer over which he would normally have leaped with the blithest assurance, but at which, in this instance, he had so strangely refused. After all, it would have been very odd if a mechanically-minded girl like Valerie hadn't even bothered to take a driving-test; and she wasn't too bad at *spoken* French—even at school. Those reports! If only—

"Big coincidence, wasn't it—about the spots, I mean?"

"No, not really, Lewis. Don't forget that both of them were sleeping with Acum; and Acum's got a beard."

It was something else that Lewis hadn't considered, and he let it go. "She's gone to London, I suppose, sir?"

Morse nodded wearily, a wry smile upon his lips. "Back to square one, aren't we?"

"You think we'll find her?"

"I don't know. I suppose so—in the end."

On Saturday afternoon the Phillipson family motored to the White Horse Hill at Uffington. For Andrew and Alison it was a rare treat, and Mrs. Phillipson watched them lovingly as they gambolled with gay abandon about the Downs. So much had passed between her and Donald these few days. On Tuesday evening their very lives together had seemed to be hanging by the slenderest of threads. But now, this bright and chilly afternoon, the future stretched out before them, open and free as the broad landscape around them. She would write, she decided, a long, long letter to Morse, and try to thank him from the bottom of her heart. For on that terrible evening it had been Morse who had found Donald and brought him to her; it had been Morse who had seemed to know and to understand all things about them both . . .

* * *

On Saturday evening Mrs. Grace Taylor sat staring
blankly through the window on to the darkened street.
They had returned from their holiday in mid-afternoon
and things seemed very much the same as she had left
them. At a quarter-past eight, by the light of the street
lamp, she saw Morse walking slowly, head down,
towards the pub. She gave him no second thought.

Earlier in the evening she had gone out into the front
garden and clipped off the heads of a few last fading
roses. But there had been one late scarlet bloom that was
still in perfect flower. She had cut that off too, and it now
stood on the mantelshelf, in a cheap glass vase that
Valerie had won on a shooting stall at St. Gile's Fair,
beneath the ducks that winged their way towards the
ceiling in the empty room behind her.

Some of them never did come home . . . never.